# Branching Out

## A Scary Good Romance

Joy Jarrett

Literary Wanderlust | Denver, Colorado

Published in the United States by Literary Wanderlust LLC, Denver, Colorado. www.LiteraryWanderlust.com

ISBN print: 978-1-956615-39-5
ISBN digital: 978-1-956615-40-1

Printed in the United States of America

# Dedication

To Jon—I'm so lucky to have you
as the hero
of our very own
romantic comedy
action
international thriller
love story.

# Chapter 1

Dusk gathered among the trees where the darkness snagged in branches and pooled around trunks. Once night fully fell, the darkness would morph into a thick, velvety blackness out here in the forest. A small tendril of dread coiled around Willow's stomach at the thought. She refused to let it take root because tonight was supposed to be a celebration. It had rained earlier, as it so often did on the Oregon coast, making it hard to believe summer lurked around the corner. The air held a chill along with the scent of pine and fir and the hoppy smell of beer.

She spotted her baby brother—fifteen years her junior— by the firepit. His friends worked to start a fire with the sort of pyromania typical of teenage boys. Connor stood a little apart from his friends in much the same way Willow did with hers. They'd invited all these people to celebrate the upcoming opening of Branching Out, their new tree house hotel, but Willow suddenly wanted a moment alone with Connor. She wove through the partygoers sitting in camping chairs and clutching red Solo cups. Freya, Willow's black lab, trotted alongside her and stopped to greet several friends along the way.

"Hey." Willow nudged her brother with her shoulder. "You missing him, too?"

"He'd have hated this." Connor bent to scratch behind Freya's silky ears. There was just enough light left to see his smile. She and Connor looked a lot alike. Same thick, dark hair, same straight noses, same deep green eyes the color of the surrounding forest. Connor's smile, though? That was their father's completely, right down to the dimple in his left cheek. Seeing it brought a lump to her throat.

"Too many people." Connor mimicked the gruff voice of their dad.

Willow laughed, having had the same thought earlier. "Yeah, he'd have hated the idea of overnight guests on his land." Her grandparents—her father's parents who'd helped raise her—didn't love the idea, either. They'd declined her invitation. *Sounds like an event for young people,* her grandfather had said. They didn't need to say neither of her grandparents could make it up the stairs of the tree houses. It made Willow sad seeing how old they'd become. They used her grandfather's fall as an excuse to move to town, but it was as much her grandma's failing memory. One more way she and Connor were on their own.

She threw an arm around her brother's waist since his shoulders were too high to reach after his recent growth spurt. That was another thing he'd inherited from their dad—his considerable height. Willow, despite her name, was short, like their mother. But she wouldn't spoil the night thinking of that woman.

She nudged Connor again. "Look what we did."

He ducked his head with a small smile. "What *you* did."

"Are you kidding me, man? I couldn't have done this without you. Really. You helped me choose the architect's plans. Made me dinner after a long day. Put in extra hours at the raptor center to pick up the slack. We did this together. You and me, kid."

His smile spread to a full-blown grin, flashing his silver braces Willow couldn't afford. For Connor, though, she always found a way.

"Dude, what the hell are you doing? You just smothered it." Connor's friend Ethan squabbled with two other boys as smoke belched from the firepit. Freya barked in disapproval.

"Come on." Willow moved away from the billowing white cloud. "Walk with me."

"Where are we going?"

"Thought you could do the honors and turn on the lights."

Connor and Freya followed her along the winding path leading back toward their cedar-shingle house.

Above them, an owl let out a low hoot.

For a quick, wild moment, Willow imagined it was the spirt of their father. With his twisted sense of humor, it would be just like him to come back as an animal he claimed he hated. Before the accident that disabled him, he'd worked in logging for Bartlett Timber. To put it mildly, he held pretty strong views on owls, specifically the Northern Spotted Owl. Still, she knew he'd admired her hard work rescuing owls and other raptors. He'd even limped along to watch some releases of rehabilitated birds. He'd watched with a smile tinged with jealousy each time a bird of prey soared back into freedom.

When Willow grew that handful of rescues into an acclaimed raptor center with ten employees, his admiration grew to full-blown pride. Despite grumbling about stupid owls, he'd been more than happy to advise her on creating a visitor building to go with the raptor center. After all, he'd had plenty of practice with that sort of thing after turning the historic Owl Sawmill on their property into a museum.

At the thought of the sawmill, Willow swallowed back a rush of guilt. Ever since her dad's death four years ago, the museum had remained closed. She glanced over her shoulder. Off to the north, a couple hundred yards away, the corrugated metal roof caught the last of the sunlight. The windows of the long building, as always, were dark.

Everything about that sawmill reminded her of her dad, and not all of it was good. The museum focused on the history of logging in Oregon. Her father had particularly enjoyed creating an exhibit devoted to the many accidents in the industry. Maybe it was cathartic for him to see he wasn't alone in his suffering, but Willow found the exhibit unsettling. If that weren't bad enough, the gleaming silver saw in the center of the museum was the site of a grisly accident a century ago that spawned the local legend of The Bandage Man. A worker had been shoved into the spinning blade. He'd survived his horrific injuries for two days before succumbing. Now he supposedly haunted the area, dressed, of course, in head-to-toe bloody bandages.

That man had been her great-great-grandfather.

It was bad enough thinking her ancestor met such a grisly end, but after her father's death and the crazy rumors surrounding it, the story became unbearable to her and Connor. She made excuses for keeping the museum closed, and some of them were even valid, like needing to use her time on the raptor center and now the new tree house hotel. But the real reason she couldn't bring herself to reopen, if she were totally honest, was that horrible silver saw blade and the story of The Bandage Man.

*It's not just a story, is it? You saw him once yourself.*

Willow shoved the thought away and turned her back on the sawmill. She and Connor reached a cheerful yellow shack that would serve as the tree house hotel's reception. A metal box on the outside of the shack housed the switch for the lights.

"Look," Connor breathed. A brown and white owl swooped down from a distant tree and flew on silent wings to land on a branch above them. Liquid black eyes stared down at them. "That's not a barred owl." A note of awe crept into his words. "It's a spotted owl."

Owls loved their property and always had, giving the old

sawmill its name. Barred owls were common, but seeing a spotted owl was unusually lucky. This one looked a lot like Cynthia—minus the white splotch on Cynthia's chest. Cynthia was the first owl Willow ever rescued after a car struck her and broke her wing. Though the fracture healed, the owl wasn't able to fly again. The now elderly bird, in excellent health, enjoyed her status as the spoiled favorite of the center.

"It's like a sign, isn't it?" Connor stared up at the owl.

"I don't believe in signs," Willow said. "But it is perfect." Freya sat on her haunches at Willow's feet. "After all, this is why we're doing all this." She swept out her arm to encompass the arc of tree houses before them and the raptor center in the distance with its two dozen birds of prey. "For our birds." She sighed in a rare moment of contentment. "All right, you want to turn the lights on?"

Connor opened the metal box. "Ready? Three. Two. One." With a click, the lights blinked on.

Willow's gasp mingled with those of their friends back near the fire. Strings of white lights crisscrossed the railings of hanging wooden bridges, staircases, and tree houses. The houses, constructed of rough-hewn wood, appeared to grow from the trees. The seven tree houses stood at different heights in a rough horseshoe around a small clearing. The lowest sat fifteen feet up and the highest soared about sixty. The center one was the largest, the only house with two stories. Seeing all of them outlined in lights was pure magic, straight from a fantasy world. Willow half-expected to see an Ewok or an elf from Middle Earth poke its head out one of the houses.

She and Connor headed back toward the fire, which had finally started properly, and rejoined the group. Freya resumed her greeting duties, a job she took seriously. Willow couldn't stop herself from smiling. Everyone had risen from their camping chairs to gawk up at the trees, exclaiming with delight.

Hayley, blonde hair bouncing in a high ponytail, bounded over and hooked her arm through Willow's.

"You made it." Willow felt a rush of comfort at the sight of her best friend. On top of working as the marketing director for the Tree Top Raptor Center, Hayley also helped at her parents' brewery, The Grumpy Owl, where she'd been waiting tables earlier this evening.

"It's beautiful, Willow." Hayley pointed at one of the tree houses. "We get the tallest one, right?"

"Yep. That's ours." Willow hunched her shoulders to her ears with happiness. "Wait until you see inside."

"Can't wait." Hayley squeezed her arm and moved off toward Tyler. He was a new employee—and Hayley's new boyfriend. Tyler was all right, but Willow knew Hayley wanted a family soon, and Tyler seemed too immature for her. He had a man bun, for God's sake.

From the shadows, Toby, the owner of Hansen Houses Construction that built the Branching Out Tree House Hotel, appeared with a beer in his hand. "Willow." His face flamed a lurid red under his shock of white-blonde hair and beard. She guessed it wasn't his first beer of the evening. "Everyone is loving this." He gave her a broad smile, and for good reason, too. Toby moved to Cedar Beach last year, with an eye to tapping into the wealthy, artsy folks in the area who might want custom-built tree houses to impress guests. For now, he made his bread and butter off home renovations, but Willow's tree house hotel would be his shining jewel of an advertisement. Willow liked the idea the hotel would fund her raptor center and also give Toby a boost in tree house construction clients.

"I think everyone will enjoy their stay." She lifted her chin toward the tree houses. "I can't tell you enough how much I appreciate all your work to get us done on schedule." Toby had pushed his crew hard. "I'm pretty much booked through the summer now."

"That's excellent news. Hey, I wanted to introduce you to my girlfriend." He waved his hand toward a group of three women clumped together with their camping chairs. One of them got to her feet and started over.

Willow's mouth went dry.

Toby grabbed the woman's hand and pulled her around to face Willow. "This is—"

"Lindsay," Willow breathed.

"Willow."

"You two know each other?" Toby swept his hand back and forth between them, slopping beer over his cup. "This is great."

Lindsay wouldn't meet her eye. "Willow, I was, uh, sorry to hear about your dad."

Seriously? Lindsay Bartlett, of all people, dared mention her father to her face?

All of a sudden, the night of celebration lost its shine. Willow glanced at Hayley making out with Tyler like a couple of teenagers. Connor sat in a chair, staring into the fire while his friends chatted without him. Her employees and friends laughed too loud, and their eyes shone from too much beer. Was it her imagination, or had the scene morphed from happy into something slightly dysfunctional?

Willow tried and failed to find the correct response to Lindsay's fake sympathy. Lindsay's father owned the logging company that destroyed Willow's dad, and she had the audacity to say she was sorry to hear about his death?

Willow snorted loud enough to be rude. "Well, thanks again, Toby. I mean, for all your hard work. And everything." She backed away from the man, tripped over Freya, and was saved by Elvis catching her by the elbow.

"Easy there." That baritone voice of his always came as a shock, considering he was maybe five-foot-six and only twenty-one.

"You okay, Boss?" Maureen materialized from the darkness beside Elvis. Of course, Willow would find her Rehabilitation Director with her intern. Those two were joined at the hip.

At first glance, Maureen and Elvis had nothing in common. Maureen was a no-nonsense skinny woman, and with her lined face and gray-streaked red hair in twin braids, she bore more than a passing resemblance to a female Willie Nelson. For years, she'd made her living driving big rigs. About a decade ago, she'd given up trucks, cigarettes, and her husband, and earned her bachelor's in wildlife conservation. Despite knowing her for five years, Willow still didn't know what prompted this woman's transformation. All she knew was the taciturn, gruff woman had a way with birds of prey that was almost mystical.

Elvis, on the other hand, was a black kid from New Orleans raised by doctor parents. Where Maureen was into country, Elvis was into jazz. Maureen ate any food that came in a box, while Elvis worked on perfecting French cuisine. Maureen had only voted in one election since 1988. Elvis joined local groups focused on social justice. On the surface, he and Maureen couldn't be any more different. But the two of them loved birds more than anything and enjoyed the most companionable of silences in one another's company.

"How's it going, Boss?" Maureen asked. Willow managed to hide her cringe at what she knew was an ironic nickname. She got the impression Maureen was constantly judging Willow's youth and every decision at the raptor center. That was okay. If Willow ever needed advice about running the center, Maureen was the first person she'd ask.

The night's festivities continued, but Willow couldn't recapture the magic from when Connor first turned on the lights. Wishing her dad could see this left her melancholy. She tried to shake it off, chatting with friends, but as the fire died down, and some of the guests crept away to their tree houses, she was relieved the night was finally drawing to a close. Hayley was sitting in Tyler's lap, but being her best friend, she always seemed to know Willow's mood. She caught Willow's eye and hiked her head toward their tree house with a questioning look.

Willow nodded.

Toby stood from his chair. "Well, it's been fun everyone, but we're off to bed." He threw a wink to the group and grabbed

Lindsay by the hand. The giggling pair headed toward the staircase of the largest tree house.

"Hey. Why didn't we get that one?" asked Austin, one of Connor's friends. "There are five in our group. Nobody else has that many people."

Connor cleared his throat and shifted in his camping chair. "We thought Toby deserved it since, you know, he built the place."

Willow knew that wasn't the reason why her brother and his friends weren't staying in the big house. It was because Connor didn't care to stay there. Willow didn't either. When Toby had proposed the Pacific Madrone tree as the centerpiece of the hotel, she'd fought him.

He pointed out it was the perfect location and size for the biggest house. She insisted all the tree houses should be built in firs and pines. Toby thought she was being ridiculous and finally won her over because her arguments didn't make much sense. If he knew her real reasons, forget ridiculous; he'd have thought she was insane.

She and her grandparents referred to that particular Pacific Madrone as The Old Tree. It was over a century old, a massive, towering giant with twisted, gnarled branches and slick, green leaves. A long lightning scar of discolored bark ran the length of the trunk, a historical marker of a severe thunderstorm from fifty years ago. In the fall, the tree produced warty, red berries. Birds and squirrels ate the berries from the other madrones on her property, but never, she noticed, from that one. The tree provoked the deepest sense of unease in Willow. That Connor shared the feeling, despite not having the same frightening experiences with that tree as her, only proved something was very wrong with that madrone.

Willow watched Toby and Lindsay's tipsy progress up the spiraling staircase. Good. If anyone deserved to stay in that evil tree, it was a Bartlett. Around and around, they climbed up the trunk. Strips of blood-red bark hung down, like flayed flesh, to reveal the white wood beneath. Exactly one time, Willow had put her hand on that smooth trunk to find out if the Pacific Madrone deserved its nickname of the "Refrigerator Tree" for having cold bark. It *had* been cold to the touch, but that hadn't been what chilled her that day as a child.

At eight years old, her animal-loving sensibilities were traumatized by the discovery of a dead squirrel at the base of the tree. Maggots swarmed the small, tragic carcass, and as Willow had stood in the cool shade, she'd had the uncanny sense the madrone was somehow responsible. That's when she'd placed her hand on the trunk to see if the tree was as cold and unfeeling as she expected. That was the moment she'd heard—

No, Willow wouldn't think of it again, and definitely not late at night when she was about to sleep near the madrone. It had only been the overactive imagination of a sensitive child seeing death firsthand. The memory chilled her again, and Willow moved closer to the last embers of the fire. Freya let out a whimper.

"Ready for bed?" Hayley's bright voice warmed her more than the fire.

"Yep, let's go." She and Hayley walked the winding path toward the tree house. Willow stumbled once, too busy watching The Old Tree. She put a steadying hand on Freya's back.

Toby and Lindsay had reached the top of the staircase, where the tree house nestled in the crux of the madrone's thick branches. Those branches ran parallel to the ground before jutting straight upward, like fingers grasping at the sky. It gave the tree house the appearance of sitting inside the hand of a giant, whose fingers might suddenly close into a fist to crush what lay inside. Willow shuddered. All of a sudden, she wanted to run to the tree, knock on that door where Toby and Lindsay had disappeared, and warn them, tell them to get out. Even Lindsay Bartlett should be warned about The Old Tree.

That was an impulse she would have to learn to ignore on a regular basis because each stay in that two-story tree house would bring in a hefty sum. She forced herself to put aside her childish fears and focus on how much money it would raise toward caring for her birds of prey.

"You okay?" Hayley asked, as they started up the flight of stairs to their own tree house. Freya clattered along behind them.

"Yeah. Just missing my dad." Because it was true, Willow didn't feel bad for omitting the other half of her bad mood.

But Hayley must have known that wasn't all of it. "Weird seeing Lindsay, isn't it?"

That too was part of her bad mood. Willow nodded.

"She looks even better than she did in high school." Hayley scowled. "God, I hate her."

"Maybe she's changed." Willow didn't believe it for a second, but lately she'd been working on being more gracious after Maureen joked that Willow was more bitter than Maureen's mother. Life hadn't been fair to Willow, and it was all too easy to give into the temptation of bitterness, but bitterness was the most unattractive trait ever. Since it reminded her too much of her mother, Willow had vowed then and there to avoid it at all costs.

Nobody chose their parents, Lindsay included. She didn't ask to be a Bartlett. She didn't choose to have an unscrupulous father who'd silenced Willow's dad with an "accident" and hired the best lawyers to make sure her dad's lawsuit never had a chance of winning. But Lindsay *did* choose to be mean to Willow at school, to call her White-Trash Willow, and enlist her volleyball team to torment Willow with taunts for the duration of the court case. Hayley, being Willow's friend, experienced collateral damage from Lindsay and her horrible clique.

Willow's money-grubbing mom returned to town during the lawsuit. After abandoning Willow at the age of one, she'd come back sniffing around in the hopes of a windfall for Willow's dad. As usual, her mom got high and went down to The Grumpy Owl, where she was arrested for being drunk and disorderly. The next day, someone plastered the mugshot of Willow's mom all over school. Seeing as Lindsay's uncle was the sheriff of Cedar Beach, it was easy to guess who'd pulled that cruel stunt.

The only good thing about Lindsay was the fact she was two years older than Willow. She'd graduated, leaving Willow mostly in peace for her junior and senior years of high school. A few kids still called her White-Trash Willow or made rude comments about her mother. The teasing stung, but it never held the same menace as Lindsay's cruelty had.

Willow shivered and reached for the doorknob. Hayley put a hand on her forearm. "Don't think about it anymore, all right? She isn't worth it."

Hayley delighted in the interior of the tree house, exclaiming over the colorful blue cushions Willow sewed for the window seat, shrieking like a little kid at the tiny two-burner stove and mini fridge in the kitchen, and testing the water in the bathroom sink. A tank held enough water for a ninety-second shower. Hayley laughed when Willow opened the double Murphy bed to reveal a blue and white quilt of otters, and Freya jumped right into the middle of it.

She and Hayley compromised by allowing Freya to sleep at the foot of the bed. They whispered in the dark for a while about how cute Tyler was—yes, even Willow could admit that. They talked about Willow's refusal to sign up for online dating and discussed what they could wear to the upcoming fundraiser at the Cedar Beach Cliff House. It felt like the old days of frequent sleepovers when they were Connor's age. Gratitude filled Willow's heart to have a best friend that could make her feel like a teenager when she was pushing thirty.

She wasn't missing her dad anymore or thinking about The Bandage Man, The Old Tree, or the odious Lindsay Bartlett when she fell asleep.

Then a scream ripped open the night.

# Chapter 2

Willow flew out of bed. Freya launched herself onto the floor and started barking. Hayley, always slower to wake than Willow, stirred under the covers. Another scream came, definitely a woman's, followed by a man shouting. Willow rushed to the window and peered out. A light was on in The Old Tree. Guilt flooded her at the realization Lindsay must be the one screaming, as if Willow's earlier unkind thoughts had summoned something terrible. Why was she screaming?

"What's going on?" Hayley sat up and rubbed her face.

"I'm going to see." Willow snatched up her orange Oregon State sweatshirt and pulled it over her head. She rammed her bare feet into her sneakers and ripped open the door and took the stairs two at a time. Freya shoved past her and streaked through the night toward The Old Tree. Lights came on in three of the other tree houses by the time she made it to the bottom of the stairs.

"What's going on?" Connor jogged down the ladder-like staircase of his own tree house, two of his friends behind him.

"I don't know." Willow turned the corner to face The Old Tree head-on, and her stomach dropped into her feet. A glowing white figure covered in bandages stood on a branch of the tree, peering into the top-floor window. Her heart pounded against her sternum. The Bandage Man.

Except The Bandage Man wasn't real.

*Crack!* The branch the man was standing on splintered and broke. Willow covered her hand with her mouth as he fell, only to catch the branch below. One of Connor's friends swore loudly in the darkness. She considered returning to the tree house to get her phone, but decided time was of the essence and plenty of people would have phones. This was her property, her situation to deal with.

Willow reached the tree. Everything was shadows and shapes in the darkness until Connor had the good sense to turn on the strings of white lights, illuminating the scene. The man dangled from the branch while Freya barked frantically under his feet.

"You suck!" Lindsay shouted from the top of the stairs. Toby clutched his belly and doubled over with laughter. She turned and slapped him on the arm. "It isn't funny. Both of you suck."

"Little help here," grunted The Bandage Man. Freya leaped in the air and snapped her teeth together with an audible *click*. He was at least twenty feet above the ground, and Freya had no chance of reaching him. Still, the man attempted to pull his legs up. The gauze bandages looked too tight to allow much movement. He began pulling himself hand-over-hand along the tree branch. The movement incited Freya into growling deep in her throat, and the man moved faster.

"Good girl, Freya," Willow murmured. Connor and Hayley joined her and several others who'd gathered around the tree to watch the bizarre event unfolding.

"That scared me so bad. You guys are so stupid." Lindsay hugged her arms over her chest and watched the man's progress.

Obviously, she knew this person. That didn't stop Willow

from shouting up. "Should I call the cops?"

"No," said The Bandage Man and Toby at the same time Lindsay said, "Yes."

Connor looked at Willow and shrugged. The Bandage Man, using what must be amazing core strength, managed to pull himself up and thread his body through the open window of the first floor, knocking the screen inside with a clatter and a muffled swear. He replaced the screen, and a moment later, he opened the front door of the tree house to join Lindsay and Toby at the top of the staircase. Willow crossed to the bottom of the stairs, her hand on the railing.

"Not cool." Lindsay punched the man in the shoulder.

The man flinched away from the repeated blows. "Ow, stop. I hurt myself."

Willow climbed the first couple of steps.

"Serves you right," Lindsay said. "You shouldn't have—are you bleeding?"

Willow completed a circuit around the trunk and had no desire to go farther up the tree. "You know I'm not liable for you injuring yourself on my property, right?" she called up. Her attorney was always drilling into her the importance of insurance and liability waivers around her raptor center and now this hotel.

"I'm fine," said The Bandage Man. "Just caught myself on the broken branch when I fell."

"If you're fine," Lindsay said, "then I can do this some more." She punched the man in the shoulder again. "You scared me to death."

"Hey, it was Toby's idea. Just a joke to scare you. You know—*Oooooo*—The Bandage Man." He lifted his arms like a mummy and wiggled his fingers. His thumb trailed a long piece of gauze.

Lindsay rounded on Toby. "Did you think anyone here would find The Bandage Man funny? After what happened to Willow's dad?"

"What?" said Toby and The Bandage Man together.

"Wait. Willow? Willow Duncan?" The Bandage Man whirled to look at her.

This guy knew her? She glanced down to Hayley, and they exchanged a look of suspicion, no doubt having both reached the same possible conclusion.

Lindsay shoved the man in the back. "Apologize to her, you idiot." He obeyed and started down the steps to meet Willow in the middle of the flight.

"I'm sorry, Willow," he said. "Even though I don't know what my sister is talking about. I didn't mean to wake up everybody or upset anyone. Except for Lindsay, obviously."

"Jake?"

"Yep."

Willow's mind flashed back to high school. Jake Bartlett, the extramarital son of Mr. Walter Bartlett of Bartlett Timber, had shown up from California like a bad penny in ninth grade to ruin Mr. Bartlett's marriage. This was on account of how Mrs. Bartlett hadn't known about Jake until then. Willow couldn't know the motivation of Jake's mother in bringing her son to Cedar Beach, but whatever it had been, she only lasted two years in town before whisking her son back to California. Jake had been in Willow's grade. Quiet and nerdy, he'd been a skinny kid with bad acne and a worse attitude who'd started a Dungeons and Dragons group at school.

That hadn't stopped Willow from developing a masochistic, Romeo-and-Juliet-style crush on the Bartlett boy. She'd conflated his quietness for mystery, and for a few months, convinced herself he must be her soulmate. He'd been the subject of quite a few fantasies that made Willow's face now flame with heat. They'd involved her marrying Jake and enraging Lindsay and Mr. Bartlett when Willow stole all the money from Bartlett Timber, ran off, and ruined their family. There may have been a few kissing fantasies thrown in there, too. It had been a relief when Jake's mother took him away the same year Lindsay graduated.

Willow shook her head to clear her thoughts. Around her, the others were drifting back to their tree houses, clearly deciding there wasn't much else worth seeing when it was almost one in the morning. "What are you doing here?" she asked him.

He hiked a thumb at Toby. The gesture revealed a red smear leaking through the bandages covering his left forearm. "We're friends from college." His voice was unrecognizable from high school, deep and rumbling to match his now considerable height.

"Look what you did." Willow pointed at the broken branch. It still clung to the trunk in a splintered mess. "That's a hazard to my guests."

"I apologize. I really am an idiot. I'll come back tomorrow and take care of it."

Willow crossed her arms and tilted her head at him. "Better yet, you can pay for a tree surgeon to do it properly."

"I can do it."

"You can do it? Properly?"

"Oh, I assure you, I can do it *properly*."

"Are you seriously trying to flirt with me?"

"No! God, no. I only mean I have plenty of experience with trees. I worked for a tree house construction company in California, okay?"

Did he have to sound so disgusted at the idea of flirting with her? And why did she care? He was a Bartlett, and if high school was anything to go by, there was nothing remotely attractive about Jake once the forbidden fruit thing was taken out of the equation.

"Fine, but I'm not liable for any injuries you incur working on my property. You'll need to sign a waiver."

Jake's mouth fell open, but perhaps not as much as it would have had it not been restricted by the bandages covering his face. "Are you for real?"

"Yes."

"He's working with me, Willow," Toby grunted from the

top of the stairs. "I have insurance, remember?" He sighed and scrubbed his hand over his face. "Look, this was all my idea. I thought it would be funny to scare Lindsay after she told me The Bandage Man thing freaks her out. I'm really sorry. Jake will take care of your tree tomorrow, okay? Or I can do it."

"I'll do it," Jake said. "I broke the branch. I'll fix it."

Willow threw up her hands. "Whatever. I just need that branch down tomorrow. You know, Toby? Tomorrow? The day when the inspector comes?"

Toby sighed again. "I am aware, yes, Willow."

"Connor, can you please turn off the lights? And go back to bed," Willow said, and then to Hayley, "Come on."

As she walked away, she heard Lindsay speaking in not-quite-hushed-enough tones. Luckily, Connor had hurried ahead to the reception shack and probably couldn't hear Lindsay.

"That was so messed up, guys," she said. "Willow's dad died in a horrible car accident. Well, I don't know about *accident*. He drove off a cliff. Everyone in town said it was The Bandage Man that ran him off the road. Just like the urban legend, you know? Personally, I think . . ."

Whatever Lindsay thought, Willow could no longer hear her, and she didn't care, anyway. She fisted her hands hard enough that her nails dug into her palms. It had been raining that night, and that coastal road was treacherous and winding.

It *had* been an accident.

Hayley squeezed her arm, and for once, Willow resented the look of sympathy from her friend. Connor cut the lights, and everything disappeared into darkness.

It *was* an accident, she repeated to herself. She hated the voice suggesting her father would have picked a rainy night so she wouldn't have to think he'd left her alone on purpose, left her at just twenty-five years old to parent her younger brother.

Her eyes struggled to adjust to the deep dark of the forest. A creeping sensation began at the base of her spine and worked its way up her back and over her scalp like skittering spiders.

Something waited in the dark behind her. A deep certainty in her bones told her whatever it was wished her harm. It pulled at her like gravity, willing her to turn around and face The Old Tree.

Willow swallowed. Beside her, Hayley picked up her pace, like she sensed it too.

The dark seemed darker, the air colder. Goosebumps broke out on her arms, despite her sweatshirt, and the urge to turn around grew as strong as a terrible itch. She remembered her grandma BiBi taking her to Sunday school at the Methodist church in town, the story about Lot's wife, who couldn't resist turning back to look. Willow imagined turning into a pillar of salt, the idea as horrifying now as it had been as a kid. She didn't turn around. She knew she didn't want to see whatever evil thing pulsed in the darkness behind her.

She and Hayley hurried, and when they reached the base of the stairs to their tree house, they were both out of breath. They jogged up the steps and into the house. Willow slammed the door and locked it, though she was struck by the sudden idea that whatever was out there wouldn't be stopped by a deadbolt.

What the hell was wrong with her?

"You okay?" she asked Hayley, who seemed equally frightened.

"Yeah, just creeped myself out. My sister's boyfriend went camping a couple of weeks ago up in the mountains. They saw a mountain lion. He told me people have been spotting them closer to the coast, too."

Willow almost laughed. She'd take a mountain lion any day over the malevolent feeling she'd sensed coming from the darkness. Even if it was only her imagination.

*Lying to yourself a lot tonight, aren't you?* Willow shoved the annoying voice out of her head and climbed into bed.

—

Willow, as usual, woke early. Saturdays were a fasting day for many of the birds at the raptor center, and those that did require feeding got their meal from a team of weekend volunteers. There was no need for her to get up yet. She tried going back to sleep, but her mind kept gnawing at all the ways this tree house hotel could fail. In order to fund the ever-more-expensive raptor center and the hotel's construction, she'd maxed out a home equity line on her house. She was using her meager savings to cover the new mortgage for now, and there wasn't much left. What if the hotel fizzled out after the bookings for the opening? She and Connor could lose everything—the hotel, the raptor center, and the only home they'd ever known. After laying there fretting for an hour next to a snoozing Hayley, she gave up and crept out of the tree house.

The air was fresh and cool as she made the short trek to the raptor center, enclosed by a rough-cut fence to give the birds privacy, and keep out Freya, since dogs frightened the animals. She entered the gate and passed by three rows of mews, the fancy falconry name for the raptor cages. In a soft voice, she greeted an array of hawks, falcons, owls, and a golden eagle.

To the south of the mews were two large flight cages where birds could exercise and practice flying. Beyond the mews was the hut, a low, hexagonal building housing everything from cleaning supplies to the freezers stocked with quail, rabbits, and rats for the birds.

Willow slipped inside the hut and found Martin and Eve, her two Saturday volunteers, laughing together over one of the dog toys they used for enrichment with the birds. Eve had her hand on Martin's shoulder. Martin was a widower in his sixties, and Eve, around the same age, had been divorced for years. Willow worried she'd interrupted some serious senior citizen flirtations, but the pair welcomed her with wide smiles. In the end, they were grateful for her help in hand-feeding a trio of orphaned barn owlets. She spent a pleasant couple of hours with her birds when she realized her guests would be leaving the tree houses soon.

For the next half hour, she stood in the gravel parking lot between the tree house hotel and the raptor center's visitor building and waved goodbye to the people who'd come to celebrate the opening of her hotel in two weeks. "Tell everyone you know about Branching Out," she told each of them, as if she hadn't already encouraged them to spread the word several times before.

The last of her party guests was driving away when a navy-blue Dodge pickup pulled in, and a tall man got out. He stood beside the truck for a minute, hands shoved in his pockets as he looked around the area. Willow squinted at the man, and he pulled his hand from his pocket to wave at her with a sheepish grin. A white bandage wrapped around his left forearm.

It hit her then with a somersault in her stomach. This was Jake Bartlett.

"Hey." He started toward her.

He'd been so scrawny and short in high school. Now he was at least six feet tall. She'd noticed his height last night, but what she hadn't seen thanks to the bandages was that Jake was now covered in lean, rangy muscle. He wore black Doc Martens, black jeans with a rip in one knee, an olive T-shirt, and a black leather wristband that should've looked stupid, but somehow didn't. It just served to accentuate his tanned and muscled forearms. A little blood had seeped through his bandage. Streaks of sun-bleached hair shot through his thick, dark waves, brushing his shirt collar, and curling around his ears. He ran his hand through that hair now and lifted his face to hers. She jolted with recognition at seeing his eyes, the one remarkable feature of him in high school. They seemed to glow from within, a stunning and unusual shade of turquoise that made Willow think of the blue dacnis bird of South America. Jake's features were strong and even. The only imperfection was a three-inch scar along his left jawline, bright white against his golden skin.

A vision of Willow kissing that scar flashed through her mind. She shook her head in irritation. Why did every Bartlett get to be so damn attractive? He looked like a male model. It was unfair. "You're here to take down the tree branch, right?" She sounded rude, and she didn't care.

If Jake noticed, he didn't care either. "I am," he said with equanimity.

"There's something weird going on with the tree."

"Weird? Like what?"

She cocked her head. "Are you any kind of tree expert? Like in a botany sense?"

"A botany sense?" He chuckled. The sound was annoyingly appealing. "I don't know if I'd go so far as to call myself a botanist, but I do know some about trees. More so about trees in California than here in Oregon, though. What's up?"

"Come and see for yourself."

# Chapter 3

"Let me grab my tools." Jake trotted back to his truck to get some supplies from the bed. He grabbed his toolbox with his good arm, looped a basket over his left, and picked up a pole saw. He winced at the pain in his forearm, regretting his hasty butterfly bandage job last night before going to sleep. The branch gouged him deeper than he'd realized, and he had a bad feeling the wound might be full of splinters. A trip to the emergency room to have it cleaned out and get some stitches would probably have been the wiser move if he weren't such a weenie about shots. He swore he could feel the skin tearing open under the bandage with his movements.

He turned back to Willow and forgot his pain at the sight of this woman scowling in front of him. Willow looked the same as in high school, yet for some reason, he'd never taken much notice of her then. Maybe because he'd been a self-absorbed geek who pretended he was more into dragons than girls to hide the sting of their disinterest. Plus, he'd been too busy feeling sorry for himself over his father's rejection to have time for any other feelings.

Willow had the same thick, dark hair, almost black in a certain light. She was short and petite, with just the right curves to make jeans and a khaki shirt look amazing. In his inexpert opinion, he didn't think she was wearing any make-up. With her round face and soft features, she looked younger than her age, naïve. Her attitude, all self-assured and tough, was anything but, and it was killing him. Sexy as hell. She might be shooting daggers at him with those green eyes, but all it did was turn him on.

So yeah, she looked the same as in high school, but also like a million times hotter. Confident, in charge, and unwilling to take crap off anyone, he was sure. In other words, just his type. Being raised by a single mother had given him a well-developed appreciation for self-reliant women, and Willow struck him as particularly independent. He cleared his throat, afraid it was becoming obvious he was staring if he didn't do something to break the silence.

Before he could speak, Willow said, "Do you have a muffin basket there?" in the same sort of tone a person might ask if someone had leprosy.

"Uh, yeah." Jake shifted the pole saw and balanced it against his right shoulder so he could hold the basket out to her. "From the Flour Power Bakery."

She took it and lifted the red and white checked cloth that came with their most expensive gift basket. What seemed like a good idea this morning now made him feel like an idiot version of Little Red Riding Hood bringing a basket of goodies to his grandmother.

"Please don't tell me you have a gluten intolerance," he said.

She covered the muffins back up. "Nope."

"It's nothing," he said, although she hadn't thanked him. Jake cleared his throat again. "Consider it an apology. Lindsay, uh, she told me about your dad and all. If I'd known, I never would've—"

"It's fine." Willow's face flushed. Whether from anger or embarrassment, he wasn't sure.

"It's not fine. It was in poor taste. So, yeah. I'm sorry."

"Okay."

A bird screeched nearby, a majestic cry he associated with purple mountain's majesty and American flags. "Whoa. Toby told me you have a rescue here. Birds of prey or something?"

She nodded. "Tree Top Raptor Center."

"That's cool." The piercing cry came again. "Was that an eagle?"

Jake watched the struggle within Willow, a battle between wanting to talk to him about the birds and wanting to say as little as possible. He could guess which would win out. In high school, she'd carried a battered leather backpack with an eagle on it. It looked like something a Vietnam vet who rode motorcycles might wear, not a teenage girl, and it had earned her a fair amount of teasing. Especially from his sister. He remembered with a cringe. He hadn't known Willow very well in school, but even he'd been aware of her obsession with birds. She'd been as shy as he was and hardly talked. When she did, it was about hawks and owls and falcons.

She was going to talk to him now. She wouldn't be able to resist. Sure enough, something shifted in her face. Her lips pressed together as if trying to hold it in, and then her mouth opened. "People always think eagles make that noise, but they don't. Red-tailed hawks do. They use their vocalization in movies for eagles. That was probably our red-tail, Albert."

"Albert. I bet there's a story behind that." He smiled. She didn't return it. "Okay, let's get to that tree."

"Yep." She turned to lead him through the winding, sun-dappled path through the forest. He wasn't a jerk, so he didn't stare at her ass, but he was human, and gave it a quick check. It was exceptional. Jake forced himself to draw even with her and keep his gaze ahead to the small clearing in the center of the tree houses. This was his first look at them in daylight.

"The tree houses are amazing," he said. "Really beautiful."

"They are, aren't they?" Her face thawed as Jake landed on what was clearly another winning topic of conversation for Willow.

"It looks like they grew out of the trees. Like something out of a fantasy world."

"Yeah, at first the architect kept giving me these mundane plans. I mean, they might have been okay for a dad building his kids a tree house, but I wanted something really special." She didn't look at him while she spoke, like she was loath to do so and was pretending he was someone else. "I sent along a message that I wanted a cross between Endor and Rivendell."

"Rivendell? That's Lord of the Rings, right?" He kept his voice innocent so she wouldn't know his childhood dog had been named Aragorn.

"Yeah. Anyway, it's like the architect and I had a mind meld. They delivered with exactly what I'd been envisioning."

"Really?" Jake rocked back on his heels and tried to hide the twitch of his mouth with vigorous nodding. "Toby and his crew did a stand-up job of making that vision a reality, didn't they?"

"He sure did. I have to give that to him. Even if he pulls stupid pranks all the time. Or makes other people do them for him."

Jake ignored that. "Do you happen to have the name of the architect? I'm going to be building my own house in Cedar Beach just as soon as I find the right property."

"Don't *you* know the architect's name?" She eyed him suspiciously. "I thought you're working with Toby."

"I'm just coming on board. Haven't met everyone yet. What's his name?"

"I don't know. Everything went through Toby. Ask him. Also, it could be a her."

"What?"

Two lines appeared between her dark eyebrows. "The architect. You asked what *his* name is, but architects can be female too, you know."

"Of course they can. But you might be interested—what the hell is that?" Jake pointed at the madrone. "This is what you were talking about?"

Her face paled, and she nodded slowly.

Jake experienced an odd mix of fascination and revulsion and crossed the remaining open space of the clearing to reach the tree. His gaze moved up, up, up to the broken branch above him. A sick vertigo overwhelmed him at the thought he'd been standing up there last night—and then hanging from the branch just below. That wasn't the only cause of the mild sickness he felt. From the broken branch leaked a long, wide trail of sap the color of blood, bright against the smooth trunk.

"Is this normal?" Willow demanded, like he was responsible. Well, he supposed he was responsible for the broken branch, but the sap being weird? Not his fault.

"I can't say I know a lot about Pacific madrones."

"Is their sap supposed to be like that? Like . . . like—"

"Blood?"

"Yeah." Her lip curled up in disgust.

"I don't know. There's a tree in Africa that does this. I read about it once in a National Geographic." Jake leaned forward, and though he didn't want to, he felt compelled to touch it with his first two fingers like a cop in a seventies film. "It's not sticky." His own lip curled, and he held up his fingers to her and rubbed them against his thumb. "It feels like blood, too."

"I hate this tree." She let out a long breath. "I told Toby not to build in it."

"Why?"

Willow looked at him for a while. "It's just—it's kind of creepy, don't you think?"

He acted like he needed to consider this, taking some time to look across its expanse of sprawling, gnarled branches. "I guess." No, he *knew*. He knew what she was talking about, but it sounded crazy. He didn't like this tree either, didn't like it on a deep and primal level, and yeah, it was creepy as hell.

He suppressed a small shudder at the bloodstained tree. It was chilly in the deep shadows of the madrone. Willow didn't say anything, and as another awkward silence stretched out, Jake noticed something. It was *silent*. With the exception of the hawk earlier, there was no sound of birds, no rustling of small animals in the forest. Above him, the madrone's slick, dark leaves swayed with a sibilant hush. There was no wind soughing through the other trees, and no explanation for the movement of the leaves in this one.

"Yeah," he said. "It's kind of spooky."

"My family always called it The Old Tree. Because, you know, it's so old." She gave him a half-smile. "When I was a kid, I thought—" Willow tapped her hand over her mouth a couple times.

"What? What did you think?"

She blinked at him, then looked away. "Nothing. I'm being dumb."

"No, tell me."

"It'll just make me sound like a lunatic."

"I promise I won't think—"

"That saw isn't long enough."

"What?"

Willow pointed at his pole saw. "The saw." She pointed up at the branch. "It's not going to reach."

"It gets longer." His face warmed. Did that sound dirty?

She smirked at him, confirming his fears. He ignored it and set to unscrewing the pole to its full length, where a curved vicious blade perched at the end. It was a great tool for sawing branches off a tree from the ground.

Well, shit. She was right. It wouldn't quite reach the broken limb, and the spiral staircase wasn't positioned right under the branch. He stared up at the tree house. "You mind if I take the screen out of the upstairs window? I can get to it that way." He set down his toolbox and collapsed the telescoping pole down so it would fit inside the tree house.

"Go ahead. You probably remember how to take out the window screen from last night." She gave him a pointed look. "Let me go grab the tree house key."

Willow started back up the path toward the yellow shack. *Don't leave me here alone,* he wanted to call after her. *Not with this bloody tree.* It was such a cowardly thought, he made himself head up the spiraling staircase. The leaves shivered in the nonexistent breeze, and that same whispering noise came again, like faraway murmuring. If he listened too hard, it would be easy to imagine words in the sound.

He stood at the top of the stairs and waited for Willow's return. From his high vantage point, he could see her disappear inside the shack, leaving him truly alone in the forest. A familiar sensation tickled his stomach. His childhood best friend in California had a basement, with a door made of paned glass. That was a bad idea if ever he'd heard one. The basement door was located across from the bathroom. As a kid, whenever he needed the bathroom at his friend's house, Jake would first make himself cup his hands on the glass of the basement door and look down the steep, dark steps. The most delicious fear would fill him with a sense of giddiness until he couldn't stand it any longer, and he'd run across the hall and slam the bathroom door.

That same rising fear filled him now, but without any of the childish fun. His impulse to run away was the same, and he just might have done so if he hadn't seen Willow reappear from the shack. He let out the breath he'd been holding and watched her progress. She looked so small down there among the trees. Her footsteps didn't make much noise on the spiraling steps as she made her way up.

She pushed past him, close enough to feel her body heat, and unlocked the tree house door. She held out a slender hand to indicate he should go inside. It was like she didn't want to go in there. He didn't feel much like it, either. The dim interior of the house was unwelcoming. He knew Willow had begged Toby to put a wood-burning stove in here, even though it meant a lot of mitigation measures for fire safety. He could see why she wanted it, though. It was May, and it was freezing in here. How would it feel in winter?

"Other than me scaring Lindsay, did she and Toby enjoy their night here?" He tried to sound casual and took a reluctant step inside.

"Toby was kind of hungover this morning, and as a rule, I don't talk to your sister."

Jake felt stupid. "Yeah, I get it. She was pretty awful to me, too. Blamed me for breaking up her family."

Willow rolled her eyes. "Of course she did. Like it was your fault for being born."

For one brief, wonderful moment, Jake felt they were on the same side. Then he paused at his betrayal, remembering he was trying to make amends with his sister. "Would you believe me if I told you she's changed? I mean, she's still Lindsay, but she's also not the same as before."

Willow's face closed off, telling him just how much hurt his sister had inflicted on her. "Makes no difference to me."

"Right. I better get that branch down. Make sure the area below stays clear." Her lips pressed together, bristling at his order. *Oops.* He needed to work on asking rather than telling.

"Nobody's out here," she said. "The cleaning crew doesn't come for another hour."

"Can you please just wait down there for me and make sure no one comes along, just in case?" And not leave me alone, he wanted to add.

"Fine." Willow didn't seem to need much excuse to beat a hasty retreat down the stairs.

He wished he could do the same. Everything in the tree house was fresh and new, decorated with yellow and white fabrics as if to ward off the gloom. But it wasn't working. Something in the very air around this tree was dark. He pushed the idea away.

With his injured arm, Jake struggled to make it up the ladder-like staircase with the unwieldy pole saw. A bedroom with pitched ceilings waited upstairs. It was even darker than the floor below, high in the thick branches and foliage, with only one window.

His arm pulsed with pain after the climb. More blood seeped through the bandage. It seemed a fitting punishment. Dress up like The Bandage Man like a complete asshat and get hurt enough to earn a real bandage. He sniffed, catching some scent. A quick glance at the rumpled bed showed where his sister had spent the night with Toby. It didn't smell like bodies, that mix of sweat and personal products. Unless Toby or his sister used rotten egg deodorant. He wrinkled his nose. Sulfur. Wasn't that what hell smelled like? He waved his hand in front of his face and crossed to the window.

The screen stuck for a few moments before giving way all of a sudden. His left arm slammed into the window frame, and he cursed at the fresh wave of pain. The red on the bandage bloomed like a flower and spread to fill the entire square of gauze. As soon as he finished this job, he'd inspect it and give it a new dressing. For now, he just wanted to get this over with and get the hell away from this tree.

Jake leaned out of the window. If anything, the smell got worse. A few feet below, the broken tree limb hung from a splintered mess of red-stained wood. The weird sap oozed from the center of it, and he suspected he'd found the source of the stench. He wasn't afraid of heights, but that same sense of vertigo hit him again seeing how high he'd been last night. He was very fortunate to have caught the branch below.

He thought of a daredevil kid he'd known from the school in Santa Cruz where his mom enrolled him after leaving Cedar Beach. The guy got unlucky with a nasty fall from his skateboard going down the rail of a concrete staircase leading to the beach. He'd landed on the edge of one of the steps and broken his neck. The guy spent a decade as a quadriplegic before killing himself shortly after their ten-year reunion. Not that Jake had gone.

Jake couldn't imagine anything worse than being trapped in his own body. High school reunions were a close second.

On the ground, Willow lifted her hand in acknowledgement. "All clear."

He shoved away the unpleasant thoughts of that poor guy and reached for the pole saw. It took some maneuvering to get it out the window and into the optimal position to begin sawing. *Rasp, rasp, rasp.* The vibrations traveled up his arms, causing a deep ache in his left one. The bandage was now saturated with blood. A gust of wind kicked up, and his eyes teared, blurring his vision. He kept going. It would all be over soon. The glossy leaves of the madrone shivered. Jake fought the current of unease that moved through him like the vibrations of the sawing.

"Stay back," he shouted down to Willow. "It's going to fall any second now."

"Yeah, I was just going to walk right under it," she shouted back.

The uneasiness lodged in his gut and coalesced into a hard ball of dread. He had the craziest notion the tree was pissed off at him, like its anger pulsed around him. He sawed faster, anxious to be done with the vile chore.

"There it goes."

*Crack!* The branch hurtled to the ground below with a rattle of leaves and twigs. A cloud of dust puffed up from the ground. The red sap oozing out of the cut end of the branch made it look like a severed limb of flesh.

He blew out a breath of relief. Wind gusted through the treetops. He rushed to replace the screen and lock the window. His arm protested again as he shimmied down the ladder with the saw. He missed the bottom step and landed on the first floor with a bone-jarring thud.

Willow was shouting outside. He threw open the front door of the tree house to find the gusts of wind had grown strong enough to make all the trees in the forest whip their branches to and fro.

"Come on," Willow said.

Jake sped down the spiraling stairs until he was dizzy. He reached the bottom when the wind blew so hard he had to grab the railing to steady himself. "Whoa."

Willow's dark hair swirled around and slapped her face like an angry octopus had attached itself to her head. It might have been funny if it weren't so disturbing. Jake staggered to her, fighting for each step. Willow shielded her eyes with her arm.

"Leave your tools," she ordered. "We need to make a run for it."

Jake couldn't agree more. He tossed his pole saw next to his toolbox and started running.

The wind died down for a second, and that's when he heard the voice in the tree.

# Chapter 4

In the brief lull in the wind, Willow stared at the tree, at the grim streaks of red sap running down the trunk, which had only grown since Jake removed the branch. She shouldn't have let him do it. As soon as he'd started sawing, she'd felt that same malevolent feeling from last night emanating from the tree. It was stupid, but she couldn't help thinking the tree didn't like what Jake was doing.

For a second, she caught a voice in the whispering leaves. *You will die.*

Goosebumps covered her arms. "No," she whispered back. Just her imagination, her memory replaying that day she found the dead squirrel and heard that phrase. Still, no reason to stick around. She ran after Jake.

Without warning, Willow was moving through a tornado of forest debris. Pine needles and small twigs stung her cheeks. The rough cedar shingles from the roofs of the tree houses began pulling up and flying through the air. She tried to run faster, but the force of the wind made it impossible to do all but stagger forward in lurches. She was grateful Connor was at his friend's house and hoped the birds were okay, that everyone working at the raptor center was rushing into the outbuildings and getting themselves to safety.

A branch thick as her arm cracked off a nearby tree and flew in her direction.

"Watch out!" Jake stepped in front of her, and the branch smacked him in the face.

"Oh my God, are you all right?"

Jake didn't answer, nor did he need to. The blood blossoming from his mouth and nose was answer enough. He held out his arm to her, and when she ignored him, he tucked her against his side and half-dragged her through the shrieking wind, sheltering her with his warm body.

"I can't see," he shouted. His eyes squeezed shut, and tears streamed down his cheeks.

Willow led him toward the house, and they dragged each other up the steps and inside. The door slammed shut behind them.

Jake reached out in front of him like a blind man. Freya trotted over and sniffed his legs.

"Who's that?" He felt around with his hands. Willow didn't miss the way they trembled. She was glad Jake had his eyes closed so he couldn't see her entire body shaking with fear.

Freya either forgot about Jake's stunt in the tree or was quick to forgive. She licked his fingers in greeting.

"You might remember my lab, Freya, from last night."

"Hey, Freya. No hard feelings, okay?" Jake fumbled to pat her on the head.

"Here." Willow helped him to the kitchen table, and he lowered himself into a chair and cradled his face in his hands.

Jake Bartlett was in her kitchen. Her heart hammered like the Oregon State marching band drumline. Half the reason was that freakish windstorm, and the other half was having a Bartlett in her house. She was a mouse who'd just let the cat into her home.

As if summoned by the thought of cats, Rex jumped into Jake's lap, and he yelped. "What's that?" He reached out to feel around. "Do you have a pet bobcat?"

She forced a laugh. "Close. A Maine coon."

"He's huge."

"Yep. Rex, leave him alone," she said.

"I don't mind. I like cats." Jake stroked Rex, and the traitor purred loudly.

Rex was usually a good judge of character, but Willow supposed nobody was perfect. Freya settled herself at Jake's feet with a dramatic Labrador groan, resting her head on his shoe.

"You're like a regular Snow White there." She ran her fingers through her hair and came away with a leaf and a handful of pine needles. "Let me get you a washcloth."

"Thanks. I think I have half a tree in my eyes." Jake sucked in a pained breath and clutched at her cat. Even for Rex, he was being remarkably tolerant to continue sitting on this stranger's lap. "What the hell was all that? I've never seen anything like it."

"Microburst or something. Don't know. I'll be right back." She dashed into the downstairs bathroom to retrieve a couple of washcloths. She caught sight of herself in the bathroom mirror. A small cut bled above her eyebrow, and her cheeks were chapped and red. If Jake hadn't stepped in front of her, she'd look a whole lot worse. Willow took a deep breath and knew what she had to do.

She returned to the kitchen to the pitiful sight of Jake. Blood oozed from his nose and smeared his top lip. His bottom lip was split and bled on to his chin. Splashes of blood dotted the front of his green shirt. Like a child with a teddy bear, he hugged Rex close to him, and her heart squeezed in sympathy.

"Maybe you should rinse your eyes at the sink?"

Despite his blind and injured state, Jake gently set Rex on the floor and got to his feet, careful to move around Freya. Willow led him to the kitchen tap and instructed him to use handfuls of water to wash out his eyes.

"Did that help?" she asked.

"Maybe. It's stopped," he said. "Did you notice?"

At first, she thought he meant the pain. Then she realized. Looking out the kitchen window, the forest stood quiet and still, like any ordinary early summer's day.

"Here." She wet a folded washcloth and handed it to him. "Um, let me get you cleaned up."

She settled him back in the chair. While he pressed the washcloth to his eyes, she used another cloth to gently wipe his mouth and face. He hissed when she dabbed at a deep gash on his forehead. She hadn't noticed it before because it was almost into his hairline. Tending to his injuries helped distract her from their terrifying experience with The Old Tree.

And the fact she had her hands on Walter Bartlett's son. *Geez, Willow, he's not the devil's spawn.* Even if Walter Bartlett might be the devil.

"Thank you," she said stiffly. "For protecting me from that branch."

He grunted. "Thanks for cleaning me up."

"I think you need to go to the hospital. You could have a scratched cornea. And that cut on your head will need stitches."

"Will it?" His shoulders hunched in alarm, and Willow was seized with the need to comfort him, but wasn't sure how. She'd been mothering her brother for years, but dealing with grown men? Not so much. And never men this outrageously handsome. Not that it mattered. Still, Willow felt herself unusually flustered around him.

"I think the stinging is going away." Jake lifted the washcloth and squinted at her from those eyes, now ringed in red. He squeezed them shut again with a wince.

"Try blinking slowly."

He followed her instructions and pulled his mouth down as if testing his face's ability to move. His bottom lip bled more freely again.

"Don't do that."

"Eyes are definitely better. Which makes me realize how much everything else hurts." He gingerly put his fingers to his mouth and examined the blood on them.

"Your teeth okay?"

He ran his tongue around his mouth and lips. For some reason, Willow blushed and looked away.

"Can I use your bathroom? I wanna take a look at myself."

He was going to regret that, she was sure. Willow showed him to the half-bath. While he was in there, she used the moment to call Maureen's cell.

"Hey, Boss, what's up?"

"Just checking everyone is safe. All our birds okay?"

"Of course."

"I've got a little situation here. I might need to take somebody to the hospital."

"The hospital?"

"Yeah, yeah. It's all right. Somebody was helping me take down a broken branch and got hurt in all that. As soon as I get back, I'll head over to the center and help clean up the debris."

"Debris?"

"Yeah, it must be a mess."

"Uh, not particularly. We're done cleaning the mews."

"There's no way you could have cleaned up all the mess already. The wind only stopped a couple of minutes ago."

"What wind?"

"From that crazy windstorm that blew up out of nowhere."

A muffled sound came as Maureen shifted her phone and spoke to someone else. "The quail can go in that freezer there." Back to Willow again. "What are you talking about?"

Willow's fingers tightened on her phone. "There's no way you could've missed it. The wind was insane. It ripped a bunch of shingles off the tree houses. Knocked down branches. In fact, that's why this guy needs the hospital. He got hit in the face with a tree branch."

"That sounds unfortunate, Boss, but don't know what to tell you. Been nothing but a few sprinkles here and there. Not even a breeze to speak of."

A tremor ran down Willow's arm, and she sank onto the kitchen chair. The raptor center was about two hundred yards from her house. How concentrated could a microburst be?

*You're still going with a microburst?* asked the snarky little voice in her head. She licked her lips a couple of times, struggling to come up with a response. Maureen beat her to it.

"Listen, Elvis wants to talk to you for a sec."

More muffled noises and then, "Hi, Willow."

"Hi, Elvis." Despite the circumstances, she smiled at his deep voice. "What's up?"

"Just got off the phone with a lady who lives right up the road. She says there's a big old owl in her back yard that's scaring her children."

"How exactly is it scaring her children?"

"She didn't say. Only that it was injured. One of its wings is dragging. Said she approached it, and it tried to attack her. She'd like if we could come get the owl as soon as possible." He paused. "Called it a devil bird and wants it gone right away."

People could get superstitious about owls. Willow knew that better than anyone.

"She said it's the creepiest bird she's ever seen," Elvis added helpfully.

Maybe it was because of what just happened out at The Old Tree, but a chill slid over Willow's scalp and down the back of her neck, something viscous and unpleasant like someone had cracked an icy egg on her head. "Well, I might be tied up for a while. Do you think you and Maureen can handle it?"

"Hey, Mo," Elvis called. "Boss wants to know if you and me can handle that devil owl?"

Willow could hear Maureen answer, "Damn straight we can."

"Thanks, Elvis," Willow said. "Tell Maureen thanks, too,

and you two be careful."

"We will. Don't worry, I already called Curtis."

"Good idea." Willow wasn't thinking straight if she hadn't reminded him to call their vet. She hesitated. "You didn't notice any crazy wind just a little while ago?"

"Can't say I did." He sounded puzzled but didn't inquire further.

They said goodbye, and Willow got up and crossed to the window over the kitchen sink. Sure enough, broken branches and leaf litter peppered her unfenced back yard and the visible forest beyond. She let out a long sigh. Did she think she'd imagined what happened earlier?

"Hey."

Willow jumped and turned around to face Jake. After his trip to the bathroom, he looked even worse. His nose was swelling, and it was clear he'd have a good shiner soon.

"You're probably right about the hospital," he said. "I'll call Toby and ask him to take me."

"He needs to be here for the inspection today."

He leaned against the counter, looking a little woozy. "Okay. I'll drive myself."

"No way. That's a bad idea. Isn't there someone else who can take you?" She couldn't stand to think of the man, but she made herself choke out the words. "What about your dad?"

He snorted. "Didn't you hear? My dad's dying, Willow. That's why I'm here."

"Oh." She should say sorry or something, except, horrible as that might make her, she wasn't sorry. That man ruined her father, and she couldn't feel too sad about Walter Bartlett dying. "That's difficult," was all she managed.

"Yeah."

"What about . . . your sister?" She couldn't bring herself to say Lindsay's name.

He shook his head. "She left on a work trip."

"Sure. No doubt scouting for more old-growth virgin forests

to destroy."

"She doesn't work for my dad's company anymore." He licked his dry lips. "She's working as a paralegal in a law firm. Going to law school to be an environmental lawyer."

"Wow. Okay." It felt like someone told her Stalin was actually the Easter Bunny. "Your dad must love that idea, right?"

Jake snorted. "Oh, yeah."

Willow tapped her hand on the side of her thigh and studied Jake. In her mind, she saw that branch barreling toward her head, Jake stepping in front of her. He'd taken it to the face. For her. She'd miss the inspection, but Toby would be here. What else could she do? "I'll drive you to the hospital."

—

Willow didn't do small talk, and Jake looked to be suffering too much for it, anyway. The first few miles of the drive passed in a silence punctuated by Jake sniffling thickly through his bloodied nose. His face was swelling more with each passing minute. Her Subaru hummed along the highway, and a light drizzle fell across the windshield. The hypnotic sounds lulled her, and the silence was more agreeable than she might have expected.

"Willow?" She'd grown so comfortable in the quiet, that when Jake spoke, it startled her. "What do you think that was about?" he asked.

"What do you mean?" She knew exactly what he meant.

"That wind." His voice came out nasal. "This sounds—okay, this sounds crazy, but it kind of felt like that wind started as soon as that branch came down."

"Coincidence." It was no coincidence.

"Uh, I don't think so." He rested his head against the passenger window. "Something weird is going on."

She recalled once more that feeling of something evil, something rotten and angry in the darkness behind her last night. She thought of the bloody sap leaking out of The Old Tree, and the feeling of dread when Jake was working on it.

Twice, she almost started to tell him Maureen hadn't noticed any windstorm at the raptor center but decided to say nothing.

"You think so, too, don't you?" he asked. "It was really weird, right?"

Willow didn't reply, but the look on Jake's distorted face told her he took that as agreement. While she wouldn't admit it, of course, it was weird. It was more than weird. It was frightening. Everything about that tree made her feel ill.

She'd been trying to avoid thinking about it, but now another unpleasant memory of the madrone came flooding back. It had been a year before her dad died. She'd found him one afternoon sitting under The Old Tree in a daze. He had a crossbow in his left hand and a gun she'd never known he owned in his right.

"Dad?" she'd said carefully. "What are you doing?"

"I told Walter," Dad muttered. His eyes were unfocused, his face drawn.

"What?" she'd asked, afraid. "What did you tell Mr. Bartlett?"

"It's happening again. At least, I think it is. Or it could."

"What's happening?"

"I can't—I can't face it." His hand had twitched on the gun. For a moment, she'd imagined him turning it on himself. Was that what he was doing under the tree? Contemplating ending it all?

"Dad, you're scaring me."

Something crossed his face then. His clouded eyes cleared, and he looked up at her as if only just realizing she was there. "Hey, Willie-Boo. I'm sorry." He shook his head. "Just lost in some stupid, depressing thoughts, but I'm okay." He'd climbed to his feet and brushed past her, not meeting her eye. "How about I grill us some burgers for dinner?"

She'd tried to ask him about it after dinner, but he shut down the conversation. They never spoke of the episode again, and Willow hadn't seen the gun before or since her father's death. The tires squealed as she turned onto the road, and she eased off the accelerator.

"There was something else," Jake said. "Right after I finished sawing off the branch."

The ocean spread like a gray silver disc as Willow guided the car down the ribbon of highway and waited for Jake to expound. Finally, she prompted him. "What? What was it?"

"I thought I heard—"

"What?" She gripped the steering wheel tighter. What she'd heard was impossible, nothing more than the brain's uncontrollable tendency to find patterns that weren't there. She'd been scared by the wind blowing through the tree's leaves, and it had triggered the memory of what she thought she'd heard as a kid. But if Jake had heard the same thing, she'd have no explanation. A shared delusion? "What did you think you heard?"

"You know, forget it."

Willow opened her mouth to ask him if he'd heard the tree talking, but she couldn't make herself speak.

The rest of the drive passed in silence, but now it felt strained. When she pulled up in front of the hospital's ER entrance, it was with a relief so profound, she wanted to cry.

He climbed out of the car and leaned his good arm on the door to peer in at her. "Thanks for the ride. I'll take an Uber back to your place later to get my truck."

He walked through the automatic doors, shoulders slumped, and disappeared inside. To her surprise, Willow found herself pulling the Subaru into a parking space.

# Chapter 5

Jake clutched the white paper bag containing antibiotics and painkillers and came out the double doors to the waiting room. God, he hated needles, and it seemed like he'd endured an unfair amount of them this afternoon. He lifted his brows a few times, feeling the pull of the stitches at his hairline. Bad call. His swollen eye pulsed at the movement. He hoped those painkillers they gave him would start working soon.

He wanted to go home more than anything, and it hit him with a shock of remembrance that he didn't really have one anymore. He moved from Santa Cruz just four days ago. Most of his stuff was in storage until he built his own house. Or maybe just a house to sell to someone else, but he was going to build one. For now, he was renting a tiny studio by the month. It was over an ice cream shop on the main drag of Cedar Beach, and its one redeeming feature was it always smelled of waffle cones. He was a bachelor, and Spartan living didn't bother him. Hell, he'd happily camp in a tent once he'd figured out what piece of land to buy here.

But right now, with his head and face pounding, he really wished he had a proper bed where he could collapse. Instead, he'd have to tuck himself up on a crappy old futon that smelled of stale pizza and was about as comfortable as a pile of cinder blocks. He pulled his phone from his pocket to call a taxi when he noticed the waiting room wasn't empty. One person was waiting.

"Willow?" She looked even more gorgeous than before. Everything pulsed with a beautiful, soft light. The potted plant in the corner, the rack of colorful magazines. "What are you still doing here? Don't you have the inspection?"

The ER was quiet, and they'd gotten him in and out relatively fast, but still. She must have been sitting there for a good two hours.

"I—uh. I wanted to talk to you. About earlier." She bit her left thumbnail for a moment. "What did the doctor say?"

"They think I'll live. No concussion. My mom always said I have a hard head." He laughed. "Nose isn't broken. Lip should heal fine. Seven stitches here." He pulled up his hair, and she leaned in to inspect the line of sutures like spider legs perched on his forehead. In her concentration, her lips parted, and he could smell her watermelon gum. It made him crazy for a second with the impulse to kiss her. He took a step back instead. "They weren't impressed by any of the damage today, really. But this from last night?" He lifted his left forearm. "This got them real excited. The doctor said it's infected. They want me to watch for any red lines around the wound. Gave me a shot in my ass and sent me home with some goodies." He held up the bag of antibiotics.

"It's infected? Already? Seems fast."

"They thought so, too, but I guess it's because there were some splinters in there."

Something crossed her face, there and gone. He wasn't sure, but it looked like disgust. Or worse, fear. Did she feel as revolted as he did at the thought of splinters from *that* tree under his skin, in his body?

He blustered on. "It's not often they see someone skewer themselves on a tree branch. Like a—like a human shish kabob."

She cradled her elbows in her hands. Definitely fear on her face. "I still don't understand how you did that."

"When that branch snapped, I fell, right?" He put one hand on top of the other and slid the top hand quickly past the bottom. "As I fell past it, I snagged my arm on the splintered sharp bit." He wiggled his pinky finger to symbolize the broken branch.

"How the hell did you not fall out of that tree?"

"Disappointed I didn't?" He grinned, his uneasiness evaporating like water on a hot sidewalk. A wave of euphoria washed over him.

"Of course not."

"Aw, thanks." He ducked his head. "I *knew* you liked me."

"No. I'm just relieved there won't be bad publicity from some idiot falling out of a tree and dying at my new hotel."

"Yeah, you're lucky I caught myself on the next branch. All thanks to these abs of steel." He slapped his belly a few times, but she didn't laugh. Uh-oh. What if she didn't think he was joking? Well, his abs *were* pretty cut, but he was trying to make a joke about the whole thing. Great. Now he sounded like a conceited bastard, which people always assumed he was. Lately, he'd been trying to downplay his looks with a scruffy appearance. That seemed to be backfiring. The older woman who owned the apartment over the ice cream shop would've rented the place to him for free if he'd let her. She'd flirted so shamelessly he was embarrassed for her. He was like some kind of lady—lady, what? His mind swam and struggled to find a word for something irresistible.

"Catnip!" he said.

"Excuse me?"

"Lady catnip." He was irresistible to the ladies, and it had caused him no small amount of trouble over the years, no matter how much he tried to offset his looks. Fortunately, the tree today had helped him out in that department. He giggled.

"What?"

"Just thinking about that saying about falling out of the ugly tree and hitting every limb on the way down."

"Yeah, you're not so pretty anymore." Willow tilted her beautiful head at him. "Hey, I'm curious. Did they happen to give you painkillers back there?"

"Yep." He cocked his own head, and it felt like water sloshed in his skull. So *that* was why he couldn't think straight anymore. "I think they're starting to kick in, too. Wait, did you just say I'm not pretty *anymore?* So, you thought I was pretty before?"

"You ready to go?"

"Born ready." Those drugs really *were* taking effect. His mom warned him everyone in their family reacted strongly to painkillers. He yawned and winced as his split lip stretched. "Thanks for waiting for me, Willow." He threw his arm around her shoulders, which she immediately shoved off. His arm fell heavily to his side. "You ever think about how you have a tree house hotel and a Tree Top Raptor Center, and your name is Willow? Like the tree?"

"No, man. Never crossed my mind once."

"Really?"

"No, not really."

"How'd you get your name?"

"My mom." Her face reddened. "She called me Willow because she said it meant I'd be strong and flexible."

"Ooh. Flexible." He waggled his eyebrows, sending stabs of regret through his forehead and aching eye.

"I'll bring the car around." She marched out the automatic doors and left him swaying in front of the reception desk. The woman sitting there gave him a small wave and a wink. He winked back with his good eye.

Lady. Catnip.

—

As soon as Willow loaded him into the car, he fell asleep and didn't wake up until Willow's crappy old brown Outback crunched onto the gravel parking lot and pulled up beside his truck. He opened his eyes. Well, he opened his eye. His right eye had sealed itself shut.

"Eduardo," he said happily.

"Eduardo?"

"My truck."

"Your truck's name is Eduardo?"

"Yep. After this friend I used to work with, because that guy was built like a two-ton truck. Doesn't everybody name their car?" He surreptitiously wiped a line of drool from his chin.

"I saw that," she said. "In case you were wondering, yes, you were snoring, too."

"I don't snore."

"Well, then, you do after painkillers." Willow turned off the engine, but she was still gripping the steering wheel, looking between him and Eduardo.

"What? What is it?" he asked.

"You clearly can't drive in your current state."

"Oh, uh. My driver's license is for California, but I'm pretty sure I can still drive in Oregon." Realization dawned. "Ohhhh. My current state." He circled a finger near his temple.

"Talk about loopy. Seriously, what did they give you?"

"Uh, some Vicodin."

"You can't handle your drugs worth shit." She gave him a disgusted look.

"My mom gets all silly on pain meds. Guess I'm the same. That's why I don't do drugs. I need you to know that, Willow." He put his hand over his heart. "I know you think I'm a dick, but I'm not. Honest. And I don't do drugs." He leaned his head against the passenger window.

"I don't think you're a dick, Jake." She sighed and turned

the engine back on. A few moments later—he must have drifted off again because he had no memory of driving there—she was parking in front of her house.

"Your beautiful house," he said.

"Okay, here's the deal. I need to talk to Toby about the inspection and check in at the raptor center. You nap in my guest room and hopefully by the time I get back, you'll be ready to go home. How's that sound?"

She helped him out of the car and into the house.

"Your house is really nice," he said, as she led him through the living room. "I love the river rock around the fireplace." He waved his hand around in a loose circle. "And it looks like you use it. Good. I hate people who have fireplaces, and they don't even use them."

"Uh-huh." Willow guided him upstairs and into the first room on the left. "Here's the guest room."

"Oh, this bed looks amazing." He stumbled forward and ran his hands over the quilt, covered with sea horses, of all things. Sea horses! "Sea horses are so cool."

He took off his shoes and started to lay down before he noticed his bloody shirt. "Oops. I don't want to get this on your pretty sea horses." He grabbed the shirt's hem and pulled it up, but it got caught on his chin. "Ow. Ow. Help me."

"Stop. Stop it, Jake."

Willow drew closer. "You smell like trees," he said, from inside his T-shirt. "And girl."

"Move your arm down."

He cooperated the best he could. At last, she got one arm and then the other out, and he was free. He collapsed back onto the double bed and winced. She studied him for a moment, then turned to the closet to retrieve a blanket, and covered him.

"Did you know you're beautiful, Willow Duncan?"

"Did you know you're high on drugs, Jake Bartlett?"

"But it's true. I thought it earlier today. Before the drugs. You're super beautiful." He patted the bed beside him. "Do you want to lay down with me? I mean, not like in a pervy way. Just maybe keep me company?"

"You're adorable, but I have to get to work."

"You think I'm adorable?" He hugged the extra pillow to his face and fell asleep with a smile.

# Chapter 6

Three long aisles of aviaries—or mews—comprised the middle of the raptor center, each fronted by a weathering yard. To the right stood the flight cages for exercising birds, and to the left was a row of permanent residents. Maureen and Elvis stopped staring at the isolation cage to watch Willow as she approached them.

"Sure took you long enough at the hospital," Maureen groused. "Why's your face all red, Boss?"

Her face was all red because holy hell, Jake Bartlett had an insane body, and she'd felt hot and cross since she'd laid eyes on it. She couldn't erase the image of him sprawled on her guest room bed, a crooked grin on his face. And wow, was he not kidding about his abs. His broad chest, lightly dusted with dark hair, that smooth expanse of six-pack. She'd wanted to run her hands down them to the belt of his low-slung jeans and start unbuckling.

It had been months since her last date. Her brain might reject a Bartlett on principle, but her body had no such qualms and was obnoxiously keen to get to know Jake's better. For a second, when he'd suggested she join him in bed, she'd been half-tempted. It shamed her now she was away from that bedroom, dominated by Jake and his strong male smell. The poor guy was injured and drugged, and she was being lecherous. No wonder her face was red.

Maureen was waiting for a response, which only made Willow's face burn more. "I was held up with a problem." Yeah, the problem was she was incredibly turned on by Jake Bartlett.

Maureen didn't look impressed by this answer, but she let it slide. "We got her," she said. "Gave us a run for our money, didn't she, Elvis? And she repaid me with this." Maureen yanked aside her Tree Top shirt by the collar to reveal a deep, glistening scratch arcing over her left shoulder.

Willow whistled. "You disinfected that, right?"

Maureen nodded. "And she got me here, but luckily, not as bad." She tilted her head to show a slight scratch on her neck. "I already named her Acantha after that story with the nymph that clawed Apollo's face."

Cynthia let out a whooping screech from her cage farther down the aisle. "Don't like that name?" Willow turned to look at the spotted owl. Maureen was a fanatical Greek mythology buff, and if Willow let her have her way, every raptor here would be called names like Andromeda or Dionysius. Although, she figured Maureen had a right to name this owl after what the animal had done to her. "That looks so painful."

"I'm lucky it's not worse. That's about the meanest bird I ever met." From Maureen, that might be construed as high praise, but the way she glared at the cage made Willow realize the woman was angry with the animal.

Maybe even a little frightened.

Willow turned to see the source of the woman's anger.

"Wow," she breathed. The owl hunched on a perch in the top corner of the mews, deep in the shadows provided by the metal patio roofing that covered the back half of the enclosure.

Set deep in a dish-shaped face, the eyes of a lion, yellow and just as fierce, stared back at her from one of the largest owls she'd ever seen. "It's huge. You're right. Has to be female at that size." In the owl world, the males were scrawny compared to the females. "A great gray owl." She'd never had a great gray at her raptor center. The tallest owl in North America, the "ghost of the forest" was too elusive, and there were too few living in Oregon. This was a rare find, indeed.

Despite its name, this particular owl had a good deal more brown than gray. Her chest was speckled, and her wings barred in gray and brown. Her wingspan would be well over five feet if she could open them both. For now, the bird held her splinted right wing folded oddly against her body. She shifted from one foot to the other, flexing heavily feathered legs ending in wicked, curved talons. The second talon on the right foot was missing. The intensity of the owl's stare was starting to unnerve Willow, and she was possessed by an odd compulsion to make sure she wasn't the first to look away.

Cynthia continued her strange, high-pitched hoots.

Maureen's voice sounded loud beside her. "Curtis said his best guess is a car hit her. Only clipped her, luckily. The woman who found her has a yard backing to the highway. Car must have grazed the owl and sent it flying into her yard."

"Anything broken?"

"Curtis says it's one clean fracture of the ulna, nowhere near the joints. He's hopeful it will heal, and she can be released one day. The missing toe is an old injury, he said."

With those yellow eyes staring with such malevolence, Willow suddenly wished this owl could be released immediately. What was wrong with her? She loved raptors, and owls were her favorite. It was probably the weird events of the day and seeing the wound this owl inflicted on Maureen, but apprehension stirred in her gut looking at this creature. Also, Cynthia's warning calls weren't helping. She'd never seen the old owl respond to a newcomer like that.

Owls, being nocturnal, held a natural association with death. Their heads could turn almost all the way around, and their nighttime activities and silent flight lent them a mysterious air. Halloween decorations would be lacking without at least an owl or two, and Willow had plenty in her own collection. Lots of superstitions revolved around owls and how they could be a portent of death or doom. Willow loved to disabuse visitors of such silly ideas and found it a point of pride to win over kids and adults alike to the charm of owls.

But this one might just make her throw all those educational talks out the window and fully embrace the idea that owls were harbingers of evil. Why did she show up now, on this very day when Willow thought she'd heard The Old Tree talking to her?

Willow scoffed at her foolishness. It was only an impressively large owl, understandably grouchy from being hit by a car. She made herself approach the mews, edging around to the side to where the owl sat. The owl's head swiveled to track her progress, never blinking or breaking eye contact.

"Hey, there," Willow said softly. "You could be a mascot for Hayley's brewery, couldn't you?" If ever she'd seen a grumpy owl, this was it. For an unpleasant moment, she thought of the menu at the brewery. The front cover sported a drawing of the Grumpy Owl, and the back of the menu described the story of the strix, another urban legend in the area. The strix was an evil owl from Greek mythology that later became associated with vampires and witches and something about eating babies. Willow hadn't bothered reading the menu at Hayley's family place in a while, so she couldn't recall the exact details. Probably for the best right now, considering this owl was staring her down like she wanted to eat *Willow*.

The bird studied her for a few heartbeats more before letting out the odd grunting hoot of the great gray. Then she opened her beak and coughed out the most enormous owl pellet ever.

"Did you see that?" she hissed at Maureen and Elvis. "That pellet is huge." A CubScout troop was coming next weekend for a stint at the outdoor archery range that Willow's father set up when she was a kid. After the archery, the scouts would have a class at the visitor building where they'd dissect owl pellets. This giant pellet would be great for the class.

Willow eased herself to the door of the mews, intent on going in and retrieving it.

"Careful," Elvis said.

Willow opened the door, grateful for the regular oiling that kept its hinges quiet. In front of the main cage was an enclosed yard that served as an airlock to prevent birds from escaping. She approached the second inner door to the cage and opened it. She inched inside the enclosure, stooped over, and picked up the still-warm owl pellet.

The owl regarded her as she might a vole, with an intense focus that made Willow want to flee.

"We'll take good care of you, Acantha." She made her voice warm, even if she felt anything but toward the owl and silently added, *so we can get you the hell out of here.*

As if reading her negative thoughts, the owl hopped along the rope perch toward Willow. She screeched, and Willow backed up to the door, but not in time to avoid getting beat on the head with the owl's good wing. Willow covered her face with her arms. She had the uncanny feeling the owl might try to claw her eyes out. Willow staggered back and slipped out the door of the cage. She slammed it shut and hurried out the second door as if the owl might pursue her.

The great gray continued to screech and beat her good wing in the air.

The northern harrier in the neighboring aviary began to flap around its mews. In a domino effect, the next bird and the next and the next hopped and flapped and screeched and hooted, joining Cynthia's cries as the distress calls snaked down one aisle and up the next until the entire raptor center filled with a panicked cacophony.

Maureen shook her head slowly in disbelief.

Like with the madrone tree earlier today, Willow experienced a sick feeling of dread. It took several minutes for the animals to calm down. She'd never seen anything like it. When the last screeches and hoots died away, a peculiar sort of hush fell over the area.

"She was right," Elvis whispered. "Devil bird."

—

Willow considered checking on Jake before she headed to the Tree Top headquarters, but she was already a few minutes late to meet Toby and the inspector. She jogged up the shivering metal steps and burst into the stuffy trailer. To her annoyance, Toby and the inspector weren't there. Hayley sat at the desk next to Willow's.

"Hey," Hayley said. "Did you see your reviews?" She turned her laptop around. "Check out this one."

"Reviews?" Willow dragged the cracked and peeling faux-leather chair from her desk over to Hayley's and sat beside her to read what her friend had highlighted.

*Five stars!!!*

*The owner of the Tree Top Lodge is gracious and accommodating. And the accommodations! All I can say is wow! I've stayed in a lot of luxury hotels and unique venues, but these tree houses are something else entirely. The experience ignites your inner child of wonder when you get to sleep high in the treetops. I cannot recommend enough. Lindsay B.*

"Lindsay wrote that?" Willow shot Hayley a glance.

She shrugged. "Maybe she feels guilty about how she treated you."

Willow snorted. "Doubtful." She tried to forget how Jake said his sister had changed. Or that their dad was dying. Because the thought now filled her with unexpected sympathy. Hating the Bartletts was a pastime of hers. She wasn't about to let it go any time soon.

The images surrounding her dad's accident came, as they

often did, in a barrage of chaotic memories. The neatly folded union pamphlets stacked on their kitchen table while her father spoke in excited tones about improving work conditions. Willow as a young girl on her father's lap as he explained fair wages. Her grandmother BiBi's face when she picked Willow up from school. *There's been an accident, Willie-Boo. Your dad was walking up to a truck coming into the lumber yard when a chain snapped, and some logs fell off.* Her diminished father hooked up to machines in the hospital. *Traumatic brain injury. Broken vertebrae. Ruptured discs.* Her grandparents' hushed voices at night when they thought Willow was sleeping. *That was no accident. Bartlett didn't like him organizing the workers.* And the disapproving faces of her grandparents when Willow's mother finally came back to town just in time for the nightmare lawsuit with Bartlett's slick lawyers who painted Willow's father as an incompetent drunk for having two beers at lunch before the accident. Lindsay tormenting her at school for the duration of the lawsuit.

And finally, snatches of memories after. Her father struggling in the hardware store to remember the name of someone he'd known for years and then forgetting why he'd come in. His periodic rages, like the time he'd swept everything off the hall entry table and broken her grandmother's carriage clock and made her cry. The stretches of depression where he didn't get out of bed for days, and BiBi brought him meals on the purple metal tray with orange kittens until he felt strong enough to come out of his room again.

Willow shook her head. One five-star review from Lindsay was a tiny water pistol against the inferno of her rage toward the Bartletts.

Toby and the inspector opened the trailer door, bringing a welcome distraction from Willow's dark memories. Toby wore a hangdog expression. Maybe *not* a welcome distraction.

The disheveled inspector wore green relish stains on his chambray shirt from his gas station hot dog lunch, a piece of information he'd felt compelled to share with Willow. His hair stuck up all over his head, and his fingernails were dirty with grime. But for thoroughness on an inspection report, Willow found the man meticulous to a dismaying degree. Not one tiny detail about the tree houses' building and safety codes had gone unchecked.

Twenty minutes later, the inspector and Toby explained the handrails on the staircases, bridges, and balconies of the tree houses failed to pass the safety regulations, thanks to a recent update six months ago that increased height requirements. All of the railings would need to be replaced. If that weren't bad enough, the wiring to the tree houses had been buried one inch shy of the prescribed depth.

While Toby's company would have to eat the cost on the project, Willow would pay the price in lost time. There was no way the custom railings and wiring would be completed for opening day weekend, when she had her first guests booked in just two weeks.

"We'll make this right," Toby said for the tenth time. "I'm short-staffed with my guys moving on to that hospital project up the coast, but I'll do what I can." Willow hadn't said much throughout the conversation. She worried if she opened her mouth to speak, she'd only cry. Hayley's sympathetic looks weren't helping matters. She wished everyone would leave so she could burst into tears. Toby and the inspector finally rose to their feet right as the metal stairs outside clanged with someone's footsteps. Willow waited for one of the staff to enter, but instead, someone knocked on the door.

The inspector opened it, and Toby shot Willow a worried look as two police officers, a man and a woman, entered the trailer. Willow swallowed hard. The face of the officer who delivered the news of her dad's car accident was forever seared in her memory. Her mind flew to Connor. He'd texted earlier to say Ethan invited him to stay for dinner. What if something had happened to him?

"Hello." The woman's tone was somber. She was the most average, nondescript person Willow could recall seeing. Average height, build, and around forty, her plain face was drawn. "I'm Officer Patterson and this is Officer Ortiz."

Officer Ortiz, a stocky Hispanic man with a thick mustache, didn't make eye contact. He shoved his sunglass on top of his head and seemed to be too busy looking around the trailer, taking in the posters of raptors and the three metal desks. His eyes, which already bore a haunted look, widened at the sight of the stuffed owl on a bookshelf, forever captured in mid-flap.

"Everything all right?" Toby asked.

"Thanks, Toby." Willow stood, allowing a little of her irritation to show. "I've got this." This was her place. When Toby continued staring at the cops, she added, "You guys can go now."

"Wait." Officer Patterson held up her hand toward Toby and the inspector. "Were either of you in this area last night?"

The inspector shook his head. "Drove from Astoria this morning. Am I free to go?"

The policewoman nodded. "And you?" she said to Toby.

"I was here." Toby shifted places with the inspector, who slipped out the door to clang down the steps and crunch through the gravel.

Willow planted her hip on the corner of her desk and crossed her arms. "What's going on, officers?"

"We're checking in with folks around the area," said Officer Patterson. "We noticed you have some sort of hotel here and wanted to check if you or your guests heard or saw anything related to a vehicular accident that occurred last night. Sometime after midnight."

Willow and Hayley exchanged a puzzled look of concern.

"No. In fact, all of us were up around midnight." Willow waved her hand to encompass Toby and Hayley. "We had an opening celebration with some friends. Someone decided to pull a stunt and scare some people."

"Really?" Officer Patterson's eyes gleamed. "How did this

individual—or individuals—scare them?"

"Is that relevant?" Toby asked.

Willow glared at him. "A guy dressed up like the Bandage Man and stood on a limb outside one of the tree houses to scare Toby's girlfriend through the window."

"I see." Officer Ortiz edged closer to Officer Patterson to make a united wall of police. "Was this individual—"

"Jake Bartlett," Willow offered.

The man's eyebrows lifted in recognition. Everyone in Cedar Beach knew the Bartlett name. Officer Ortiz continued. "So, Jake Bartlett. He was a guest here?"

"No."

"After the prank, did he remain on your property?"

"He went back to his place in town." Toby's voice took on a defensive edge.

"Presumably he drove?" Officer Patterson asked.

"Yep," Toby grunted. "What's the deal with this car accident?"

Patterson sent her partner a questioning look, and Ortiz nodded.

Officer Patterson blew out a long breath, like she needed to gather herself before telling them something unpleasant. To Willow's satisfaction, the cop addressed her rather than Toby. "You know the ravine running along the western edge of your property?"

"Of course." The ravine was formed by a creek that eventually fed into her land. It had been damned up to form the log pond by the old sawmill. For some distance, the creek had paralleled an old railway track for shipping lumber. The railway track no longer existed and had become the highway running past Willow's house. "The Saddle Creek bed."

"That's it. Dispatch got a call from a woman last night. When her husband didn't arrive home from a party, she got concerned and followed the likely route he would have driven. She noticed tire tracks on the asphalt leading to broken foliage on the roadside. With the creek running so low, she was able to spot her husband's vehicle in the bottom of the ravine."

"Did he survive?" Willow, arms crossed, cupped her elbows tightly in her hands.

"The victim was deceased," Officer Patterson said.

This sounded all too familiar. A man driving at night goes off the road and crashes to his death. It wasn't the oceanside cliff her father had driven off, though. The ravine wasn't particularly deep, but she supposed at high speeds, if the man had hit a tree, it could be fatal. She tried, and failed, not to imagine someone's broken body in the wreckage of a car, and when she did, her mind made the man her dad. Hayley must have noticed Willow's distress because she came over and put a comforting hand on her shoulder. Willow flashed her a small smile of thanks.

"You didn't hear any noise of someone braking hard or a crash or anything out of the ordinary?" Officer Ortiz asked, moving his gaze between Willow, Hayley, and Toby.

All of them shook their heads.

"That's so sad," Hayley said. "But I'm not sure what it has to do with us?"

Willow silently agreed. A man drove off a road and died. It was a tragedy, but not exactly a mystery. Maybe he'd been speeding or under the influence or fell asleep at the wheel.

"There was"—Patterson puffed out her cheeks—"an irregularity."

Ortiz grimaced. "I'll say."

Willow waited, growing more impatient with every passing second. The two officers seemed to be in a silent standoff about who would reveal this irregularity. "Yes?" she said, when she could take it no longer.

Officer Patterson lifted her average face to look Willow in the eye and deliver some more-than-average news. "The victim in the car doesn't appear to have died from the accident."

Willow sensed Hayley stiffen beside her before she spoke. "Are you saying he was murdered?"

"We're launching a full investigation to determine the cause of death." Ortiz shifted his weight, and his gun belt squeaked with the movement.

"You can't say if there was a murder?" Willow's voice shook. "Practically on my property?" This was not the kind of publicity her new hotel needed.

"This is an ongoing investigation. We're not at liberty to discuss it," Officer Patterson said smoothly. "When you get a chance, we'll need the contact info for all the guests who stayed here last night. And Jake Bartlett."

For a moment, Willow considered telling the officers Jake was in her house. She held her tongue for several reasons. He might have left already, and if he hadn't, he probably wasn't in a fit state to deal with the cops. It had been a rough day, and he would look like a mess to the police. The more she thought about it, the stranger it would sound to explain a freak windstorm had pummeled Jake in the face with a branch. She didn't feel like explaining it to anyone herself.

"Here." Toby picked up a pen and paper from Willow's desk and scribbled. "This is Jake's number. He's a good guy."

Officer Patterson wrote down all their names and contact info and then retrieved some cards from her shirt pocket and handed one to each of them. "Get me the guest info when you can and call us if you think of anything you saw that was unusual. Or if you *see* anything unusual."

"Like what?" Hayley asked.

"Anything unusual," Officer Patterson repeated as she opened the trailer door.

*You mean like bleeding trees that whisper threats and cause freakish wind storms? Devil birds? Stuff like that, Officer?*

"And be careful," Officer Ortiz said, following her out.

"Of what?" Willow asked.

"Just—be careful, okay?" He flipped his sunglasses down and let the door slam behind him.

Toby looked at Willow. "That was weird as hell."

And that, Willow thought, was a huge understatement.

# Chapter 7

Jake opened his eyes but found only one would cooperate. His face throbbed to his heartbeat. Where was he? He experienced the stomach-dropping sensation of having no idea where he was for several seconds as he lay in the dark.

Something landed on his bare chest with a soft *thump,* and he jumped. Then the thing on his chest started purring, and he remembered in a flash of clarity. Rex the cat. Willow Duncan's house.

He groaned. On the plus side, his head was clearer. On the downside, that was because the painkillers had worn off. The pain surged through his head and face. Thankfully, his arm felt better. He pushed himself up to sitting and the cat, rather than run away, curled on the bed beside him. The room out was chilly, which probably explained the cat's friendliness. A glance at the clock told him it was eight p.m. He'd slept *that* long?

Willow was right. He really *couldn't* handle his drugs worth shit. What must she be thinking? Even though the two of them didn't have much history, she wasn't exactly hiding the fact she loathed him for being a Bartlett. Not that he could blame her. He was surprised she hadn't kicked him out already. Maybe she'd forgotten he was here.

A breeze rattled the blinds through an open window. It wasn't quite nightfall, but with the blinds and the thick forest outside, he couldn't see more than dim shapes in the room. A chest of drawers, a corner chair, and the dark outline of a closet. Jake reached for the lamp on a nightstand when the cat started growling, a low, I-mean-business noise that made him sound like a miniature panther.

"It's all right." Jake wondered why the cat would suddenly turn on him, and then, to his horror, saw the closet door sliding open with a soft rumble. A pair of red eyes appeared high in the closet, as if something perched on a shelf inside. Those eyes bore into him with such malice, every hair on his body stood on end.

Rex and Jake got to their feet at the same time and raced each other to the door. Jake ignored his aching head and rushed into the dark hallway toward the light streaming up the staircase.

"Hello?" he called past the lump of fear lodged in his throat. "Willow?" His feet pounded down the steps in time to the pounding in his head and heart.

"Jake?"

He came to a stop in the living room. Willow was curled on the leather couch under a green plaid throw blanket, reading a book. Her dog, Freya, lay with her head on Willow's feet. At his appearance, Willow pushed the blanket aside and stood. The black lab gave him a wounded look that he'd disturbed her.

"Are you all right?" Willow asked.

"There's—there's something in the closet upstairs."

"What?"

"I saw red eyes."

"Red eyes?" She raised her dark brows at him.

"I know it sounds crazy, but I woke up, and the closet door started opening, and there were these—these eyes. Red eyes. Do you have another cat?"

"With eyes that glow red?"

"You got a lot of birds around here? Could it be a bird?"

"Okay. Let's go check it out." Her voice held a skeptical note that brought back an unpleasant memory.

He'd been a teenager when his mom brought him to Cedar Beach with the terribly misguided hope of him getting to know his father. She'd rented the two of them a tiny cottage in town. Every other week, he'd gone to stay at the giant Bartlett house on the hill to enjoy a few days of indifference from his father and outright hostility from Mrs. Bartlett and Lindsay. One night, he'd come downstairs to find his dad working late. While his father sat behind an imposing desk, Jake explained he'd heard strange noises in the attic above his room. The loud scratching coming from the ceiling above his bed frightened him, but at fifteen, he'd tried to share this news as casually as possible. His father could tell he was scared, though, and smirked. "Aren't you a little old to be afraid of monsters and ghosts?"

His father had fetched a flashlight, gone to the upstairs hallway, and pulled down the ladder to the attic. His father slapped the flashlight in Jake's hand and motioned for him to climb up. When Jake hesitated, his father had said, "I won't have a coward for a son. If you're afraid of something in life, the best thing to do is face it." He'd pointed at the black square in the ceiling. Jake had been terrified, but he'd made himself climb the ladder. Jake spent about five seconds looking around the dusty, insulated attic before attempting to come back down. His father had blocked his way down the ladder and insisted he look around some more. It was the first time Jake really felt hate for someone.

Jake never found anything, but every shadowy strut of the attic had sent his pulse racing. By the time his father allowed him back down, he'd been in tears that still shamed him to this day. He'd returned to bed, and the scratching had started again. He hadn't slept all night. Eventually, a pest control guy discovered a nest of squirrels in the attic. Jake still couldn't believe how loud a squirrel could be.

Willow, with Freya at her heels, led him up the stairs as his father had all those years ago. He came into the guest bedroom behind her, and she flipped on the overhead light. She strode over to the closet. The door was ajar, and she slid it back the rest of the way to reveal shelves of board games. It was the usual fare. Clue. Battleship. Monopoly. Some German-style board games like Settlers of Catan, Agricola and Carcassone. Games Jake loved to play with his friends back in Santa Cruz.

Definitely no monsters.

A few winter coats and empty hangers hung on the closet rod. The top shelf held a lone cowboy hat and some trophies. Jake forced himself to take a few steps closer to see what they were. Standing atop each trophy was a golden figure of a person holding a bow. He caught Willow's name and the word *Archery* in a glint of light. Why hide them in the guest room closet?

Willow slid the closet door shut again. "See? All good."

"I swear the door started opening, and I saw something in there. Look. Your dog doesn't want to come in." Freya stood at the doorway, her head lowered.

Something shifted in Willow's face—a flicker of fear—but she composed her features into calm. "You had some strong painkillers earlier. I don't know what to tell you, man. Could you have been dreaming?"

"No! Your cat was flipping out, too."

Willow's mouth turned down. "Rex was in here?"

"Yeah. He was on the bed with me."

Her frown deepened. He could tell she didn't like her cat chose to hang out with him. "Probably something spooked Rex, and you were half-asleep. Coming off those drugs, your brain was playing tricks on you."

He rubbed at the left side of his face, avoiding his swollen right eye. He hated the way she looked at him. "You're probably right." She wasn't, but he couldn't deal with this anymore, not with the pain in his head. He needed to lay down again.

"Get yourself together, okay?" she said. "The police came around here earlier asking questions about a car that crashed into the ravine behind my property last night. They want to talk to you since I mentioned you were here."

"What? Why would they want to talk to *me?*"

"I don't know, Jake. I had to explain to them why I was up late last night, and *you* were the reason."

"But what would I have to do with a car accident?"

A heavy sigh lifted Willow's shoulders. "It sounds like the man in the car accident maybe didn't die from the accident."

"What do you mean?" Something unpleasant skittered down his spine. "Like somebody killed him?"

"I don't know. The cops weren't exactly forthcoming with details."

Jake didn't want to be here. Not in this guest room near that closet, not in Willow's house, and not on her property where trees attacked him, and people apparently got murdered. "Something weird is going on here."

"Yeah," she said flatly. "And it all started when you showed up." Her gaze traveled over his torso, and he registered he was still shirtless.

He picked up his shirt off the chair and pulled it back on. His head popped through the neck hole, and he caught Willow staring. She blushed so hard—he was surprised she didn't burst into flames. Under normal circumstances, he might've been tempted to wink at her—not that he could wink now—but it wasn't the time for flirting. Not with all this crazy shit going on.

"I don't think you should be alone here," he said.

"In my own house?"

"Something bad is happening here, and you know it." As if to underline his point, Freya let out a low whine from the hallway. "Do you have any family or friends you could stay with?"

"Because there was some wind?"

"Yeah, Willow. Some wind." He let the sarcasm drench his

words. "Not to mention a bleeding tree and red eyes in that closet." Jake pointed harder at it than he meant and knew he looked pissed. He *was* pissed, though. Why was Willow being so stubborn? "Aren't you even a little scared?"

"No," she said, and he knew it was a lie. "You hungry?"

"No." That was also a lie, but he could tell she wanted him gone. He'd imposed enough already. He started to rub his hand down his face again and thought better of it. "Thank you for taking me to the hospital and letting me crash in your guest room. I apologize for the inconvenience and anything I might have said earlier when I was, as you say, loopy." A memory surfaced. Uh-oh. Had he told her she smelled of trees and *girl?* He hoped he'd dreamed that, but had a feeling he hadn't. He remembered a few of his comments, and now he was the one blushing. "I should get out of your hair." He edged into the hallway, eager to be away from that closet, even if it did look innocuous with its selection of colorful games. He hadn't imagined those red eyes. He hadn't. "Tomorrow, I'll take care of that tree limb. Cut it up and haul it away, okay?"

"It's fine, Jake."

"I insist."

She studied him in a considering way, and he could tell from her expression that whatever she saw, she didn't like. She lifted her hand and touched a finger to his jaw to turn his head. His breath hitched in his chest at the feel of just one single finger of hers on his body. "Can you see out of that eye?"

"No, but luckily I've got a second one." He eased away, and her hand dropped.

"I'll take you home. Driving as a cyclops probably isn't the best idea, and you must feel awful."

"No, you've done enough."

"Where are you staying?"

"An apartment over the ice cream shop."

"Okay, easy. I'm going to pick up my brother in town anyway, so it's no big deal."

He wanted to refuse, but a wave of aching exhaustion swept over him. Plus, if she drove him, she'd be out of this house for a while at least. He hated the idea of leaving her here alone. "Thank you. That—that's really kind of you."

They stood staring at each other for a beat longer than was comfortable.

"Let's go. Don't forget your meds." She nodded at the white bag on the nightstand and brushed past him into the hall where Freya waited. The contact sent a thrill coursing through his body, overriding the pain for a few seconds, the electric rush of it better than any drug. He wondered if Willow felt it, too. If so, she gave no sign and headed downstairs.

He hurried down after her into the living room. While the house was homey, it was also in need of attention. Everything looked a little worse for the wear. The baseboards were scarred, the walls scuffed, an armchair sagging, a light fixture broken. He doubted Willow had much money, and what she had was obviously not going toward new furniture and home renovations.

Willow led him through the kitchen where red checkered curtains hung in the window over the sink and the window of the back door. Next to the door hung a white board covered in a scrawling grocery list and a note under the To-Do's that said, *Be kind to yourself.* Something squeezed in his chest. Had Willow written it to herself or her brother?

"Your brother," he said behind her.

She stopped with her hand on the doorknob. "What about him?"

"Is it just you and him here?"

"Yep." She held open the back door, and he patted Freya goodbye before going out.

Willow would be alone out here with only a teenage boy? "What about your mom?"

Willow laughed, though it held no amusement. "Don't even know if she's still alive. Once it was clear your father's lawyers were going to screw my dad, and there'd be no money for her, she split town again. She didn't come back until about a year later to dump Connor on my dad and grandparents. Haven't heard from her since." She crunched across the gravel to the driveway at the side of the house.

"Wow, that's horrible."

"About my mom or your dad?" Her voice was venomous, but Jake didn't allow himself to react.

"Both."

Her gaze met his over the top of her Subaru. He tried and failed to read her thoughts. Was she deciding if he deserved her wrath for the Bartletts?

"You're raising your brother?" he said.

The muscles of her jaw tightened. "I don't need your pity, Jake." She climbed in the car and slammed the door.

Jake got in, and the only sound was the buckling of seat belts and the jingle of keys in the ignition. He cleared his throat. "I don't pity you, Willow. I admire you."

"People do what they gotta do, right? It doesn't make them heroes."

He was taken aback at her angry tone and decided it was safest not to reply. Willow turned on the radio to some alternative station and drove faster than was prudent on the dark, twisting road.

Jake shifted in his seat. Maybe distracting her with conversation would make her slow down, but what to talk about? "Oh! How did the inspection go?"

By the light of an oncoming car, he saw her forehead furrow. "Not good." She told him about the railings being too short by three inches, and the cables being too shallow by one. The cables weren't his fault, but the railings? He inwardly cursed himself for his stupidity. Why hadn't he pulled the regulations again?

"The grand opening is in two weeks, and the houses are fully booked," she said. "Toby said there's no way it'll all get done by then. A bunch of his crew went up the coast to work on that new hospital. He said all the railings need to be replaced. Looks like

I might be canceling a bunch of reservations and getting my first one-star reviews."

"I'll do it," Jake said. "I don't have to replace the whole railings. I can extend the top rails."

She took her eyes off the road longer than he'd like to look at him. "In two weeks? Single-handedly?"

"I'll do my best," he said. His mind already spun with the best options for addressing the problem, the necessary supplies needed to create higher top rails, and how to make it look good at the same time.

"That would be . . . amazing." Her tone was grudging, and more than a little doubtful. He got the impression Willow didn't like accepting help from people—and she didn't trust them much, either. "But I think you should rest up for a few days."

"I'll see how I am in the morning."

They didn't say anything else until the car glided onto Pacific Avenue, the main drag in town and his new address. A couple of restaurants, a real estate office, an art gallery, gift shops, and a medical clinic rolled by.

She stared straight ahead as she braked for some early-season tourists who poured out of a pizza joint and into the street. Otherwise, the town was quiet and empty at this hour on a Sunday night. "Jake?"

"Yeah?"

"At the hospital earlier today, you said you thought you heard something. When all that wind kicked up."

"Uh-huh." He didn't want to think about that just now. Maybe not ever. He shivered, remembering that sibilant voice, the sound of leaves rubbing together, of branches sliding against each other. Willow guided the car down the street and parked illegally on a yellow curb near the ice cream shop.

"What was it?"

Jake put his hand on the door handle, and the proximity to a fast exit gave him the courage to tell her the truth. "I heard a voice. Like a whispering voice. Coming from the tree." He lifted his chin, refusing to tell her it sounded crazy. He knew what he heard, and he also knew something really weird was happening at Willow's.

Willow watched a couple coming out of the shop with waffle cones piled high with ice cream. "What did it say?"

"It said, 'You will die.'"

Her hands tightened on the steering wheel, and she nodded. "Okay."

"Okay?"

"Yeah. Thanks for telling me."

"Willow, what's going on with that tree?"

"Don't worry about it."

"Except I do. You're all alone out there and—"

"I'm not alone. I've got Connor. And a big dog."

"And a giant cat." Jake smiled, and his lip stung. His smile faded. "Seriously though, will you please consider staying with somebody?"

"I can't leave my birds. Someone always needs to be on site."

"Can a friend come and stay with you, then? It's—"

"Not your problem."

"Hey, I'm going to be working out there for the next couple of weeks near a possibly homicidal tree, so it kind of is."

"Look, let Toby deal with bringing everything up to code. The railings aren't your problem, either, okay?"

"Actually, they are."

Willow twisted in her seat to look at him. "What?"

"You know that architect you had a 'mind meld' with?" He pointed at his chest. "Me. And I'm the idiot who designed your railings too short. So tomorrow, I'll be at your place bright and early to get to work remedying my mistake." He clutched his bag of medications. "If there's anything you know about that tree you're not telling me, I'd sure appreciate you sharing."

Willow stared at him from those pretty green eyes. "*You're* the architect?"

"Yep. Jake Bartlett designed your Branching Out Hotel."

He wanted to add, *so put that in your pipe and smoke it,* but refrained.

She nodded some more. "Well. Okay. I guess I'll see you in the morning. If you're up to it."

"And the tree?" he prompted.

There it was again. That ripple of fear over her features. After a long pause, she said, "I don't know, okay? Maybe—try not to break any more branches off it." She reached out to stop him from getting out. "How's your arm?"

Her gaze dropped to his bandaged arm. Did she think it, too? That there was something awful about having splinters from *that* tree in his flesh? "I think it's a little better. Must be the antibiotics." He rattled the paper bag in demonstration before climbing out. He ducked his head back in. "I'm sorry about your railings. Thanks again for driving me home."

"Thanks for taking a branch to the face for me," she said. "Get some ice on it."

He waited, not quite letting himself hope for anything else.

At last, she said, "You suck at railings." Her mouth twisted in a sexy half-smile. "But you sure do design a cool tree house."

The happiness her words brought faded quickly when he imagined her driving back down that dark, winding road with Connor, just the two of them going inside that big house. "Willow?"

"Yeah?" Her voice was curt.

"Be careful." He pulled one of his business cards out of his wallet and held it out. "Call me anytime, okay?"

She did nothing for so long he was about to give up and withdraw his hand. Then she took the card, her face serious and thoughtful. "Thanks, Jake."

He started up the stairs to his apartment when his phone beeped in his pocket.

It was a text from Willow, and he smiled.

*Here's my number if you need me, okay?*

# Chapter 8

Willow's head spun with the day's events. Connor wouldn't expect her for another hour. She pulled away from the curb and drove a block down to pull into a tiny parking lot. A few brave souls sat outside The Grumpy Owl at picnic tables, huddled under propane heaters. A low brick wall enclosed the patio in front of the two-story brick building. Flower boxes of pansies and geraniums festooned the windows. Five wooden owls perched along the roofline, and above the front door was a huge stainless steel metal owl, with a scowling face and two painted yellow eyes. Light and peals of laughter spilled from the open doorway. It was a brewing night, and the air was heavy with the smell of hops.

Stepping inside the brewery was a little like coming home. Being a Sunday night early in the tourist season, it wasn't too busy. At the front, some late diners were finishing dinner in the restaurant area. Farther back were the high-tops and the long bar. To her right, bright copper gleamed from the brewery. Willow waved hello to the bored hostess and made her way to the bar, the smell of fish and chips mingling with beer.

Hayley's mom chatted with two middle-aged women drinking white wine at one of the high-tops. Despite Hayley putting in some hours at Tree Top, she was still pulling pints of beer for a trio of men about their age at the far end of the bar. A quick flick of Willow's gaze in their direction told her none of them could hold a candle to Jake's looks.

Where did *that* thought come from? Willow climbed onto a barstool and let out a long breath. She was only human. She wasn't immune to the effects of spending a good chunk of her day with one of the best-looking guys she'd ever met. Didn't Jake just know it, too? Except . . . he hadn't really acted like that. She sensed he knew he was good-looking, but in a chagrined kind of way. He might act confident, but underneath, she glimpsed some reservoir of uncertainty. Willow had been trying to dislike Jake all day, first for his idiotic Bandage Man stunt, then for being a Bartlett, but he wasn't what she expected—an arrogant jerk who knew he came from money. Willow wasn't even sure she could call him a Bartlett when he'd spent most of his life unaware who the Bartletts were or what that meant. As far as she could tell, he hadn't got any of his father's money either. And he was a far cry from the pretentious, nerdy guy she remembered from high school.

Jake was *unexpected.*

Jake was the architect. Her architect. He'd designed her tree houses. She didn't know how to feel about that. When she'd seen the plans, seen Toby and his crew bring them to life, she'd had this feeling whoever designed those tree houses really *got* her. And it had been Jake Bartlett. Why had she ever told him she'd had a mind meld with him? She buried her face in her hands and wished she hadn't given up alcohol in college. She didn't want to end up like her mother, but one shot of whiskey would sure be nice right about now.

Willow glanced at the two televisions mounted above each end of the bar. One played a Mariners game, and the other ran the local news with the caption, *Possible murder victim scavenged by animals.*

"Whoa." She recognized the stretch of road by her house. "Hayley. Get over here."

Hayley rushed over. "What? So impatient. I got your usual right here." She pushed a Shirley Temple across the bar.

"No, look." Willow pointed at the television, which now showed a white sedan wrecked in the bottom of the ravine. The footage switched to the sheriff at a podium. He was tall and thin, with salt and pepper hair and deep lines creasing his forehead. Hayley turned up the volume, and she and Willow stared open-mouthed at the screen.

*"At this time, we're asking the public to come forward with any details relating to the accident on May 20th or any information pertaining to the victim, Mr. Mitchell Schmidt. The cause of death is still pending, and there's enough—abnormalities—surrounding the car accident to suspect foul play."*

An unseen reporter shouted from somewhere at the back of the room. *"What were these abnormalities?"*

The sheriff frowned. *"I'm unable to discuss details at this time. The circumstances surrounding this individual's death were suspicious enough to warrant an investigation."*

*"What circumstances lead you to believe he may have been murdered?"*

*"Again, I'm not able to comment on that at this time."*

A female reporter in a red suit stood in the front row. *"Can you tell us what you do know about the accident?"*

The sheriff scratched the top of his head. *"Uh, the car was found at the bottom of a ravine, and the victim was, unfortunately, deceased."*

*"Is it true the man was eaten by something?"* asked a young reporter.

The sheriff appeared caught off-guard by this question. He glanced at someone off-camera before replying. *"Uh, a wild animal or animals opportunistically scavenged the individual."*

Another reporter waved his arm. *"When you say the man was scavenged, it almost sounds like you're saying he was eaten? Sheriff, was this man eaten by wild animals?"*

*"Uh, that is, well, yes, portions of the man were, uh, scavenged by wild animals."*

The same reporter shot to his feet. *"I've heard the man's hands and face were eaten off."*

*"Was he dead before he was eaten?"*

*"No further comment."* The sheriff lifted his hands from their death-grip on the podium. *"Let's have respect for the victim's family during this difficult time, please."* He brightened, as if comfortable knowing what to say next. *"And know our entire sheriff's office sends their thoughts and prayers."*

He tried to slip away from the podium before a forest of hands flew straight into the air.

*"Sheriff, what wild animal?"*

The man paused, looking exposed in his new position several feet away from the podium. *"That's still under investigation."*

*"Is the public in any danger, Sheriff?"*

The Sheriff lifted his brows. *"From wild animals? Very unlikely. No one should be alarmed. This was an opportunistic—and isolated—event. As always, just be aware. With coyotes active in our area, it's always a good idea to keep small pets indoors. In the meantime, anyone with new information relating to this accident should contact the sheriff's department."*

The news moved to the weather forecast.

"Great," Willow said. "Right behind my house, some dude was murdered and *eaten* by a mystery animal, but I shouldn't be alarmed. That's the perfect end to an incredibly weird day." *Please let all these events be unrelated.* "Like the weirdest day ever."

Hayley glanced down the bar at the three men, and seemingly satisfied they were all right, she leaned on her elbows. "What's going on?" she said in a low voice. "Tell me?"

Willow did, starting with Jake protecting her from that branch, their trip to the hospital, the great gray owl Maureen and Elvis picked up, and ending with Jake seeing scary eyes in her guest room closet.

"Whoa, whoa, wait. Jake Bartlett is hot now? And he was shirtless in your house?"

"Really?" Willow tore off a corner of a napkin. "I tell you a tree is talking to us, and that's your leading question?"

"Uh, yeah. When's the last time you had a boyfriend? Wait, remind me, *have* you had a boyfriend?"

"Ha, ha." It wasn't funny though. Willow's life revolved around Connor and her raptor center. There wasn't much time for reading or seeing friends, let alone dealing with an entire relationship. She'd had a brief—thing, for lack of a better word— with a paternal forty-two-year-old guy last year. It didn't take a genius to realize her dating a much older guy a few years after her father died might have meant she had daddy issues. It didn't take a genius, but it still took *her* a couple of months to put it together, an embarrassing fact that made her squirm on the barstool now. Once that realization soured her on the relationship, she'd ended things amicably. There had been nobody since. Before that, no guy lasted more than a year. The older guy hadn't been scared off by Connor, but anyone close to her age was.

Willow figured once Connor graduated high school, she'd focus on herself. If that involved dating, great. If not, she had her birds who needed her. Sometimes, late at night, when she lay alone in her big double bed, she wondered if she'd even know how to date. Maybe she was meant to be alone. Loneliness had become like an old injury. The pain of it was always there, dull and in the background, and only flared up in the right conditions, like holidays or a friend's wedding.

"You should totally ask him out," Hayley continued.

"He looks like a male model."

"And that's a negative?"

Willow shrugged.

Hayley put her hand on her hip. "Don't you dare think for one second he's out of your league."

"I'm not even playing in any leagues, Hayley."

"If you were, you'd be in the premier one."

"Thanks." Willow smiled at her friend.

"Ask him out."

"He's a Bartlett."

"Oh, whatever. He can't help his mom had a brief lapse in judgment once. It happens to us all."

Willow wished she could shrug it off as easily as Hayley. She imagined it, for one brief, shining moment. She and Jake, on a date—or even in a relationship. She imagined the relationship developing. She would never leave Tree Top, so the only fantasy that made sense was Jake moving into her house. If her father hadn't been cremated, he'd be rolling over in his grave at the idea of Walter Bartlett's son living in his home. She shoved the idea away. It was crazy anyway. He was *Lindsay's* brother.

"How did he know?" she asked softly.

"How did he know what?" Hayley asked.

"What I thought I heard from the tree? He said he heard the same thing. How could he know?"

"Since I don't believe in talking trees, I'm gonna go out on a limb here—get it, a limb?" Hayley slapped the bar top and guffawed. "And I'm going to say that you must have told him at some point before that."

"I didn't."

"You must have. You told him and planted it in his subconscious. What other explanation is there unless you expect me to believe a tree verbally threatened you today?"

She sighed and ripped off another corner of the napkin. "I guess you're right." Willow *had* started to bring up the subject of her childhood scare, but she didn't remember sharing exactly what she'd heard. She must have though since she also didn't believe in talking trees. It was the most logical explanation. It had been a long day, and the order of things was getting muddied in her mind. "Can I see your menu?"

Hayley frowned. "Just tell me what you want."

"Can I see it?"

"Nothing's changed but the prices. You know that menu inside and out."

"What's the big deal? Why can't I see it?" Sometimes Hayley was so trying.

One of the guys at the end of the bar signaled Hayley. She slapped a menu in front of Willow in a distracted way and headed toward the men.

Willow flipped it over. The menu was wet. Willow used her sleeve to wipe off the laminated back. She hadn't looked at the menu in years. Hayley was right. It hadn't changed, including the block of text on the back with the title *The Legend of the Strix*. It had been ages since she'd read it, though she remembered the basics. Her father hated this story and said it creeped him out. Willow blamed it on his accident. Before that, he'd watched horror movies and used to infuriate her grandmother by scaring Willow with ghost stories. After the accident, that stopped. He'd seemed more fearful, more childlike in his fears. Traumatic brain injuries changed people in so many ways.

Willow shook off the sadness and read the words again.

*The coast of Oregon is no stranger to urban legends. The Bandage Man gets most of the attention these days, but many years ago, a different, more frightening story plagued the people living in the stretch of woods near Cedar Beach. For that tale, we must travel back to the time when logging camps boomed along the coast where rivers met the sea. At several logging camps, victims were found in the woods, partially eaten, their bodies exsanguinated. (Hey kids! That word means all the blood was drained from their bodies!) It wasn't long before people noticed numerous owls appearing in the trees before the killings occurred. A cook who traveled between camps noticed someone always died whenever a young Hungarian woman stopped by to sell her medicines. Could she have anything to do with the grisly murders? In all, six men, two women, and one child died over several months. Was it the work of a deranged serial killer, or something else entirely? Dreadful shrieks and screams came at night and struck mortal terror into the hearts of the lumberjacks. Whispers among the immigrant workers hinted at a horrifying creature from the old stories. Was it possible the strix had come to America in hopes of new opportunities as well? The strix dates back to Greek mythology and continues to crop up throughout medieval history. A hideous owl by night and a beautiful woman by day, the strix devours the flesh and blood of humans, seeking that of infants above all else. Long associated with witches and vampires, indeed spawning the word strigoi in Romania for vampire, the strix are not easily defeated. Branches of hawthorn keep them at bay. To kill them, nothing less than cutting off the head or driving a stake through the heart will do the trick. But beware. Many believe killing a strix may very well be the last thing you do. Fortunately, our own Grumpy Owl has never been known to eat a single human. So why not enjoy a pint of Grumpy Owl Pale Ale today!*

No wonder Willow's dad hated this story. It was pretty unpleasant, all in all. Was any of it true? Had people been found dead in the woods in such a horrific state? Willow snapped a quick photo on her phone.

She rubbed her knee. God, that news story. *Something* had eaten that man in his car. Strix weren't real, of course, they weren't—but then, what *did* eat that man? Coyotes? A pack of rabid raccoons? Come on. She'd never heard of such behavior. A strix made more sense than that.

Willow shook her head, wondering why she was letting her brain go down this ridiculous road. That great gray owl had freaked her out, and okay, she couldn't stop thinking about its scientific name of *Strix nebulosa*, but it was just an owl. Not only that, if she wanted to be logical about her silly fears, what did the owl have to do with the crazy stuff with the tree?

Idly, she remembered BiBi noticing all the berries on some hawthorn trees not far from where the raptor center now stood. When Willow was a kid, her grandmother commented that some people made jelly out of them. Willow carefully collected the small fruit for what felt like hours. When she proudly presented her haul to BiBi, she'd told Willow she was too busy for that sort of thing. Willow had eaten a few and found them horribly tart.

Willow polished off the last of her drink, ate the maraschino cherry, and left a generous tip on the bar she knew would annoy Hayley. She stood up and lifted her hand in farewell. Hayley held up her finger to indicate Willow should wait, but she kept going.

Outside, no one remained at the picnic tables. The street was empty and dark. Mist rolled off the water, wisps of it hanging just above the buildings. It was cold outside compared to the warm, yeasty air of The Grumpy Owl. She pulled her blue waterproof tight around her.

Something made her glance over her shoulder at the brewery. As usual, those five wooden owls perched along the façade of the brick building. For a brief moment, Willow caught the gleam of two red eyes. She blinked, and it was gone. Nothing more than her imagination. She turned the corner of the building. A streetlamp illuminated half of the parking lot, and the other half lay in the shadow of the brewery. Willow's footsteps ground on the rough asphalt, and the waves crashed on the nearby beach. She strained her ears, though for what, she didn't know. She dug for the keys in her pocket and broke into a jog.

A prickling between her shoulder blades told her something was watching her. She sprinted the last five yards to her car. She hit the unlock on the key fob, checked the backseat for ax-wielding maniacs, and launched herself into the driver's seat. Like an idiot in a horror movie, she fumbled her keys and dropped them on the car floor. She hit the lock button on the doors and folded herself in half with a grunt to fish around on the floor mat at her feet.

*Thump.* So light, but there all the same, the sound of something landing on the car roof on the passenger side. Willow's stomach shriveled, and her fingers scrabbled around, frantic. Scratching, soft and low, reverberated through the roof. Something was on top of her car. She should get out and investigate. Probably just a seagull.

If her head wasn't full of that stupid strix story, and there were other people around, maybe. A strong instinct for self-preservation told her getting out of the car would be a bad idea. Willow's fingers closed around the keys, wedged between her seat and the console. She straightened and jammed them into the ignition. Unlike a horror film, the car didn't stall. It roared to life as much as an old Subaru could. She blew out a shaky breath and put the car into reverse.

A couple of years ago, Willow had installed an aftermarket backup camera after she almost ran over Freya in her driveway. She glanced at the screen but saw nothing except the grainy image of the brewery's empty parking lot.

She backed out of the space and heard nothing else. Pulling onto the street, she allowed herself a small sigh of relief. Probably was a stupid seagull. A couple of blocks later, her short-lived relief evaporated when something screeched across the roof toward the driver's side. She put her foot on the gas and glanced out her window, watching for something to fly off her car.

Nothing.

Willow took the upcoming left turn as hard as she dared. The screeching moved back across the roof toward the passenger side, but she didn't see anything out that window either.

"Get off," she muttered. She slammed on the brakes. Nothing slid down her windshield, and not moving made her feel like a sitting duck. She gunned the car with a squeal of tires and the smell of burning rubber. In her rearview mirror, she caught sight of a large, dark shadow, there and then gone, whipping into the sky. It was too fast to make out the shape, only a shadowy flutter as if a sheet had flown off the car.

What the hell was that?

Given she was on a residential street, she slowed marginally. Her hands trembled on the steering wheel. Two blocks down, she hung a right. She didn't want to pick up Connor in this state. *Get it together.* Willow took several deep breaths and slowed further before pulling into the drive of Ethan's house to park behind their old minivan. The porch light was on, and their dog, Peaches, was barking inside. The open living room curtains revealed the changing lights of a television. Windows glowed in the houses up and down the street. She was safe.

Still, it took no small dose of courage to open the car door. She hastily backed away a safe distance and turned to check nothing was on the roof. Even in the light of the streetlamps, the damage was clear. Long, deep scratches gouged the brown paint down to the silver metal beneath.

Not that Willow ever believed the sea gull theory, but if she had, this evidence ruined that idea. What could do that to the paint? She ran her hand along the cool metal. The scratches ran the width of her car, back and forth.

"Hi, Willow." Willow jumped at the sound of Ethan's mom at the front door. "Everything all right?"

"Yeah, Stacy, thanks." Willow pulled her hand from the roof and moved away from the car to face the woman. She gulped hard, like she could swallow away the fear as easily. The only problem was, the fear lodged in her stomach already. "You mind telling Connor I'm here?"

"Sure, let me get him." Stacy turned and hollered over her shoulder. The woman, with the same bright red hair as her son, stepped out on the porch, wearing black yoga pants and a faded Seahawks sweatshirt. "You want to come in?"

"I'm good, thanks. And thanks for having Connor over."

"Always a pleasure."

Willow believed it. Connor had been best friends with Ethan

since first grade, and the two boys practically lived at each other's houses. Willow enjoyed having Ethan over, too. She opened her mouth, ready to invite Ethan back to their house, but it was a school night. Even if Stacy would agree, it was a dumb idea, with the worst of motivations. Did she think Ethan was going to protect them? He might be a big, oafy man-child, but he was only fourteen, the same as Connor. If something weird *was* going on—and she wasn't ready to admit that—the last thing she should be doing was inviting another child onto her property and endangering him.

No. The wind that hurt Jake had been nothing more than a microburst. That great gray owl was aggressive because her wing was broken. And whatever landed on her car earlier had been nothing more than a— "A stupid bird," she muttered under her breath.

"You sure you don't want to come in?" Stacy called. "I heard the creepiest noises earlier."

Willow drew closer to the porch. "What kind of noises?"

"Maybe you could tell me, being a bird expert and all. It was a screeching noise. Sort of like a bird, but also like a woman crying, too." Stacy shuddered.

There it was again. A chill slithering down Willow's spine. "Sounds like a fox." She kept her tone light and watched a moth circling the porch light. She wouldn't think of the story on the menu.

"Maybe." Stacy looked doubtful. "But it sounded more like a bird. You know, like one of those eagle cries?"

*Dreadful shrieks and screams came at night.*

Connor appeared at the screen door and saved Willow from correcting Stacy about red-tail hawks making that noise. Her brother opened the door under a hail of Nerf-gun darts as Ethan cackled in the living room. A dart stung Willow's cheek.

"Ethan, knock it off!" Stacy shouted. "Ow!" She jumped, grabbed her backside, and returned inside.

Willow grinned at Connor. This was just the ordinary family

life distraction she needed.

"That hurt, young man," Stacy said from inside, and Willow and Connor laughed. Stacy poked her head back out the screen door. "Bye guys, see you later."

"G'night. Thanks, Mrs. M." Connor headed toward the car, his backpack slung over his shoulder.

Willow hurried after him, readying an excuse about driving under a low tree branch to explain the scratches on the roof. She held her breath as Connor approached the passenger side. He was plenty tall enough to see the top of the car, but he slid in and didn't notice.

She studied the backup camera intently as she reversed out of the McEnroe's driveway. All she saw was a regular neighborhood street. "You have fun with Ethan?"

"Always do." Connor smiled. Willow was so grateful for Ethan's joyful friendship with her brother, which had helped him through some tough times. His smile faded. "You all right?"

"Yeah, why?"

"You just look—tired. Or something."

Shit. Why did the kid always have to be so observant? "I'm always tired, right?" She tried to laugh.

"You have a nice day?" Connor never asked that question politely. He always wanted to know how Willow was doing.

"Yeah, it was fine. Just a little excitement." In the most boring, factual way possible, she explained how the branch fell on Jake, how she took him to the hospital and let him sleep off the painkillers in the guest room. She obviously left out the freak windstorm, the talking tree, the car in the ravine, and the red eyes in the closet. And she definitely didn't say a word about something landing on the car roof a few minutes ago.

"That was really nice of you to take care of this guy," Connor said. "Especially after what he did last night."

"Hey, just did what needed to be done."

"You always do, right?"

Willow glanced over at him slouched in the seat, frowning

under his mop of shaggy hair. "Why do you sound annoyed about that?"

"I'm not annoyed. I'm worried."

"About what?"

"You, Willow." He looked at her, staring back with the same green eyes. "You're always taking care of everybody else, but sometimes I wonder. Who's taking care of you?"

"Me. I'm taking care of me. You don't need to worry about that, okay?"

He shook his head. "Sure. Once you stop worrying about me."

# Chapter 9

Jake wolfed down the microwave meal he'd made. Swedish meatballs and overcooked noodles with enough salt to bring on an instant stroke. He gulped down his antibiotic with a Coke and stared at the painkiller. His face ached, and his arm pulsed with his heartbeat again, worse than ever. What the hell. Without Willow around, he didn't have to worry about making a fool of himself again. He washed down the pills with the soda and crawled onto his futon.

It was uncomfortable before. In his current state, lying on the futon was about as inviting as settling into an iron maiden. He pulled the blanket over himself and lay in the dark. Despite his exhaustion, despite all the weird shit that went down today, the thing his mind kept buzzing about was the railings for the tree houses. He didn't owe Willow, not really, everything considered. More like the other way around. If she knew about any of that, though, she'd flip out. He still wasn't a hundred percent sure he'd done the right thing. He wasn't responsible for his father's actions, but he couldn't stop feeling he needed to atone for them somehow for the sheer fact he was a Bartlett, too.

Since she didn't know what he'd done, and never could, it meant from her perspective, *he* owed *her*. None of it mattered anyway, because he *wanted* to help her out. Not to mention, he *had* screwed up the railing height.

Something about Willow pulled at him. She'd hate knowing that underneath her prickly exterior and cynicism, he sensed a deep sensitivity to her. Alone out on all that land, raising her brother, running a bird rescue, and opening a hotel. It was admirable.

He also wanted to protect her, even if that made him a caveman, and even if she thought she didn't need it. Maybe she didn't. Women could take care of themselves. But didn't everyone need someone? Need that one person to always count on? Who did Willow have? She struck him as so vulnerable. Part of it was her small stature and sweet face, but it was more to do with the sadness he saw in those green eyes. It couldn't be easy being abandoned by her mother. Jake knew a thing or two about the damage inflicted by a parent's rejection. Fortunately, he still had his mother. He couldn't imagine how devastated he would be if he lost his mom, like Willow had lost her dad.

She was alone in the world, and he couldn't stop himself wanting to be there for her in whatever way he could.

Jake was a Bartlett though, and the nasty history between his dad and hers couldn't be erased. Because of that, he could never be the person she counted on. He liked Willow already, and under different circumstances, he could imagine something developing there. Chalk it up to one more thing his asshole father had ruined. Sooner rather than later, he'd have to make a trip up that hill to pay his father a visit.

He'd like to visit his dying dad about as much as he wanted to see The Old Tree again, but his mom's words echoed in his mind. *This is your last chance with him.*

Jake sighed and punched the bed beside him. It was what

it was.

He couldn't pursue anything with Willow. He could, however, fix her railings and do his best to make sure she could honor those tree house reservations in a couple of weeks.

He would do a double top rail, and by the time he finished, it would look amazing and unique. Jake fell asleep calculating the cost of supplies.

—

Jake woke up gripping the doorknob. He blinked one eye while the other struggled to open. Why was he all the way across the room, standing in front of his apartment door? He'd been dreaming.

No, judging by the pounding of his heart and the fear clutching his chest, it had been a nightmare. He couldn't shake the idea something was wrong. He looked around his studio. He saw boxes, the small café table with two chairs, his futon, a coffee table, a bookcase, and his surfboards leaning against the wall. There was nowhere for anyone to hide, and all seemed as it should. If he strained his ears, he could just about hear the sound of the ocean across the road. Why this crushing sense of doom?

The nightmare returned in a tumbling barrage of images, more vivid than any dream he could recall. He'd been walking through a dark forest toward a sickly light, pulsing like a heartbeat in the distance. It was the purple of a black light, only darker, as if darkness itself had become light. It filled him with the most awful, icy dread. Still, his feet kept moving against his will, pulling him ever closer to the source of that light. Mixed with the dread was a longing unlike any he'd ever known. His arm ached and pulsed with the beat of the light, but with every step, the pain in his arm lessened while the fear ratcheted up.

Strange screams came from the surrounding trees, and wherever he looked, red eyes in the branches above followed his progress. Hungry eyes. Their gaze alone gobbled up some life force inside him. Jake moaned, terrified and yet also hungry himself. Something was there with him, just out of his line of vision. Something dangerous—no, more than dangerous. A lion was dangerous when hungry. This was something *evil* in its appetite, and it was watching, ready to devour him. If he only moved his head to the side he'd see it, but he was powerless to do anything but walk. He tried to turn and run away, but his legs kept marching on. He grew closer to the light and at last saw its source.

The Old Tree.

It stood—a black silhouette against the dark sky—deep within its trunk, that sickly light pulsed and throbbed. He didn't want to see what was inside. More than anything. If he did, it would be the end of him, and he knew this with every fiber of his being. But once again, his legs betrayed him. Step by step, he came closer and closer until the toes of his shoes bumped into the trunk. Even in the dark, the blood-red sap was visible. He leaned forward and, to his horror, began to lap up the sticky substance with his tongue. As he did, the trunk split open to reveal—

He didn't know. He'd woken up. Thank God he'd woken up. He'd never sleepwalked in his life before. Jake ran his trembling hand through his hair, trying to ignore the pulsing pain in his head and arm. He shuffled to the kitchen sink and got a drink of water. He had the worst idea his body had been trying to take him to The Old Tree in real life, and he shivered.

"Just a nightmare," Jake muttered. Those painkillers were something else. He picked his phone off the box he was using as a nightstand. 2:47 in the morning. In the phone's light, he saw something on his arm. Trying not to panic, he fumbled for the lamp and blinked his good eye in the sudden brightness.

"What?" He pulled at the edge of his bandage. From underneath the gauze square, squiggling red lines branched out in every direction.

*Branched out.* Jake swallowed at the phrase his brain had

chosen. Carefully, wincing as the tape caught his arm hair, he peeled up the bandage.

He yelped and fell back against the futon.

Red lines of infection snaked over his forearm to create the perfect outline of the trunk and gnarled branches of a tree. *That tree.*

# Chapter 10

Willow woke up with icy feet. She'd forgotten to wear socks to bed. Eighty-year-old BiBi had better circulation than her. She lay in bed, staring up at the twin skylights in the sloped ceiling. Her grandfather had put those in, saying he loved to wake up with the sun. Willow needed to get up early every morning to work at the raptor center, so she didn't mind them, and she loved seeing the night sky. The mist from earlier had blown away, leaving a clear view of twinkling stars set in midnight blue. It looked cold, and *she* was cold. Reluctantly, she threw back the covers and crossed to her dresser—well, BiBi's dresser—to grab a pair of socks.

Even after two years, it felt weird sleeping in the master bedroom that had been her grandparents' room for her entire childhood. Her dad's room had been on the main floor, which Willow turned into an office a year after his death. She knew her dad didn't go in for any sentimental crap and would be pleased she used his room as the de facto headquarters for her life. She could always pop into the trailer to speak with employees, but her real planning for the raptor center, and now the hotel, and really anything to do with her and Connor's lives, took place in that office. Her dad had added built-in bookcases, and she'd kept all his old books there to remind her of him. Connor had taken Willow's old room with a Jack-and-Jill bathroom to the guest room next door.

The bedroom still had her grandparents' heavy wood furniture set, and she swore she still caught the smell of BiBi's rose-scented perfume on warm days. It made her both happy and indescribably sad. She'd take her grandparents to lunch soon before the summer tourists flocked in droves to the coast.

Willow pulled the socks on and climbed back into bed, willing her brain not to go into overdrive. She snuggled under the covers with a sigh. It might be a night to employ some of the relaxation techniques that the therapist gave her when Hayley insisted she talk to someone two years ago.

Willow imagined herself at the beach, her breath rolling in and out with each wave. She wouldn't think of that great gray owl hitting her with its wing. Breathe in. Breathe out. She wouldn't think of cops in the trailer, or murder victims, or whispering trees. In. Out. She wouldn't think of something landing on her car earlier tonight.

*Thump.* The same soft noise came again, as if conjured by her memory. Willow's eyes flew open. On the skylight directly overhead perched an owl. Its talons scrabbled for purchase on the slippery glass, the sound like fingernails on a chalkboard.

Why would an owl land there? It was huge, as big as that great gray. It found some sort of equilibrium, and its massive feet splayed out. The owl tipped its head forward and peered down at her.

She loved owls. She had a tattoo of an owl in flight, only visible when her hair was in a ponytail, its wings spanning the nape of her neck. Owls inspired her raptor center, even if hawks made up most of her rescues. If Willow went in for that sort of thing, she'd consider the owl her spirit animal.

Like with the other owl today, this one scared the hell out of her. More like an *evil* spirit animal.

Freya stood up in her dog bed and growled. Willow's heart pounded. This wasn't normal. Owls didn't behave like this. Willow snatched up her phone and turned on the flashlight, directing it up. Something in her gut recoiled at the sight of those owl's eyes. Red tapetum lucidum reflected back the light from her phone. Red eyes. Like Jake claimed to have seen.

It was another great gray owl. They called them the "ghosts of the forest" for a reason, namely because they were so rarely sighted. Willow had never had one at her raptor center, and now one showed up injured and another landed on her skylight? What were the odds? What were the odds that the soft *thump* on her car roof and this soft *thump* on her skylight should be exactly the same?

Her mouth went dry as she remembered the words on The Grumpy Owl menu. Ridiculous. Strix weren't real. *Strix nebulosa, Strix nebulosa, Strix nebulosa,* came the infuriating refrain in her head.

"Go!" She kept her voice low so as not to wake Connor. "Get out of here."

It kept staring with those unblinking eyes, and Freya kept growling. Willow glanced around the bedroom. She needed something to reach the skylight. She whipped open the dresser drawer and scooped up a handful of sock balls. She launched one toward the skylight, but it came a few inches shy of hitting the glass. The owl didn't move; it remained a dark shadow against the starry sky. She cocked her arm back again, calling on the muscles that helped her achieve first place in her college mixed archery team, and threw the socks as hard as she could. The sock ball whacked against the center of the skylight.

The owl didn't flinch. One foot scraped a little on the glass, but it continued staring down at her. The power of its gaze made Willow feel like a mouse. A surge of anger hit her. If it wouldn't leave, she'd go sleep in the guest room. She crossed the bedroom, refusing to look up at the skylight again, and ripped open her door.

"Willow!" Connor shouted. Terror shot through his voice.

What now? "Coming!" Willow stumbled along the hallway, Freya at her heels, and plowed right into Connor with a shriek. She grabbed his upper arms. He was trembling. "What is it? Are you okay?"

"I saw him. He was here."

"Who?"

"The Bandage Man."

Willow's already racing heart flipped over in her chest. Connor had been ten when their father died. Old enough to hear the rumors around town about The Bandage Man scaring their dad into driving off the road. Young enough to start believing them. For months after, Connor slept with his bedside lamp on, terrified he'd catch a glimpse of the ghost who might've killed their father. The light had always kept his fears at bay when he was younger.

She flipped the hall light switch. Nothing happened. "You must've been dreaming. A nightmare."

Connor shook his head. "I saw him. A man in white bandages."

"Where?" The word came out angry. "I'm not mad at you," she added. She was mad at the idea—and maybe a certain Bartlett who'd caused this fear to resurface—but she wasn't mad at her brother.

Connor pointed to the guest room. "In there," he whispered.

Willow rushed right past the fear and into the guest room so she wouldn't lose her nerve. The ceiling light didn't work in here either. "Shit. Circuit must've tripped." Her grandfather built this house in the sixties, and the wiring was about as steady as the man himself, who now used a walker. Usually, though, the circuit tripped when it was overloaded, like when Willow used her hairdryer and the microwave at the same time. Why would it happen now? *The wiring is old, that's all.*

"It's freezing in here." Before she could blame it on a ghostly presence, the blinds rattled against the window frame. "Why the hell is this open?" She crossed over and lifted the blinds to shut the window. The screen was gone with only a wide rectangle open to the night beyond. As she reached up to close the window, the most god-awful shriek came from the roof.

People talked about their blood freezing in their veins when they got scared. Willow felt like someone had turned her blood to lead. Her limbs instantly grew heavy with dread. The sound was just as Stacy had described. Bird-like, but with a horrifying human voice thrown in, like a woman screaming. Freya barked from the hallway. Willow slammed the window shut and locked it too, for good measure. For all she knew, owls that sat on skylights and stared at people might be capable of opening a window as well.

"What was that?" Connor hung back in the hallway, his face a pale moon in the darkness.

"Just an owl." Not the scream of a strix, because those weren't real.

"That was an *owl?*"

"Yes." Willow decided not to tell him she'd seen the owl standing on her skylight minutes before. "When Jake was in here, he said he saw red eyes in the closet. An owl must have got in through the open window and gone back out again. I saw it on the roof earlier." The idea of that owl inside her house made her skin crawl.

"I've never heard an owl make that noise." Connor crept closer to the guest room doorway. "Why would an owl come *into* our house? Maybe it has something to do with *him*. The Bandage Man. I saw him, Willow. Standing right there." He waved his hand to indicate the doorway. "He was looking at me." He sounded close to tears. "Except he didn't have any eyes."

"It was only a nightmare." She hugged him against her side. "Stupid Jake and his stunt last night must've planted it in your subconscious."

"It wasn't a dream." Even in the dark, she could see the stubborn set to his jaw, the way he tipped his head and pressed his lips together. With a jolt, she realized she did the same thing.

"Well, he's gone now, okay? I'm going to flip the circuit breaker."

"I'll come with you."

"Sure." She kept her tone easy, and she was glad for the company.

Willow and Connor made their way downstairs with Freya, through the living room, into the kitchen. They left Freya inside and crept out the side door and down the steps into the garage. The motion-sensor light came on to show an overstuffed space full of everything from boxes to old furniture to Christmas decorations. No room for a car. Sorting through her grandparents' and father's things wasn't high on her list of priorities compared to the demands of the raptor center. Looking at it now, in the dead of night, she wished she'd made it a higher one. The light only spilled so far into the jungle of objects filling the garage. She pushed through the maze of her grandfather's sawhorses and woodworking tools to get to the circuit breaker on the wall.

Something scraped in the far corner. Willow's head snapped in the direction of the noise. A stack of boxes up to the ceiling blocked her view of that area. Behind the boxes stood a wooden Santa cutout Grandpa made. The thing was only a couple inches thick but stood six feet high on its stand. It rested at a wonky angle with one hand out so that he seemed to be waving at them.

"Ouch!" Willow stubbed her toe and looked down at an old lawnmower.

"Willow," Connor breathed behind her. "It moved."

"What?"

"Santa," he hissed.

Willow saw the old Santa's hand sliding down. She gulped, and the lights went out to plunge them into pitch-black. Connor's hand found hers and, to their credit, neither of them screamed.

Instead, Willow's body decided to freeze in absolute silence.

Something scraped again, followed by a loud crash. Connor's hand squeezed hers hard. It was just the boost of courage she needed. She pushed him back toward the kitchen door. Freya started barking from inside the house, and Willow stumbled over the stupid lawnmower.

The light came back on in the garage. Connor ran the last few feet and ripped open the kitchen door. Freya bounded out, barking staccato barks. Her hackles stood in a ridge down her back. Willow looked around and saw the Santa figure had fallen to the ground.

"It's all right, Connor," she said. "Santa just fell over. Probably had too much nog." She tried to laugh, but it caught in her throat.

"Come on." Connor waved her up into the kitchen with the sort of panic reserved for someone trying to get somebody out of shark-infested waters.

"Hang on." Willow shoved her way back through the sawhorses, over the mower, and past a shelving unit with dried-up old paint cans to reach the circuit breaker and reset the tripped circuit. No way was she going back upstairs without working lights. Then, for Connor's sake, she crossed the garage to the now prone Santa and lifted him up and shoved him back in place.

She stepped away and saw something lying on the concrete floor. Her stomach dropped with a sickening lurch of horror. A single large feather, striped gray and brown, lay on the floor. Had that been there before?

Over the years, she'd collected feathers from the birds at the center. Most of them went to the museum in the visitor building, but her grandmother kept some in a box. BiBi wanted to frame some, but never got around to it before moving into the condo. Maybe the box was out here in the garage, and the feather came from there? She glanced at the stack of boxes. One was labeled "Arts and crafts" in her grandmother's scrawl. That must be where the feather came from.

How many times tonight would she have to ask herself, *What are the odds?*

She looked around, straining her ears. Freya had stopped barking. She heard nothing. She bent, picked up the feather, and set it on top of the boxes.

"What are you doing?" Connor said.

"Just picking up some stuff."

"Uh, not exactly the time to clean the garage, Willow. Get back in the house."

Willow obeyed this time. Freya was overjoyed to have her back inside.

By the time she herded her brother and dog back upstairs, her heart rate had slowed. Connor had a nightmare, that was all. When they were walking around in the garage, knocking into piles of stuff, they must have caused a slight domino effect that made the Santa fall over. The feather came from her grandmother's box. The owl on the skylight . . . had been weird, sure. It was getting harder to rationalize the disturbing events of the past twenty-four hours.

Willow didn't believe in paranormal explanations for things, but neither did she like discounting a growing body of evidence.

Even though there was school the next day, Willow told Connor he could watch some old episodes of *The Office* on her tablet. No one could be scared while watching the antics of Jim and Dwight. He might be fourteen, but Connor didn't complain when she tucked him in and pushed back his messy hair to kiss his forehead.

"I'm right down the hall if you need me. You just had a crazy dream, okay? Everything's okay." *No. It's not.*

"Okay," Connor said, already lost in an episode. He was snuggled deep under the covers. It didn't escape her notice he had his bedside lamp on still.

"Love you, bro."

"Love you too, Willow." He looked up. "Can you close my

door?"

She didn't blame him for not wanting to stare into the dark hallway. She shut his door and went down the hall where the guest room light had come on when she flipped the breaker. Willow reached for the light switch when, again, something on the floor caught her eye and made her freeze.

She went over and examined it. Her heart kicked up into high gear once more as she picked up the object and held it pinched between her thumb and finger. It was a strip of bloody bandage. Oh God, Connor really had seen the Bandage Man and—

*Jake.* She remembered his injured arm being bandaged. It must be from Jake. See, she told herself, there's always a perfectly mundane explanation for everything.

Willow didn't get back to sleep that night.

# Chapter 11

Jake woke up unrefreshed, his mouth sticky, and his mind hung over from a night of painkiller-induced nightmares. He rolled over, and agony lanced through his arm. His arm! He sat up and studied it in the white light of an overcast day spilling through the gap in the beige curtains. The red lines of infection still made the outline of the tree on his skin. That part wasn't a dream. His arm felt like he'd plunged it into a fire ant nest. A doctor needed to look at this. Somehow, he'd drag himself a few doors down to the clinic.

—

"Even half an inch past those lines and you get yourself to the hospital, understand?" The doctor rolled backward on her stool and gave him a stern look.

"I understand." The doctor had marked the red lines on his arm with a black marker, which only highlighted how much they really looked like a tree—*the* tree. The physician was a no-nonsense woman with a short, gray bob and had summarily poo-

pooed Jake's idea that his infected arm had taken on the shape of a malevolent Pacific madrone. She'd raised her eyebrows and remarked he had a fever. "Ever heard of pareidolia? The human mind tries to find patterns everywhere."

God, he hoped she was right.

"Thanks for getting me in so early." He stood, and his ass smarted where she'd injected him with a mega-dose of antibiotics.

"I mean it. If those lines move at all, you—"

"Get to the hospital. Aye-aye." Jake attempted a small salute but was too tired to pull it off effectively. He plodded out of the clinic when his phone rang.

"Hey. It's Willow. Just wanted to see how you're doing."

"I've been better." In fact, he couldn't remember a time he'd felt worse. He told her about his arm, including how it looked like The Old Tree, and gave her a run-down of his doctor visit.

She was silent for all of half a second. "I want to see it. I'll be there soon. Don't go anywhere."

That part was easy.

—

Jake fell asleep on his vile futon until Willow's pounding on the door woke him.

"Jake? You okay? Open up, or I'm calling the cops." Bleary-eyed, he shuffled to the door and opened it. "Wow. You look like crap."

"Thanks," he croaked. "Come in."

Willow pushed inside. She wore the raptor center uniform. Her hair was swept up in a high ponytail, and a tattoo of an owl in flight peeked out from beneath it on her neck. Even in his sickened state, he was overcome by the urge to kiss her there.

"Let me see it," Willow said. Jake held out his arm, and she swore creatively. "Well. That—that is peculiar."

Jake didn't have the energy to respond to her vast understatement with anything more than a nod.

"Hey, you got anyone to look after you? I don't think you should be alone."

"In my own house?" He smiled with grim satisfaction at the opportunity to throw back her own words at her.

She rolled her eyes. "Seriously. Is there anyone?"

"Toby's working."

"I know. He's at my place. So, um, any other friends?"

He sank onto the futon. "I don't really know anybody else in town. But I'm fine, Willow."

She studied him for a long, uncomfortable moment. He resisted the urge to squirm under her gaze. "Fine, my ass. Here's the deal. You can come back to my place, or I can drop you off at the hospital."

Equal parts shame and relief flooded him. Relief because he knew he couldn't look after himself very well at the moment. Shame because he was scared to go back to that guest room.

As if reading his mind, she said, "I'll set you up on my couch, okay?"

—

Jake hadn't realized he'd fallen asleep until the car bumped over the gravel drive and woke him.

"Here we are." Willow came around to help him out like he was some sort of elderly invalid. Fair enough. He felt a hundred years old.

Except he actually felt a little better. That shot of antibiotics must have helped already. "I got it." He waved her away and started toward the back porch.

"Take it easy, okay?" She took him by the arm and led him inside.

By the time she got him settled on the couch with a pillow and blanket, he was feeling almost human again.

She stood in front of him with her hands on her hips, having no idea how sexy she was in her confidence. "How about some toast?"

To his surprise, his appetite was back with a vengeance. "That would be great."

"Tea all right?"

"Yeah, thanks so much." After a few minutes laying there waiting for her return, he cautiously sat up. He could hold his head upright without it hurting, and the screaming pain in his arm receded to a small hum.

She came into the living room carrying a tray with a plate of toast and a steaming cup of tea. "You okay there?"

"Yeah. I feel better. A lot better." His voice came out strong, and he stared at her in surprise.

Willow stared back at him, and her mouth fell open. The teacup rattled on its saucer. "Your face."

"What about it?" Startled, Jake ran his hand down his cheek. Nothing but two days of stubble.

"It—it looks fine now."

Jake blinked. He blinked *both* his eyes. "What?" He touched his lips and felt no swelling or pain.

She set the tray on the coffee table with a loud clatter and bent to peer closer. "Any chance you're an amazingly fast healer?"

"I mean, I'm relatively young—and definitely virile." He waggled his eyebrows at her, but stopped when she didn't look amused. "Sorry." He cleared his throat. "I'm healthy enough, but this is kind of extreme. How do I feel so much better?"

"Your black eye—it's just . . . gone." Gently, she touched under his eye.

His body thrilled to her touch, and he averted his gaze so she wouldn't see what her proximity did to him. That's when he noticed.

"Willow," he breathed. "My arm."

The tree was almost gone. Under the doctor's black lines, only a faint red outline remained.

"What? How? I don't understand." Willow blinked at Jake, and he was once again struck at how beautiful she really was. All of his injuries seemed to have healed in a matter of minutes, and it was like his body went, *Hey, you're all good now. Let's think about sex. Like, immediately.*

Willow sank onto the couch beside him, and her leg brushed his. She put her hand on his forehead, the contact making his entire body flame with desire. "Warm, but not feverish."

Warm? He was burning up.

Jake reached up and grabbed her hand in his, lowering them both to the couch between them. Her wide green eyes fixed on him, and her gaze lowered to his lips as she licked her own. The regulator clock ticked on the wall, and the tension grew with each passing second.

"Jake." She eased her hand away.

"I'm sorry. I—I don't know what I was thinking."

"What's happening here?"

He was confused whether she meant his injuries healing or his attraction to her, but the answer was the same either way. "I have no idea." Jake rubbed the tops of his thighs. He told her about his nightmare, about waking up with his hand on the doorknob. "It's crazy," he said. "In my dream, I knew something evil was *inside* the tree." He barely caught himself from dramatically adding that, thanks to those splinters, the tree was inside *him* as well. That maybe it could communicate with him. Which was beyond crazy.

"Something weird happened to me last night, too. I got a visit from an . . . owl."

He got the impression *the owl* wasn't the word she wanted to say. "What do you mean?"

Her account of an owl perching on her skylight filled him with a cold horror that didn't make sense. It was odd, sure, but not outside the realm of normal possibility. "Hm," he said intelligently.

Then she told him about something landing on her car earlier in the evening as she drove to pick up her brother.

Jake clenched his fist in his lap. "What the hell is going on?"

Willow didn't respond, and the silence stretched on. "Do you know, Willow? Is there something you're not telling me?"

She rubbed her hands down her face. "I don't want us getting caught up in some sort of hysteria."

"Do I sound hysterical?"

"You know what I mean. Like a—like a shared delusion. I need to think about this rationally. Scientifically."

"I get that, but shouldn't we exchange information and ideas if we want to figure this out?"

"We're letting our imaginations run wild. I saw an owl. You had a bad dream. It's ridiculous."

He let out a long sigh. "You want to be scientific? Why don't we go take a look at that tree?"

Willow jumped to her feet, and he missed the nearness of her. "Let's go."

—

"Guess we were too distracted with the windstorm to notice *that*," Jake said. A fissure about a foot wide and four feet long had cracked open under the broken branch of The Old Tree at the base of the trunk.

"Or it wasn't there before."

He avoided looking at Willow because every time he did, all he could think of was how much he wanted to kiss her. Which showed what an idiot he was. Some sort of frightening paranormal insanity was going on here, and all he wanted to do was grab her and shove her up against a tree and kiss her. Not that tree. Obviously, not *that* tree. But any other tree. She was bending over and looking at something on the ground. Oh, man. He wished he weren't wearing these loose-fitting shorts. If she turned around, she'd see exactly how much he liked the view.

He looked at the bloody sap, and the sick feeling it gave him calmed him right down. "What are you looking at?"

"Feathers." She turned around, clutching one in her hand. It was long and striped. "Do you see them? Owl feathers. There are more over by the tree."

They both seemed reluctant to go near it, but hadn't that been the point of coming out here? To look inside the tree and see what they might find? Jake didn't want to get any closer, though. He sensed that same evil from his dream emanating from the tree like a rotten smell, and the closer he got, the stronger it was. In fact, it literally smelled like sulfur.

Willow took a few steps toward the trunk.

It was just like his nightmare, although he was moving closer to the tree not against his will, but to prove to Willow he was as brave as she was. Or he hoped he was. With every step, his fear increased, but his body felt even better than it had in her house.

His arm didn't hurt at all now. He glanced down and gasped. "It's totally gone." He held up his arm for Willow to see.

She put her face so close to his arm, he could feel her warm breath on his skin. He shivered. She looked up at him, and her throat convulsed with a loud swallow. They both turned and looked at the tree, at the dark crack in the trunk.

"Guess I better take a look," she said.

He stepped in front of her. "Let me."

"Why?" She tipped her head. "Because I'm a girl?"

"What? No. I'm just trying to—" How could he finish that sentence without offending her? He wanted to protect her? Be a gentleman? Keep her safe? All of those were true, and he knew she wouldn't like any of them. Inspiration struck. "Look, I'm the idiot Bartlett who broke that branch in the first place, okay? Whatever's going on here, it's my fault. I don't want to put you in any danger. Let me look, all right?"

She studied him for a long moment and nodded with something he hoped was respect. "Okay. But I'll be right behind you."

He turned and faced the tree. He'd thought that evil feeling was like the smell, but now it was also like a noise. So low as to not be audible, but vibrating all the same in his ears, his chest, and setting his teeth on edge. A wave of nausea washed over him, and every muscle in his body strained against his attempt to move toward that gaping hollow.

Willow touched his back. "Jake. You okay?"

No, he wasn't okay. He could feel it. Something hateful in this tree. He turned around. "Is—is there something we should have with us? For protection?"

"Like holy water?"

He smiled through the nausea. "A few garlic cloves, at the very least."

"Mm, now you're making me want spaghetti."

Jake blew out a long breath. "Okay, I'm stalling." He pulled out his phone and turned on the flashlight. "Here I go."

Willow put her hand on his back again, this time in support, and he leaned forward through the buzzing, through the rot, through the sick dread in the pit of his stomach. The white light of his phone illuminated the empty hollow in the trunk. The space was maybe two-foot by two-foot and extended several feet up inside. He shined his light around. Bloody sap coated every surface of the fetid hole. It smelled of damp and mold and— "Death," he mumbled.

"What?"

"Nothing." He tamped down the urge to gag. "There's nothing in here." Moving his light over the ground, he saw two more feathers and three small, white objects. "Wait, I see something." He pushed his head farther into the gap to reach them and couldn't stop himself from gagging. He grabbed the feathers and scooped up the white things before staggering back to retch.

"Are you all right?"

Jake held up his finger and retched again as he stumbled a few steps away. He wasn't going to puke in front of Willow, and though it was a close thing, he managed it.

She came up beside him and waited. At last, when he caught his breath and was confident he could open his mouth without vomiting, he said, "I found something."

He opened his hand to reveal two more owl feathers and the three white objects in his palm.

Willow touched one of them. "Those look like—"

"Bones. Like from a giant human finger."

"No, not a finger." She pointed toward the ground. "It's a human toe."

Jake arranged them in order from largest to smallest in his left hand and stretched his right index finger alongside it. "Yeah, obviously not a finger. Wonder who's missing a toe?"

Willow paled at his terrible stab at a joke.

"What? What is it?" he asked.

"It's just—" She covered her face with her hand. "Nothing. This is crazy." Without warning, Willow whirled around and rushed toward the tree with a groan. Jake watched her flash her own phone light around the hollow before backing out and retching as he had done. She lurched away from the tree and hunched over with her hands on her knees, breathing deeply.

"There's nothing else in there." Willow straightened up with her hand over her mouth. Tears filled her eyes.

"Hey, it's okay." It was a stupid thing to say because it wasn't okay, clearly.

She shook her head. "Yesterday, I was just worried about getting everything up to code so I could open my hotel. Today I'm wondering how to solve *The Mystery of the Evil Tree* like some sort of demented Nancy Drew book. Because I sure as hell can't have guests stay in *that*." She stabbed her hand, palm-up, in the direction of the tree. "If I don't get this hotel off the ground, I'm going to lose the raptor center *and* my house. Do you know how hard it would be to re-home two dozen birds of prey?"

Naturally, Willow's concern was for her birds before herself. Tears slipped down her cheeks. Against his better judgment, he pulled her against him. She stiffened before relaxing into him. He kept the hug a short, comforting embrace.

"We're going to figure this out, okay?" He smiled at her.

"The good news is, now I'm all better, so I can get started on those railings."

She sniffed and wiped her face with the backs of her hands. "That would be really helpful, Jake." She blew out a shaky breath. "I've got to get over to the raptor center to do some rehab with a hawk before the Cub Scouts get here. Is there anything you need from me to get started?"

"I'll check in with Toby. He can take me on a lumber run with his contractor's discount."

"Okay, thanks." She lifted her chin. "I have no idea how to even start dealing with all this, but I have to solve this problem. I *have* to."

Jake had never seen anything as compelling as Willow's fierce face.

"And we will."

She gave him an inscrutable look. He suspected she didn't like his use of the word *we*.

"Can I see those?" She waved her hand toward the bones he held, and he dropped them into her palm. She stared at them and shook her head.

"What is it? What are you thinking?"

"Just a crazy theory. I'll share more later, okay? I need to get going."

She turned and started up the path. He watched her figure grow smaller until she disappeared out of sight to cut across the parking lot to the raptor center. She might not have realized it yet, but they were in this together now.

He pulled down the sleeves of his shirt to avoid any awkward explanations about the black ink and went to find Toby. He and a small but freakishly strong Romanian guy on the crew named Adrian were busy digging the trench for the underground wires.

"How's it going, man?" Jake asked.

Sweat dripped off Toby's red face, and he grunted.

"I'm sorry to bug you, but I need to pick up some lumber with you for the railing project."

Toby swiped his arm over his forehead and hopped out of the ditch. "I could use the break."

"You know it's only ten a.m., right?"

"You wanna help dig, smart guy?" Toby glowered at him, and Jake laughed.

"No way. Architects don't dig ditches."

Toby punched him in the bicep hard enough to make him wince. They walked toward the parking lot, and Toby slid him a sly look. "So, you and Willow hooking up or something?"

"Not that it's any of your business, but no." Jake couldn't face explaining everything to Toby, and he was sure as hell glad his friend hadn't known about his injuries before.

"Your truck was here when I pulled in this morning. How come?"

He sighed. "Long story. Rather not get into it if that's okay with you."

Toby held up his hands. "Sure, whatever. But just so you know, Willow doesn't have a boyfriend."

"I am aware."

They'd reached Toby's truck, and he unlocked it for them. "You're aware she doesn't have a boyfriend, and you're one irritatingly good-looking son-of-a-bitch, and your truck was here first thing this morning—kind of like it was here all night—and you were in her house for some reason, but to be clear, you're not hooking up?"

"Look, even if I wanted to—"

"Oh, you want to. I can tell."

"Wouldn't matter. I'm a Bartlett, remember?"

"So?" Toby shoved his large frame behind the steering wheel, and Jake got in the other side.

"What do you mean, so?" Jake practically ripped the seat belt out of its anchor, pulling it over himself. "You do know the rumor is my dad set up a hit on Willow's dad? That it was no accident at all that injured him? My dad wanted to stop Mike Duncan from moving forward with his unionizing talk.

And when the guy tried to sue my dad, he twisted it all around and made him look like a drunk. He basically ruined Willow's dad. I didn't even know about it at the time. Lindsay told me everything recently."

Toby pulled the truck out onto the road. The trees stood so thick on either side, it was like driving through a tunnel.

"Everyone knows what Walter Bartlett did," Toby said quietly. "It sucks. But he's not *really* your dad, is he? More like a sperm donor. Anyway, you can't blame people for what their parents do."

"Maybe, but I can't blame Willow if she wouldn't want to date the guy whose *sperm donor* almost killed her father."

"You *do* want to date her, you sly dog, you. You like her. Like, like her, like her," Toby said in a singsong.

Jake's mouth twitched. "Would you stop?"

"No, I won't, actually. I like Willow a lot. And you—well, you're not half-bad yourself. I can see you two together. Figure out how to show her you're nothing like Walter Bartlett, okay?"

Was it really possible? Jake had felt it before, in her house on the couch. A sexual tension he was sure he wasn't imagining. He pulled at his bottom lip, thinking.

They were a mile down the road from Willow's when he realized his arm hurt again.

# Chapter 12

Willow's brain was on overdrive as she walked across the parking lot, thinking about The Old Tree and its connection to the strix, how it seemed like the creature had escaped from within the tree itself somehow. The human toe bones and the missing talon on the great gray owl—could it really mean the strix was real? A shapeshifting monster changing from human to owl and back again? How long had it been inside the tree, and why did it only now appear since Jake broke off the branch? Her mind fluttered and struggled like a bird with a broken wing, but she couldn't make any sense of it.

She was grateful for the distraction of Rufus, the short-eared owl. She cut across the back of the raptor center to the last row, where Rufus waited. He perched in his mews, looking healthy and alert. He watched her with a dopey expression before realizing her intentions and flapped his wings in alarm. Too late. She'd had years of practice and was able to wrestle him into a carrier with a minimum of fuss.

"You'll like this," she said to him. She lugged the owl to a large flight cage, went inside, and opened the door of the carrier. She backed away and gave Rufus the space and time he needed, but he didn't need either. He quickly hopped out and began doing wing stretches in an uncanny impression of someone doing yoga. Clumsy yoga, but yoga.

People were surprised to find birds-of-prey had their own personalities, and if she were honest, she'd have to describe this guy as Rufus the Dufus. He was a messy eater and wasn't above taking an undignified bath in the shallow tub of water in the bottom of his cage, an unusual trait in owls. Short-eared owls sported black patches or lines around each eye, which usually gave them a menacing air. But on Rufus, the angle of the lines wasn't right, and his eyes somehow looked framed in long lashes, giving him a silly, vacant expression. The feathery tufts of his "ears", usually not so noticeable on the species, stood up in a messy spray on his head. Now she'd gotten to know him this past week, it made sense Rufus had flown into someone's front window one evening.

Fortunately, he hadn't broken anything. He suffered nothing more than some contused chest muscles, and he'd been quietly recovering and was now ready to literally stretch his wings. She predicted he'd be ready for release within three or four days, tops.

Rufus decided his warm-ups were over and, with an inelegant flapping, took to the air to make a wobbling circuit of the flight cage.

"Looking good, isn't he, Boss?"

Willow jumped and turned to see Maureen and Elvis standing outside the flight cage. She immediately gasped. "Maureen. What happened?"

The woman touched her neck, where the scratch from the owl had obviously become infected and seeped a disgusting yellow fluid. "It's nothing. I put some antibiotic cream on there. I'm fine."

Behind Maureen, Elvis was shaking his head and giving

Willow a meaningful look. He cleared his throat. "Maybe Maureen should get checked out. You know? By a doctor?"

Willow crossed to the chain-link fence and peered closely at Maureen. The red on the woman's neck was spreading up toward her face. "How's your shoulder?"

Maureen jerked the collar of her shirt up and scowled. "I said I'm fine. Got a strong constitution, don't I?"

"She wouldn't let me see it either." Elvis shook his head in disapproval.

"Might be a good idea to see a doctor." Willow recoiled from Maureen's glare.

"I hate doctors." Maureen shifted so the scratch on her neck wasn't visible.

"Devil owl," Elvis said.

Willow couldn't stop herself from saying, "Maybe so."

"Well, good news. She ain't our problem anymore," Elvis said.

"What do you mean?" Willow was vaguely aware Rufus had landed on one of the high perches behind her. "Did she die?" She felt guilty hearing the hope in her voice.

"No, Boss." Maureen fixed her with a hard stare. "You gotta see this for yourself."

———

Willow squinted in confusion at the empty mews. "How is that possible?" The wire mesh of the cage was torn and twisted to leave a gaping hole about a foot wide. "A person did that, right?"

Elvis gave her a look that said she was an idiot. "Oh sure. Somebody came in here last night and decided to bust out a great gray owl and steal away with it. Sell it on the great gray black market."

Maureen chuckled, but the sound quickly died away.

Willow frowned at her intern. "You think an *owl* ripped open the side of this cage?"

Elvis shook his head. "No, not an owl. A devil bird."

Maureen nodded her agreement.

"You know, that's not really funny anymore," Willow said.

"You see us laughing?" Maureen's grim expression was made more so by the livid red patch creeping up her jawline.

"I'm just glad she's gone," Elvis said.

"She could still be hanging around nearby," Willow said. "That owl came to my house." In the dark, up on the skylight, Willow hadn't noticed the missing talon, but the owl had kept sliding, struggling on the smooth glass. The missing toe had probably made it harder to keep her balance. "She landed on my skylight last night."

"You kidding me?" Elvis's deep voice shot up two octaves. "That owl was looking in your house? At night? For real?" He shuddered.

His reaction doubled Willow's fear. It was harder to convince herself she was silly for being so frightened when someone else felt the same.

"Let's hope she was just saying goodbye," Maureen said. "There was something really wrong about that owl."

"She was just an owl," Willow said. She didn't believe that anymore. Not for a second, but seeing the steady, stalwart Maureen as freaked out as Elvis about the great gray was unsettling Willow.

"That was no ordinary owl, and I, for one, hope I never lay eyes on her again."

"Take the rest of the day off, Maureen," Willow snapped.

"I told you, I'm fine to—"

"Get yourself checked out with a doctor."

"Okay." She saluted with a dangerous glint in her eye. "*Boss.*" The woman strode off down the aisle of mews.

"Maureen, wait, I was just—" Willow couldn't bring herself to say it and let the woman go.

*I was just scared.*

—

Willow regretted sending Maureen away by the time she and Elvis finished cleaning out the last mews. Her back ached, and she smelled of sweat and bird droppings, or mutes, as they were called. She needed to shower and get ready for her Cub Scout class.

"I'll finish up here," Elvis said, when Willow moved to gather up the cleaning supplies.

"Thanks." She managed a weary smile. "I'm gonna go get cleaned up." She tossed a brush in an empty bucket and started off. She took two steps when Elvis put his hand on her arm.

"Willow?"

"Yeah?"

"Be careful, all right? Something ain't right around here, you know? You got that guy getting his face eaten off down in the ravine and crazed owls landing on your skylights." He shook his head. "I don't like it. That's all. I do not like it."

*That makes two of us.*

—

Willow and her education coordinator, Brenda, moved between the tables of boys in the visitor building. The roof of the round wooden structure rose to a central peak, giving the interior the feel of a giant tent. Taxidermy birds of prey soared through the open space above. Exhibits lined the circular walls, moving clockwise through time, beginning with some of the earliest fossils of true avians and ending with a rotating board showing photos of the latest rehabilitated releases. The center of the room held long tables for field trips and classes, another modest money maker for the raptor center.

Willow refused to run raptor flight "shows" or put her birds on display for entertainment. She did have a few educational ambassadors that interacted with the public—like Cynthia who was always gentle—but most of her money was raised by the fees to the visitor building, where students could dissect owl pellets, touch feathers, and experience her raptor camps, which might be forty-five minutes, a full birthday party, or even an overnight event called the "Night of Flight." Scout troops loved that one, and the only accommodation necessary was space on the floor for their sleeping bags.

These Cub Scouts were here for the owl pellet dissection class, and Brenda had already given the children a run-down on using the tweezers and various tools to pull apart the pellets to discover the undigested bones of the owls' meals. In order to figure out what that meal entailed, they'd provided the boys with bone diagram cards to match against their finds.

Brenda's children were all in their teens. She often said she liked running events with the younger kids because she missed having them. This, however, was a hefty dose of younger kids for the end of a never-ending day. Willow's head ached at the cacophony and smell of twenty rowdy third-grade boys. Why did they shout at each other when they were sitting at the same table? On the other hand, their happy chatter was just the elixir she needed for all the crazy paths her thoughts kept taking.

Willow gave a jaw-cracking yawn as her sleepless night caught up with her. She sipped a Diet Coke and hoped the caffeine would kick in so she could keep up with the boys. They squealed in delight and disgust as they dissected bones from their pellets and set them on their cards. One black-haired boy, quieter than the rest, refused to join in. Brenda settled him in a corner with a magazine about eagles, and he sat cross-legged and content.

"I found some bones!" A chubby boy with glasses waved something over his head. Willow pegged him for trouble earlier when he'd snatched the largest owl pellet from the tub. It was the pellet coughed up by the great gray owl yesterday.

"Hey lady," he said to her. "What's this? It's not on my card."

Willow hurried over to stand behind him and see what he clutched in his hand. The boy smelled of chocolate and dirt.

"Here." He dropped whatever he held in her hand, with the air of a cat who's proudly brought in a dead rodent. "Which bone is this?"

A white cubical bone, stained from being in an owl gizzard, landed in her palm. "Hmm. Well, it's definitely not from a mouse." She studied it closely, heart pounding, not wanting to admit what she was looking at, while the boy continued to pick through his pellet.

"Ewwwww. What's this?" He picked something up with his tweezers and shoved it in her face. "Guys, guys! Look at this."

Reluctantly, Willow took what was pinched between the tweezers and dropped it in her palm next to the small white bone.

"It's a fingernail!" the boy shouted.

Willow's heart rammed into overdrive as she stared at the items. A phalange—a finger bone—lay in her hand next to a fingernail, both of them obviously human.

"Can I see those?" Willow reached for the tweezers and the boy handed them over. She poked through the owl pellet and spotted the white of bone. She plucked at it with the tweezers and stared in astonishment.

Not bone. A tooth. A human incisor.

Horror, heavy and cold, spread through her body as she remembered the reporter's question last night. *You mean his hands and face were eaten?*

But owls don't eat humans, Willow thought stupidly.

———

Willow bagged the bone, fingernail, and tooth with the pellet and slipped out of the visitor building to call the police. Officer Patterson sounded very confused by what Willow had found, but promised she'd be over the next morning to take a look.

Willow tried to stay calm and push through the second half of the class. She fibbed to the boy with glasses and told him what they'd found only looked like a fingernail and was probably a mouse shoulder blade. But eight-year-olds were smarter than she gave them credit for, and he wasn't buying it. Instead, he kept telling everyone about the fingernail, and not even the special owl sugar cookies she and Brenda brought out for the boys could shut him up.

Finally, the last of the parents picked up their offspring to leave Willow and Brenda alone to clean and close the building, a task made more exhausting by Willow's efforts to evade Brenda's curious questions. How much should she disclose to her employees to keep them safe? But safe from what, exactly? She'd sound insane if she started telling her staff a strix was on the loose in the area *eating people*.

Strix weren't real. They were a myth. A monster from Greek mythology. The more logical explanation than a killer Greek myth was the possibility an owl had opportunistically scavenged the car accident victim.

Except owls didn't scavenge. Owls did *not* eat people. That was crazy.

Crazy or not, Willow couldn't stop herself looking over her shoulder as she exited the visitor building into the drizzly evening. She passed through the tree house hotel area on her way home. The scent of fresh-cut wood hung heavy in the air. A glance at The Old Tree revealed the broken branch was gone, presumably hauled off by Jake. Other signs of his activity were apparent. Lumber was stacked under a blue tarp. To her amazement, one of the tree house staircases already possessed a double railing. It was the shortest tree house, and therefore the shortest staircase, but still. She was impressed. The double top railing gave the staircase an intricate look, adding to the magical quality of the tree houses.

The drizzle turned into a steady rain, and she ducked her head and rushed up the pathway toward her house. As she turned her back on The Old Tree, she felt a tingling down her spine. Something was watching her. Behind her, something scraped and dragged, the sound barely audible beneath the pattering rain. Willow's breath quickened, as did her pace.

*Don't look. You don't want to see.* A few steps later, she couldn't resist a backward glance. There and gone so fast, she wasn't sure if she'd imagined it. A flash of movement near the cracked hollow of the Old Tree's trunk. Willow ran for her house, stumbling up the path. She let out a startled cry when the solar-powered lights lining the trail flickered to life in the near-dark.

She arrived at the back steps and heaved a sigh of relief. A pile of corded wood lay stacked against her house, drawing her attention before she noticed Jake sitting with Connor on the back porch, their two chairs pushed together as they looked at some papers in Connor's lap.

She jogged up the steps. "It's really raining now. Why don't you get inside?"

"Why?" Connor said, not even looking up from his papers. "The porch is covered."

Jake must have seen something in her expression, because he immediately stood. "You heard your sister. Let's go in. I'm hungry anyway."

Willow hoped it wasn't obvious she was urgently herding them inside. Once in her kitchen, with the door locked, her breathing evened out. She shucked off her wet jacket and hung it on a hook, taking a moment to gather herself by washing her hands at the sink.

She peered out the kitchen window, searching for any movement in the surrounding forest. After reassuring herself, she turned to face Connor and Jake. Jake stood by the table, somehow sucking the air out of the room with his presence. He wore dark blue jeans and a snug, long-sleeve black T-shirt with a Cedar Beach Surf Shop logo, and a pair of scuffed brown Caterpillar boots. His hair was rumpled and damp, and he looked amazing. Why was he here? "What are you two up to?" she asked, keeping her voice light.

"Just rocking it with some quadratic equations." Jake smiled, but she read the question in his eyes. *Are you okay?* She shook her head ever so slightly, and he continued in a cheerful tone. "I was grabbing some tools from my truck when I heard Connor on the porch saying some very unkind words about math."

Willow shot her brother a look. "You mean he was swearing about his homework?"

Jake shrugged. "Let's just say he was expressing his frustration in creative ways. Thought I'd see if I could help."

"He's like a math genius." Connor grinned. "And he surfed all the time in Santa Cruz. He said he'd take me kitesurfing this summer."

"Okay, slow up there," Willow said.

"Hey, Connor," Jake said, "didn't you say you have a review packet?"

"Yeah, it's in my backpack upstairs."

"Why don't you go get it?"

"Sure." Connor dashed from the room with more enthusiasm for math than Willow could have imagined was possible.

"You don't have to help him," Willow said as soon as he was out of earshot.

"I like math. And Connor seems like a good kid."

"He is." She didn't know why, but her tone came out defensive. "I don't quite understand why you're here, though? Are you trying to protect me or something? Because I can take care of Connor and me fine."

Jake nodded. "I'm sure you can. More like I'm here to protect myself."

"What are you talking about?"

He crossed the space between the table and the sink in several long strides. She'd have backed up, except she was already standing against the counter. This close, she could see his long lashes and the lighter streaks of pale blue like lightning in his eyes. His breath smelled of spearmint gum. He looked over his shoulder before dropping his voice. "Toby and I were driving toward town earlier. We got about a mile and my arm—" He pulled up the sleeve of his shirt. A muscle in his tanned forearm jumped, and so did her heart. "My arm started throbbing, and the red lines reappeared in the shape of the tree again."

"What?"

"By the time we finished buying the lumber, my fever was back. I could barely get myself in Toby's truck to make it back here."

Willow touched his arm to trace the black lines of the marker, the skin underneath unblemished. His breath hitched when she touched him, and she licked her lips in a nervous gesture. As soon as she did, she wondered if he'd misinterpret it. She glanced up and caught him staring at her mouth.

"Willow." His voice was husky, and his face hovered only inches from hers. God, did she *want* Jake Bartlett to kiss her?

She couldn't back up, so she slid along the length of the counter to put some distance between them, refusing to think how much she longed to kiss that scar on his jawline. "Your arm looks fine now."

The spell was broken. Jake cradled his left wrist in his right hand and looked at his arm. "Yeah. Just like before, the closer I got to your place, the better my arm felt. The better *I* felt. The lines started disappearing again."

Connor's feet pounded on the stairs.

"I—I hope you'll let me stay here until we can figure this out," he continued in a hurried voice. "I don't know what else to do. I had to go back to the hardware store for some extra brackets, and the same thing happened. Every time I leave, I get sick. Every time I come back, I'm fine. I can camp in your yard or pay for a tree house. Whatever you want. But please, can I stay here for now?" His gaze moved to a backpack in the corner she hadn't noticed. "I brought some stuff."

What else could Willow say? She took a deep breath. "Yes, of course you can stay here." She hesitated and dropped her voice low. "Just before I came inside, I thought I saw something disappearing into The Old Tree. Maybe you should stay in the house."

"Sure."

She hated herself for it, but she couldn't deny she was glad. Like some sort of damsel in distress, Willow was glad a man would be staying here.

And not just any man. Jake *Bartlett*.

# Chapter 13

"You're sure I can't help with dinner?" Jake asked again.

"No." Willow checked on her cooking rice. "You're helping Connor."

She experienced an unpleasant twinge of jealousy watching Jake work with her brother. Whenever she tried to help Connor with his math, he'd start out huffing, then move on to surly comments, and finally escalate to slamming his book shut and storming out of the room. But Jake had Connor laughing over polynomials, and every few minutes Connor would let out a, "Ohhhh, now I get it."

Now Willow was the one huffing and surly, slamming vegetables onto the chopping board and cutting up carrots with more force than necessary. It had been a day, that was for sure. What had she gotten herself into agreeing Jake could stay? And where, exactly, was he going to sleep?

The image of Jake in her bed flashed through her mind. Fortunately, the steam from the rice could be used as an excuse for her flushing face. She snuck a peek at Jake, brushing his hair out of his eyes and grinning at Connor. The onions made a satisfying sizzle when she dumped them in the pan. Sizzling hot like Jake—*stop it.*

She drew a deep breath to calm herself. Yes, possibly a strix was on the loose. Yes, Jake's arm developed red lines in the shape of The Old Tree and became sick whenever he left her property. Yes, Jake would be staying in her house. And all right, she could admit she was attracted to him. She could handle all of it. It was good Jake was staying here. She could tell him about the human finger bones in the owl pellet. Together, they could figure out what the hell was going on and how to stop it. Then he could finish her railings, leave her property, and get the hell out of her life.

It struck her that under different circumstances, the scene could be considered quite homey. The windows fogged up with condensation from the steaming rice, blocking out the view of the Old Tree. Rain lashed the house, and every once in a while, distant thunder rolled. The scent of cooking onions and ginger and soy sauce filled the air. Jake and Connor sat at the kitchen table in a pool of yellow light from the wooden light fixture her grandfather had carved into four owls, each holding a bulb. Jake's thick, wavy hair gleamed with the highlights she now knew must be from surfing in Santa Cruz. Connor's own black hair shined with his youth. The two of them laughed at another math pun. Freya lay under the table at Connor's feet, and Rex meowed at his empty food bowl in the laundry room. It was a domestic, ordinary, and cheerful scene that was somehow louder and bigger than Willow's and Connor's normal existence.

She didn't like how much she liked it. It would mean admitting something was missing from the family she'd created for her and Connor. She might even have to face that their lives could be a little lonely at times, with no man in her life and no father for Connor.

Willow forced away the uncomfortable thoughts. "Dinner's about five minutes away. Can you clear that off, Connor?" She waved at the mess of papers strewn across the table. "And please feed Freya and Rex?"

Connor gathered up his math homework.

"Can I set the table?" Jake asked. "It smells delicious."

Willow pointed. "Silverware drawer."

Her brain couldn't wrap itself around the fact Jake was in her kitchen, rummaging through her cutlery and setting her table for dinner. He was even folding the napkins into some complicated pocket that he slid the silverware inside.

He caught her looking at the napkins. "Years of being a waiter."

"Years?" Willow cracked the eggs in the pan with the rice and vegetables and the resulting hiss was loud enough to drown out any answer from Jake.

He waited for the noise to subside. "Yeah. Ever seen that movie Endless Summer?" He rubbed the back of his neck. "I chased summer—and the waves—around the world and funded it wherever I could by waiting tables."

"Must be nice to have that kind of freedom." Willow winced at the bitterness in her words and slid her gaze to Connor to make sure he hadn't heard, but he'd gone into the laundry room to feed the pets. The sound of kibble hitting metal bowls and a scarfing dog followed.

Jake followed her gaze. "Unless you want to count those two years with Lindsay, I didn't really grow up with any siblings." He gave a small smile. "You two are lucky to have each other."

Willow couldn't help but smile back. "I don't know what I'd do without Connor." She glanced at the laundry room again and then at Jake. "I'd do anything to keep him safe."

Both of them looked out the window toward the Old Tree, and Jake rubbed his arm.

Connor popped his head back into the kitchen. "I'm gonna get something to show Jake." He pounded up the stairs, clearly caught in the grips of some serious hero worship.

"There's something I have to tell you." The words tumbled

out as she quietly told Jake what she'd found in the owl pellet.

"Wow." Jake blew out a long breath. "That's crazy."

"What's even crazier is, I'm having a hard time coming up with any explanation besides something out of—out of an urban legend or a myth. It's insane, right?"

Jake shrugged. "I mean, I don't think any explanation for what's happening here is going to sound sane."

"We *have* to figure this out. And keep him safe." She stabbed her spoon in the direction of the living room and the sound of Connor thumping down the stairs.

"I'll do my best to keep Connor—and you—safe, okay?"

His resolute expression stirred a feeling that scared her, though she wasn't quite sure what it was. She couldn't think of a reply in her muddled state, so she busied herself dishing up the fried rice into deep white bowls.

Connor bounded into the kitchen, carrying something in his fist. "Hey, Jake. Look what I found at the beach last weekend." He threw himself in a kitchen chair, and Jake dropped down beside him. Her brother uncurled his fist to reveal a jagged shark tooth.

"Whoa, that's wicked! May I?" Jake held out his hand to take it from Connor. "I had a run-in with a shark once when I was surfing. Got the scars to prove it."

"Whoa, are you serious?" Connor picked up his fork in anticipation of dinner.

There was a lot of *whoa*ing going on.

"And you want to take my baby brother out kitesurfing?" Willow set the bowls on the table, and Connor dove into his fried rice with the voracity of a shark.

"What happened?" Connor asked through a mouth-full of rice.

Willow sat down with her own bowl. "Don't talk with your mouth full."

"It was in Santa Cruz at Pleasure Point," Jake said. "Just a nice easy day of longboarding with my friend Devin. It was late in the afternoon, and he's straddling his board behind the line-up, right? And my ride's over. The waves just closed out on me, and I'm in the soup. All of a sudden, he starts yelling, 'Shark! Shark!' at the top of his lungs." Jake scooped up a big forkful. "Oops, almost talked with my mouth full." He winked at her brother, and then, because he was obviously smooth enough to avoid ruffling Willow's feathers, he added, "This is delicious, Willow, thank you so much."

She got the impression Jake was enjoying spinning out his tale. Connor was hanging onto his every word.

"What happened?" Connor rammed in another bite.

"My buddy's screaming, waving his arms." Jake demonstrated by waving his own arms over his head. "People are clearing out of the water as fast as they can. Moms are scooping up their kids—any kids, all the kids. Everyone's fleeing in terror."

Connor was so enthralled with this story, he actually stopped eating mid-bite, his fork dangling halfway to his mouth. Willow wasn't surprised at his fascination. Connor had started surfing last year, and her brother had become enamored with anything to do with the sport.

Also, she may have found Jake's story kind of interesting herself.

"My heart's going like this." Jake put his hand under his shirt and mimicked a crazy beating heart. The action lifted his shirt enough she caught a glimpse of those amazing abs of his. "The water's waist deep. I'm off my board and wading as fast as I can. I see a little kid, a girl maybe six or seven, trying to get to shore. I grab her. I've got my board under one arm, her under the other. And I just see this gray fin rising out of the water coming straight toward us."

"No way." Connor's mouth hung open. "Were you shitting yourself?"

"Connor!"

"Sorry. Were you crapping yourself?"

Jake's generous—and fully healed—mouth turned down at

the corners, and he nodded in consideration. "I think it's fair to say I was suffering from a little touch of outright panic. Just a tiny, really tiny bit of mortal terror." He looked at Willow. "This is like the best fried rice ever."

Willow tamped down the rush of pleasure at his compliment. Rex jumped up on the table and sat in front of Jake. "Rex, down! Sorry. He's a shameless beggar."

"I don't mind." Jake ran his hand down Rex's back, and the cat jumped from the table to land beside Jake in the empty fourth chair. "Look at him." Jake laughed. "He's wondering where his bowl is."

"Come on, Jake, what happened next?" Connor literally sat on the edge of his seat and squirmed.

Jake lifted his leg, stopping inches from putting his foot on the table—no wonder he didn't care about a cat when he practically plopped his shoe in their dinner—and rolled up his jeans to show Connor a long scar snaking down the outside of his left calf. Willow couldn't help but notice his calf was tan and leanly muscled, like the man's delectable forearms. Maybe her freshman self in high school had been a prescient genius to have a crush on a guy who ended up being the hottest man she'd ever seen.

"Twenty stitches," he said.

Connor stared at the jagged scar. "A shark did that?"

Jake rolled down his jeans, chuckling. "Nah, dude."

*Dude?* Willow lifted her brows at him.

"It was my surfboard fin. A wave caught my board when I was thrashing around, trying to get away from that shark. Flipped up, and the fin caught my leg."

"What about the shark?" Connor asked.

"The shark? It must've been ten feet long . . . and turned out to be an inflatable floatie some kid had brought to the beach."

"Wait. There wasn't even a real shark?"

"No. Crazy, right? My friend felt terrible." Jake shoved some more rice into his mouth.

"It wasn't really your friend's fault. Maybe they should outlaw inflatable sharks at the beach. That's dangerous."

Willow couldn't remember the last time she'd heard Connor string so many sentences together.

"I agree, Connor. They should totally make it against the law."

Connor gave that small, shy smile he did when he was pleased, showing off the tiniest glint of his braces. "When can we go kitesurfing?"

Willow opened her mouth to protest, but Connor's face was so hopeful, she pressed her lips together with a sigh.

"Maybe we can start off just surfing first." Jake glanced at Willow with a questioning look. "We could go to Short Sands. You got your own board? Or you can borrow one of mine?"

"I have two." Connor said it with such satisfaction that Willow got a lump in her throat. Connor worked hard at the raptor center, and she paid him like any other employee. He'd earned the money for those surfboards, and they were his most precious point of pride.

Like Connor was hers.

"Aren't you out of school soon?" Jake asked.

"This is my last week before summer vacation."

"Cool. I'd be happy to take you out this summer. Would that be okay with you, Willow? Maybe once I earn your sister's trust, we could try kitesurfing down the road?"

Willow looked up from her bowl, where she'd been pushing around a stray pea. Three male sets of eyes stared expectantly back at her: Connor, Jake, and Rex. The cat did a slow blink as if to say, *Go on.*

Jake reached over and squeezed Willow's hand, and her pulse hammered at his touch. "I understand if you say no, but if you let me take him, I'll be really careful. I promise. We won't go out if conditions look scary, all right? I'll look after him like he's my own brother."

"Let me—let me think about it," she said.

"Please," Connor whined.

"She said she'd think about it." Jake waggled his eyebrows at Connor. "Why don't we butter her up by doing the dishes?"

He'd won over her cat, made her brother happy, and now he was washing her dishes.

*But he's a Bartlett.*

Right about then, she couldn't seem to care.

# Chapter 14

Jake washed the last plate and handed it to Connor to dry. Willow was working on her laptop at the kitchen table. Her screen faced away from him, but whatever she was looking at, she didn't seem to like it. Her thick, dark brows drew together in a furrow. God, she was so gorgeous and had no idea. He imagined walking over and kissing her on the forehead to erase that worry.

Except there was a lot to worry about right now.

"You wanna play on my Xbox?" Connor asked him. "I have this new alien game."

Willow stirred at the table. "Jake and I actually need to talk about the tree house railings. Do some planning." She gave him a significant look.

Connor collapsed inward like an inflatable tube man at a car dealership.

"But you can go play," Willow added.

"All right." His voice was dejected.

"Or you could do some more math review for your final."

Connor disappeared so fast, Jake thought he glimpsed a cloud of smoke in his wake and laughed. "That was effective."

"Hey, I haven't been Connor's guardian for the past seven years without learning a few tricks. Even if I don't know what I'm doing most of the time."

"Seems like you're doing a good job." Jake flipped a chair around backwards and sank onto it, resting his elbows on the back.

"Thanks." She sighed. "I just hope I'm not screwing up this kid. I put him in therapy after our dad died, but it only lasted a few months. Our mom abandoned him, too. It's just so much for one boy, and he's stuck with only me. What if I'm making him all warped?"

"He doesn't seem warped to me. He's polite, smart, funny. Worked hard on his math." He grinned. "I like him. And he surfs like me. You know—"

She pointed her finger at him. "I haven't made up my mind yet, okay?"

"Am I so transparent?" She gave him a wry look. "Fine. That just shows what a good big sis parent you are, looking out for him like that."

She tipped her head back toward the ceiling and blinked furiously. Her delicate neck worked with a swallow. Without thinking, he reached out and put his hand on hers. "I can tell how much you and Connor love each other. I think you're probably doing okay."

She eased her hand away and used the back of it to swipe away a tear. "Sorry. I don't even know why I'm talking about this with you. I don't really have anyone to share with and—" She winced and covered her face with her hands. "God, I sound pathetic. I'll shut up now."

"Look, I get it. My mom was a single parent, remember? Unless you want to count Walter." He put as much disdain as possible into his father's name. "She tried to hide it, but I knew she was always agonizing over whether or not she was a good parent. And look at me." He tipped his chin up and spread his arms wide. "I turned out pretty amazing, right?"

Willow studied him like she was really considering that question. His face warmed under her scrutiny, and his grin faded.

"You know what?" she asked. "I think you might be all right." She dropped her gaze. "You want to hear something crazy?"

"Always."

"I had a crush on you in high school."

"What?" Jake snorted and jerked his head in denial. "No way."

She covered her face again. "I shouldn't have told you that."

"No, it's just—do you remember what I was like in high school?"

"Oh, quite clearly."

"So—what exactly did you like?"

She licked her lips in that sexy, nervous habit he'd noticed. "To be honest, just to keep your ego in check, I think it was just a forbidden fruit thing."

He nodded and tried to look pensive. "Forbidden fruit. I dig it. What an asshat I was. I was so insecure about my size and looks and tried to cover it up by being a know-it-all dick. Thank God for my D&D group. Do you play?" He waved his hand away. "Never mind. You were always too cool for that."

Willow burst out laughing, and he wondered if that was the first time he'd heard her laugh. It transformed everything about her, lighting up her eyes and making her look even prettier. "Are you kidding? You think *I* was cool? Me? White-trash Willow?"

"White-trash Willow?"

She picked at her thumbnail. "That's what your sister called me. It caught on."

Jake rested his chin on his forearms propped on the chair back. "She was really horrible to you, wasn't she?"

"The worst."

"She's sorry now. She's told me many times she wishes she

could go back and be a different person then."

"I wish she could, too."

"You *were* cool, though, Willow."

"I wasn't."

"You were in your own way. You dyed your hair purple and blue and were sort of goth-y and emo and into your raptors and stuff. You didn't take shit off anyone or care what they thought."

"I did care," she said quietly. "I just had to act tough to survive." She tucked her shining hair behind her ear and jutted her chin up to meet his gaze. "Eventually, all that acting tough translated into *being* tough, and here we are."

"Like I said. One cool chick."

"Me? You're the surfer dude with the perfect hair and the cool leather bracelets."

"I still play D&D."

"D&D's super cool these days."

"Maybe we can play together sometime." His voice came out gravelly, and he heard how suggestive his words sounded.

Something pinged, and Willow looked at her phone with a scowl.

He straightened. "What's up?"

"It's my intern, Elvis. He's worried about one of my employees. He tried checking on Maureen earlier, but he can't get a hold of her." Willow proceeded to tell him how Maureen had been attacked when rescuing a terrifying great gray owl with a missing toe, which gave him pause. A devil bird, she called it. He didn't like the news that it escaped last night and must have been the one perching on Willow's skylight.

"What the hell's going on?" he asked.

Willow took a deep breath, as if gathering her courage. "You ever heard of something called a strix?"

"Strix?" A memory tickled the back of his brain. "Yeah. That's a D&D thing. You want to know what dice roll is needed to defeat it?" He laughed, but her worried face shut it down, and he raised his hands palms-up. "Sorry. Thought some D&D

mockery might lighten the mood."

"Listen. I know this sounds crazy, but my friend Hayley's family owns The Grumpy Owl. Here's their menu with the story of the strix." She held out her phone to him with the photo pulled up.

Jake squinted at the tiny text on the screen. "Okay, that's not at all like in Dungeons and Dragons."

"I've done some research online, too. This strix thing is like a cross between a witch and a vampire that can shapeshift into an owl. Those human toe bones—and the great gray owl with the missing talon. It's almost like proof they're the same being."

Jake cupped his jaw and stroked his fingers over his stubble, nodding slowly. "So, they just, what? Go around eating people or something?"

"I guess. I can't believe we're talking about this like it's real."

"Something is happening, and it's real. Let's not discount any ideas or possibilities." He drummed his fingers on the back of his chair. "Okay, let's say it is a strix monster. What does that have to do with the creepy-ass tree out there?" He pointed toward the window. "Did anything about strix also mention trees?"

Willow stared at her laptop screen. "Only that hawthorn branches keep strix away."

"Okay. Behind curtain number one, we have a big owl on the loose, possibly eating people, who may or may not turn into a human. Behind curtain number two, a tree oozing blood that causes windstorms and sickness and gives off super bad vibes."

"And tells us we're going to die."

"Oh, man. How did I forget that little gem? Okay, and a tree that threatens us with death. Let's not forget the tree cracked open to reveal a vomit-inducing hollow where I'm pretty sure the Headless Horseman might live."

Willow frowned. "Not the Headless Horseman." She looked thoughtful. "I think the strix lives in The Old Tree. Remember the toe bones were in there? They share a connection somehow."

"Let's burn the fucker to the ground, then."

"That tree seems to be keeping you feeling all right at the moment."

"Maybe if it's gone, this curse, or whatever it is, will disappear, and my arm won't be an issue anymore. I say we burn it."

"Along with the biggest tree house—the centerpiece of my hotel that has to succeed so I don't lose everything I care about?"

"Dumbass Toby. Why did he build in that tree?"

"I tried to talk him out of it."

"Yeah, but he's a stubborn bastard. And to be fair, that's a huge and convenient tree. Okay, back to my fire idea. Hear me out." He swept out his hand like he'd found the solution to world peace. "What if we made it look like an accident? Do you know any firefighters we can bribe?"

"I don't have any money for bribes."

"How about sexual favors?"

Willow rolled her eyes. "This isn't funny." But she smothered a smile with her hand. "I have no idea how to solve this problem."

"I know. I'm actually the most terrified I've ever been in my life, but humor's my defense mechanism, so you're going to have to deal." He waggled his eyebrows at her. "Some people even find it charming."

"Are you really flirting with me right now?"

"I really am. Flirting is another one of my defense mechanisms."

"You certainly have a lot of those."

"Yep." He leaned forward, staring into her green eyes. "It wasn't just the drugs, you know."

"What wasn't?" She licked her lips again, and his heart kicked up.

"When I said you were beautiful. You really are."

"You already said that." A blush swept up her neck and over her cheeks.

"I know, but it's true, and I like seeing you blush."

Willow cleared her throat. "Um, we should probably figure

out where you're going to sleep tonight."

"The living room couch is fine."

"I was thinking the guest room. Or are you too afraid of the closet?"

"Not really funny right now."

"Sorry," she said. "Humor is also *my* defense mechanism."

"But not flirting?" He let his gaze sweep over her.

She shrugged. "I've never been good at it."

A heated silence spun out, and he cleared his throat. "Well. Thank you. For the guest room. And I promise to be on my very best behavior while I'm staying here."

Willow slowly leaned forward in her chair until their faces were only inches apart. "Maybe I don't want you to be on your *very* best behavior." Her gaze flicked to his mouth.

"Your flirting seems fine to me." Jake reached up and cupped her face, rubbing his thumb over her jaw, and simply studied her features, the light smattering of freckles over her nose. He slid his hand to the back of her neck, relishing the feel of her heavy, silken hair. Her eyes darted back and forth between his own, and her swallow was loud.

"Are you going to kiss me?" she asked.

"Do you want me to?"

She nodded, slowly.

He traced his fingers behind her ear. "I know I'm a Bartlett, but I want you to know it's in name only, and I—"

Suddenly her mouth was on his, and he forgot what he was going to say.

# Chapter 15

Willow had been forced to stand to reach Jake's mouth over the table, but the guy might've talked all night if she hadn't acted. Now she was stuck in an awkward crouch over him. Even so, she didn't want to pull her lips from his. They were warm and firm, kissing her back with gentle want. Her back was protesting the angle when he solved the problem and pulled her in one motion into his lap to straddle him in the backwards chair. He shifted to pull her snugly against him, trapping her between his body and the chair back without ever breaking the kiss.

And wow, could the man kiss! As it spun out—impossibly slow—she grew dizzy with it. The heat of his mouth, the slide of his tongue over hers; it was like a drug. His hands stroked down her hair, and she threaded her fingers through his. The chairback dug into her spine, and she shifted in his lap. At the movement, Jake groaned into her mouth, and his hard arousal was obvious in this position. His hands shifted to her hips and squeezed, as if he fought against the need to grind himself against her.

It was, quite simply, the hottest first kiss Willow had ever shared with a man, and the realization sounded a klaxon in her head.

*What the hell are you doing?* It was too fast. Connor was upstairs. They needed to be solving this strix problem. She hardly knew Jake—and oh, now he was kissing trails down her jawline to the place where her pulse hammered in her neck. His hands, rough from his day of work, slid under her shirt, his palms grazing up her back to elicit a shiver.

Something vibrated against her hip, but it was a distant thing, none of her concern. Once, twice, and on the third time, Jake broke apart from her, tipping his own hips back to retrieve the phone from his pocket. This new position only thrust the hard length of him against her even more. It was embarrassing, but she was panting.

Jake glanced at the screen and swore.

Willow swung her leg off him to stagger gracelessly to her feet. Her legs trembled, as did her hand when she ran it through her hair, messy from Jake raking his fingers through it. "Everything all right?"

Jake shook his head once. "Hello?" The caution was heavy in his voice. He stood and began to pace around the table. Freya got up and followed him.

Willow hurried to the stove and grabbed the kettle to make some tea. The kitchen felt steamy enough as it was, and the last thing she wanted was a hot drink, but she had to do something with her hands and sort out her muddled thoughts. All the blood in her brain seemed to have made its way further south in her body. It must be the shock of everything going on. It had clouded her judgment completely.

"You don't think he should go to the hospital?" Jake's voice rose with alarm.

His dad. It must be. Willow blew out a long, shaky breath and turned to set the kettle back on the stove, the control clicking like a metronome until the blue flame lit with a small *whoosh* and a whiff of gas. She turned to see Jake's face scrunched up with an emotion she couldn't decipher. Anger? Fear? Both?

"Okay. Yeah, no, I get that," he said. "Yeah." Long pause. "Um, yeah, tell him okay." Jake nodded. "Okay." More nodding. "Thanks. Bye."

Willow leaned against the counter and crossed her arms. She opened her mouth to ask what was going on, but all that came out was, "Want some tea?"

"No." Jake ran his hand through his hair over and over.

Willow waited, ashamed that her body still wanted nothing more than to grab this man and drag him upstairs to her bedroom when he was so distressed.

"That was my dad—Walter's—hospice nurse." Jake patted Freya's side, seemingly unaware he was doing so. "He's, uh, taken a turn for the worse tonight."

If anything could douse the fire of her lust, it was the stark reminder Jake's father was Walter Bartlett. *Jake* was a Bartlett. What on earth had she been thinking kissing him like that? No, not just kissing. They'd been in the middle of a hot and heavy session, and she wasn't sure she would've stopped it if the phone hadn't done it for her.

"My d—Walter—he's on hospice care because of his COPD. It's pretty bad. He could last a few more months, or the nurse said he could have a really bad flare-up and go at any time." Jake's face crumpled and recomposed itself. "I haven't seen him in over three years. She told me to prepare myself for a shock when I visit. He—he, uh, lost a lot of weight she said."

She still couldn't bring herself to feel sad about Walter Bartlett dying, and maybe that made her a terrible person, but she *was* starting to care for Jake, who was visibly upset. "I'm sorry," she said, and meant it.

Jake's mouth twisted in a harsh expression. "Walter smoked for years. Didn't stop until he went on hospice. On top of that, one of his doctors told me he didn't do his lungs any favors by working in a lumber mill his whole life. His office was upstairs at the mill, but he was always walking around on the mill floor. No mask, just breathing in the sawdust."

"I remember." Sometimes, BiBi would take Willow to the mill to surprise her dad with a special lunch. Several times she'd caught sight of Mr. Bartlett's tall figure prowling around the mill, and even as a child she hadn't missed the way the workers straightened their backs when he walked by, their bodies rigid with apprehension. One time, she and BiBi arrived just as Mr. Bartlett approached a group of laughing smokers outside. He'd joined them with his cigarette like he was one of the workers, but the other men's and women's eyes grew wide, and their gazes slid to the ground.

Jake let out a heavy sigh. "Anyway, the nurse said he's got pneumonia. They're treating him with antibiotics, but she said it might be a good idea to see him soon." He tapped his fist against his thigh. "Like tonight, soon." His mouth twisted. "Lindsay's headed back from her trip, but for now, I guess I'll have to do."

"Anything I can do?"

Jake closed his eyes and shook his head. "I hate to leave you and Connor alone, but I won't be gone long."

At first, she thought Jake meant because it would be difficult to see his father, but then it all came crashing down on her again like a pile of two-by-fours. The wound on Jake's arm, the red lines in the shape of The Old Tree, the fever that overtook him whenever he strayed far from it.

"We'll be all right. It's you I'm worried about. Are you—are you ready to see your father?"

"Hey, that's why I came back to Cedar Beach, right? Sounds like if I put it off any longer, it will be for nothing." He looked stricken at the idea.

Willow wondered how she would feel if she found out her mother was dying and was surprised how upsetting the thought was. She suspected it was more to do with the idea that any chance of her mom magically healing all the trauma she'd inflicted on Willow in some Hallmark movie moment would die, too—though the loss of the woman herself saddened her. A parent was a parent, even if just in a genetic sense, and losing one represented many things, all of them painful. "Guess you better go, then." She plastered a smile on her face. "Can I get you anything before you leave?"

His gaze drifted to her mouth, and heat crawled up her face at the memory of what they'd just been doing. Something flickered across his own face. Not embarrassment, exactly. She might be reading too much into it, but it almost looked like regret. He took a step back, like he was physically trying to separate himself from the situation. Which was good because she knew it couldn't happen again. Even if Jake weren't a Bartlett, there was too much other crazy stuff going on, and she had to keep her wits about her to protect Connor, her birds, and her home.

So why did it feel so bad when Jake slipped out the back door with no more than a wave?

———

A minute later, Connor appeared in the kitchen. "I saw Jake's truck driving off. I didn't know he was leaving, or I'd have told him goodbye."

"He'll be back." Willow pushed her hair off her forehead, hoping it wasn't obvious why it was so messy. She quickly explained Jake's dad was sick and maybe dying.

"That's sad," Connor said.

"It's Mr. Bartlett," she snapped. It was like having Jake out of sight brought back her feelings of hatred for his father with a vengeance.

"It's still sad when somebody's dying, right?"

Willow rubbed her cheeks to hide her shame at her brother's compassion in the face of her complete lack thereof. "You're right." She cleared her throat. "So, uh, Jake's going to be staying with us for a little while."

Connor's previous hero-worship evaporated into instant suspicion. "Why?" He gave her a careful look. "Are you dating him or something?" The question started off angry and ended on a hopeful note.

"No! No, it's just more convenient if he stays here." She explained about the railings needing to be higher and that Jake was the architect.

"Jake designed our tree houses? That's pretty cool."

"You're okay with him staying here?"

"Sure, if that's what you want." Connor sounded confused, which was understandable. He might like the guy, but having Jake stay with them was a whole different story. Willow was just relieved he wasn't asking more questions. Her little brother didn't need to know the real reason Jake was staying or hear about all the frightening events happening.

Freya growled. The noise of breaking glass came from the living room, and the dog ran toward it in a frenzy of barking. At the moment her brother rushed after Freya, Willow had a terrible feeling Connor was about to see for himself exactly what was going on around here.

"Connor, wait."

Willow dashed after them into the dark living room, where the front window was a mess of broken glass. Shards of it twinkled all over the antique buffet table under the window and sparkled on the rug in front of the couch. The lamp Willow always kept lit lay on its side, the bulb broken to leave the room in darkness, cut only by the light spilling from the kitchen.

Willow grabbed Freya's collar and dragged her to the laundry room to keep her away from the glass. That didn't stop Freya from continuing her ear-splitting barking, and worse, occasionally dropping into low, menacing growls. The lab frantically scratched at the door, rattling it with her efforts to escape. "Stop, Freya. Stop it." The dog ignored her and kept scratching.

Willow returned to the living room to find Connor holding a large branch. Her heart pounded wildly in her throat at the sight of the unmistakable glossy leaves of the madrone still attached to it.

"Don't touch that." Willow hurried to his side.

"What?" Connor held the branch like a staff.

"Drop it, okay?" The last thing she wanted was for him to get a splinter from that tree. She shook his arm in emphasis until he let the branch fall onto the floor.

Connor glared at her. "Why are you being so weird? And how did this even happen?" he asked. "It's not like it's windy out." He pointed to the window, and Willow followed his gaze.

Wicked pieces of broken glass surrounded a jagged hole, letting in a light breeze of chilly, damp air. He was right. There was no strong wind. Nothing but blackness was visible through that hole, but Willow knew exactly what stood in her front yard. A stone birdbath, a couple of weathered Adirondack chairs, a glimpse of the ribbon of highway running below the house— and several large trees, including an ash growing too close to the house that required regular trimming. None of those trees, however, were Pacific madrones. There was no natural explanation for how a branch from a madrone tree crashed through her living room window.

The evil that was stalking Willow might as well have tied a note on the branch for how clear the message was.

*I'm coming for you.*

Willow ground her teeth together and took a deep breath through her nose. "That branch must've been ready to fall from the ash tree. I'll trim it back next winter." Hopefully Connor wouldn't notice the branch wasn't from an ash. "Let's get that glass cleaned up and cover the window."

"There's plywood at the raptor center," Connor said. "Left over from making that quarantine mews."

"Good thinking." It struck her how often Connor was a source of help to her these days.

It took all of Willow's willpower to turn her back on the window, to not rush out into the night and scream at whatever was trying to scare her. No, not *trying* to. Succeeding. She could admit she was afraid, but she wasn't about to give whatever was out there the satisfaction of knowing it. Plus, she didn't want to leave Connor alone.

Her number one priority was protecting her brother. He was already halfway to the kitchen and returned a minute later with the broom, dustpan, and a plastic bag.

"I'll clean it up," she said. "I don't want you to cut yourself."

"Willow, I'm not a baby." He shook his head at her with a half-frown, half-indulgent smile. "I've got this. You go get the plywood, okay?"

She debated which was more dangerous, leaving Connor alone in the house with the broken window or bringing him out into the night. She tapped her fingers on her mouth.

"What are you waiting for?" he asked. "Go." He was carefully picking the pieces of glittering glass off the buffet table, and he stopped to shoo her away.

Unless she wanted to explain her concerns to him—*Oh, hey little bro, forgot to mention a killer flesh-eating owl is on the loose*—she'd be better off hurrying to get the plywood. Besides, she reasoned, Freya would be here with him.

"You got your phone close by?" she asked.

"Am I a teenager?" he deadpanned.

"All right. Call if you need me. I'll be right back."

Willow could never have imagined herself thinking it before, but she wished she knew what became of that gun her dad was holding that day under The Old Tree. What had he been doing out there? Did the tree, or the creature within it, have some hold over him? She shoved the thought from her mind. She needed to focus on grabbing the plywood and getting back to Connor as fast as possible.

She opened the front door and glanced around, acutely aware of being unarmed. What could fight a strix, anyway? She eyed the coatrack of hats and jackets as if it held some sort of weapon. Garlic? Holy water?

No, you idiot, you told Jake earlier. Hawthorn branches.

And she had hawthorn trees on her property. Willow smiled grimly. She'd get some branches of her own and fight fire with fire, so to speak.

Willow stepped outside and spared a glance at the broken window. Connor was visible, far too visible to her tastes, busy with a broom. She crept around the corner of her house like a small woodland creature, keeping her back to the wall as she edged toward the driveway and her car. She scanned the trees, expecting the pale, silent flap of wings at any moment, but she saw and heard nothing.

She slipped into the car and reversed down the drive before heading up the road to the entrance to the raptor center. The car nosed out, again reminding her of a scared mouse darting out of its hole. Without meaning to, she gunned it and fishtailed on the gravel before lurching onto the asphalt. A short way up the road, she turned left into the raptor center entrance.

It was only nine-thirty but felt much later in the darkness of a moonless night. A light drizzle fell. To the far right of the raptor center was a service road to the back. Her headlights swept across the aisles of mews as she turned, and a few birds hopped in their cages at the disturbance. She swung the car onto the narrow road, lined with shrubs. Their branches scratched and thumped the side of her car, making her yelp. It seemed to take much longer at night than in the day to get to the hut at the back of the raptor center. Next to the hut sat a squat work shed with the plywood.

Willow clutched her keys in one hand and her phone with the flashlight on in the other as she climbed out of the car. She looked in every direction but saw nothing. An owl hooted nearby, and her stomach clutched until she realized it was Yolanda, her barn owl. She let out a shaky breath and approached the shed to unlock the padlock on the door.

A chain hung from a single bulb, its weak light doing nothing to illuminate the far corners of the shed. It was a space about the size of her living room, with a small window at either end.

Workbenches lined three sides. Willow spotted several offcuts of plywood leaning against the far wall. She started toward it and tripped over the handle of a rake to sprawl on the rough floor. Her palms stung at the impact, and she crouched a moment to catch her breath.

As she climbed to her feet, she caught a movement in the far window above the plywood. Her pulse sped up, and she glanced at the door. There was no way to lock the shed from the inside.

The movement came again, and she sighed in relief. It was only the wind blowing the branches of the nearby trees. Willow hurried to the plywood and picked up a piece. It was heavier than she'd expected, and she had to make a separate trip for each of the three pieces she figured would be sufficient to cover the living room window. On her last trip, she pulled a simple bow saw from the pegboard on the wall.

Time to find those hawthorn trees by the creek. She stood by her car and peered into the dark. The drizzle turned to a steady rain, and she was chilled through, her hair plastered against her head. She regretted not wearing more than a T-shirt under her jacket. Was this the best idea? Was she really going to traipse into the woods by herself at night in the rain?

But if it were true, and strix *were* repelled by hawthorn, then surely it was worth the risk. There was no point wasting more time debating it while Connor was alone at the house.

Willow drew a deep breath and plunged into the trees. Behind her, Yolanda—*please let it be Yolanda*—hooted again. She gripped the bow saw and looked all around. The faint sound of running water grew louder under the soft sound of rain falling through the trees. It was so dark, she worried she might fall into the creek, even with the phone light. She spotted some trees that looked promising and used an app to snap a picture of one of the leaves.

*C. douglasii or black hawthorn* popped up on her screen. Bingo. She set her phone on the ground with the flashlight pointed up to illuminate her work. She quickly sawed at the branches, choosing finger-sized or smaller. The rasping noise made her nervous because she couldn't hear anything else above it, nor could she see anything outside the bright circle of light from her phone. It took an eternity to cut through each branch, and the darkness pressed in like a physical presence until she couldn't take it anymore. Instead of the dozen cuttings she'd wanted, she settled for eight.

Willow gathered the branches against her chest, struggling to carry the bow saw and use her light to navigate while gripping her car keys. Up ahead, what scant light there was glinted off the car's windshield. Almost there. She quickened her pace when her phone light turned off to plunge her into darkness.

A current of air stirred above her head. She glanced up in time to see a huge great gray owl glide silently into a nearby tree. Willow broke into a run and didn't stop to pick up a fallen hawthorn branch. She reached the road and her car, quickly unlocking it to toss the branches onto the passenger seat with a clatter. She dove behind the wheel and slammed the door. The satisfying click of the locks made her feel safer.

Her breathing was loud and ragged, and the metal of the car key dug into her fingers. No way was she dropping it again. She shoved the key into the ignition and started the engine, throwing the car into reverse.

In the grainy image of her back-up camera, the road behind her wasn't empty.

Willow shrieked at the sight.

# Chapter 16

Jake pulled into the steep driveway of his father's house on the hill. Naturally, it was a log house, two-stories with three dormer windows on the second floor. It might be built of the lumber that made his fortune, but Walter Bartlett's house was about as rustic as a celebrity's cabin in Aspen or Jackson Hole.

One dormer window glowed, and a faint light on the first floor came from the living room. Otherwise, the giant house was as dark and foreboding as the feeling in Jake's gut. He got out and closed the truck door to stand in the cool night. The ocean crashed onto the rocks below, covering up the sound of his heavy breathing. He was really going to do this. He was going to visit his dying father.

Jake's arm ached, and he knew it wouldn't be long before it grew into a deep throb. It was hard to tell how much of his sick feeling was the illness creeping in again or his fear of facing what waited inside that house. Right about now, he'd rather face a strix in The Old Tree than go in there. With heavy feet, he clomped up the porch steps and lifted his hand to knock, but the door swung in before he could do so.

He hadn't given much thought to his father's hospice nurse, but she wasn't what Jake had expected—maybe someone middle-aged and matronly. Instead, a young Asian woman with electric blue hair opened the door. He stepped inside the stuffy house.

"Jake, right?" She pushed her red glasses up her nose and gave him an encouraging smile.

He only nodded. Words couldn't escape his tight throat.

"I'm Olivia. You want anything to drink before we go upstairs?" she asked. "Water? Coffee? A shot of whiskey?"

Jake tried to laugh, but the sound came out strangled. "I'm good." He glanced around, surprised the house was messy. Papers and books were strewn over the couch, the baby grand piano, and the coffee table in the living room. Olivia led him through the gourmet kitchen where his father never cooked. Soft under-cabinet lighting revealed that here, too, every available surface was covered in more books and papers. It was like some mad, absent-minded professor had taken over his father's house.

Olivia must have noticed his interest because she gave a small laugh. "He doesn't want the cleaners here anymore. Just me and another nurse."

"What is all this?" Jake took a step toward the granite island and picked up what looked like a magazine. "'Journal of Paranormal Science'?" His heart stuttered in his chest. He slid aside the glossy journal and picked up a book. *Myths of Eastern Europe.* A yellow sticky note on a stack of papers read, "Tree Spirits" in his father's slanted, angry scrawl and was underlined three times. "What the hell?" he muttered.

Olivia shoved her hair back from her forehead. "Yeah, your dad's into some pretty weird sh—stuff." She shifted her weight to stand taller, as if reminding herself to be more professional. "It's not unusual for dying people to take a sudden interest in more spiritual concerns, or to want to explore the supernatural.

It can provide comfort, the idea there's more to this world than what we see."

Comfort wasn't the word Jake would use. He couldn't imagine his father being interested in anything like that. Not that he knew Walter that well, but still. He was a man of industry and commerce, more concerned with money and material—not spiritual—wealth. At this exact moment, Jake wished more than anything he could believe there *wasn't* more to the world than what he could see, than what could be explained by science and reason. His arm pained him, and he was sure if he shoved up his sleeve, the red lines would be back. It served as a reminder he couldn't afford to tarry. He rubbed his hand over his forearm. Heat radiated from it. His body ached more with every passing second.

Olivia paused at the bottom of the back stairs. "You ready?"

Jake nodded and followed her up to the landing. It was even hotter upstairs. Ahead, faint light spilled from the cavernous master bedroom. The soft *whoosh* of an oxygen machine reached his ears, and Jake swallowed.

He recalled the last time he'd seen his father. Thanksgiving, a few years ago. It had been, to his initial consternation, just the two of them for the meal, which Walter had had ordered from a boutique restaurant in the next town over. The food was delicious and the company was surprisingly good. Without an audience, it turned out his father felt no need to bully Jake. They'd talked about Jake's studies in architecture and his adventures kitesurfing, and his father spoke about his most recent trip to Bolivia, even gifting Jake with a small stone talisman from his travels. After the obligatory pumpkin pie, his father suggested a game of chess with Jake, who hadn't played much before. His father patiently explained the basics of the game, and for the first time in his life, Jake imagined having a relationship with him.

That's what made it all the crueler when his dad's new girlfriend showed up. It didn't take long before Walter returned to his bullying ways, pointing out Jake's dumb chess moves and even expressing doubt Jake would finish his architecture degree. "He'll be back to his beach bumming soon enough," he'd said, laughing heartily in the face of his simpering girlfriend with the overdone plastic surgeries.

Why was he even here? One single meal summed up the only good time he'd ever had with the man in that room, and even that had been ruined on the same night.

"Hey, it's all right," Olivia whispered, and Jake stirred from his frozen stance in the hallway. She laid her hand on his arm and frowned. "You feel all right?"

"I'm fine." His voice came out a croak. "Just—not looking forward to this." He waved toward the open bedroom.

"Your dad told me things haven't been ideal between you."

"That's one way to put it."

"Whatever's happened in the past is in the past. I'm sure you'll have to process that, but in this moment, you only have right now with him. He felt it was extremely important he see you, and I'm sure he'll appreciate you honoring that request." She smiled. "I can be here the whole time if you want, or I can wait downstairs." She tilted her head. "You sure you're okay? Physically, I mean?"

Jake was not okay in any sense of the word, but what he needed to do was face his father and get the hell back to Tree Top, where Willow was waiting for him and where he'd quickly feel better. "I'm good." Remembering the girlfriend at Thanksgiving, he added, "You can wait downstairs."

"Okay, but I'll be nearby if you or Mr. Bartlett need anything."

"Thanks."

Jake watched the young nurse turn away with some reluctance, waiting until she disappeared down the stairs before entering his father's room. It was stifling, like stepping into a sauna. Low light came from a bedside table. A massive four-poster, king-sized bed made of burl wood dominated the room. But where was his dad?

Jake startled when his father stirred on the bed, horrified his dad had been there all along. He was so small. Jake hadn't seen him at first. He rested against a pile of pillows, huddled under a thick burgundy comforter. Jake was built like his dad—tall and rangy. Walter Bartlett hadn't been a broad, hulking man, but he'd always had a presence that made him seem bigger than he was. Now he'd shrunk to skin and bones, a tiny figure who looked like a little boy in a giant's world, lost among the land of bedding to make no more than the smallest of mounds in its landscape. The only sound was the soft *click* and *whoosh* of the oxygen.

His father tried to speak but broke into a coughing fit that went on for several minutes. Jake's legs trembled with the urge to run from the room, but he fought it. Walter, still coughing, waved him closer, and Jake lurched toward the bed as if jerked on a string.

Jake never called him Dad, and Walter just felt weird. "Hey."

"Jake," he rasped. He reached clumsily for Jake's hand and grasped it in his icy, bony one. Jake tried not to recoil. How could Walter's hand still be cold in this blazing hot room? "You—don't look—so good." His words came out in pants, each syllable hard won.

The chill from his father's skin crept up his arm to where pain pulsed with his heartbeat.

"You don't look so hot yourself." Jake didn't hide his scrutiny of the man. His face was pale and blotchy, his eyes sunken, and the blue tinge around his mouth was obvious even in the low light.

"What'd you—expect? I'm dying, kid."

Jake didn't know how to respond.

"Don't worry—not right now. I'm too mean—to die—for a little while yet." He laughed, which turned into another coughing fit, mercifully shorter than the last. "This is my third bout—of pneumonia this year. I'll pull—through, you'll see." He squeezed Jake's hand, then released it. "Hey, don't look—so disappointed. I'll die—eventually."

Jake looked down at his shoes.

"Don't tell me—you'll be sad—when your old man's—gone?"

Jake lifted his head. "For the rest of my life, I'll be sad. Sad that we never had a relationship."

The words, in the simplicity of their truth, must have hit home. Walter flinched like he'd been struck. His oxygen *click*ed and *whoosh*ed a few more breaths before he spoke. "Me—too, Jake. More—than you can—imagine."

Jake's body was growing weaker by the moment at the effort of standing up and trying to appear normal. If he didn't get back to Willow's soon, he might as well crawl into the bed next to his father and join him. "Is this some kind of deathbed confession of yours when you beg for my forgiveness, and I tell you it's all okay?" Jake sounded exhausted, rather than angry.

"I don't—expect that," he gasped out. "Don't—deserve it."

Jake thought of his mom's advice to go see his father before time ran out, but what did she think would be accomplished by this? Some real-life version of the Johnny Cash song, *A Boy Named Sue?* All he felt was a crushing sense of sadness, of needless waste that this man before him was little more than a stranger. Suddenly, it was all too much. The overwhelming heat of the room made his head spin, and without thinking, he pushed his sleeves up out of habit.

His father gasped, and his eyes widened in dismay. With surprising strength, he grabbed Jake's wrist and pulled his arm closer. "No." The word was a soft wail, and the chill from his father's hand spread throughout his body at the sound. "You've—been—marked."

Jake yanked back his arm and pulled down his sleeve. "Marked?"

"Mike always—said—there'd—be—more." He took a labored breath. "No. Not my son." His fingers grasped at the blankets. "Not Jake." His gaze took on a faraway look before snapping back to Jake. "You have to—" He stopped to take another breath. "You have to—listen." He reached for Jake's hand again, and Jake's fingers tightened reflexively, both afraid and eager to hear what Walter would say next. "To—survive—this—you—have—to—" He started coughing again, and Jake stared in helpless horror as his father's face grew bluer. He was about to get Olivia when he heard steps on the stairs.

She entered the room and nudged Jake out of the way to take his place. "Hey, Walter," she said with false cheer. "Let's get you up a little higher, okay?" In moments, with brisk efficiency, she had Walter propped up on the pillows. It disturbed Jake how easily this small woman could move his father around, proof of how frail he'd become.

Walter tried to gesture or point, but all he managed to do was to flop his right hand off the bed.

Olivia picked something off the nightstand. "Yes, I was just going to get your inhaler for you." She held it up to Walter's mouth. He shook his head, but she ignored him. "Take a nice, slow breath. That's it, nice and easy."

After a couple of puffs, his father licked his lips and waved his hand toward Jake. "I—want—"

"No," Olivia said. "I want *you* to rest."

Walter shifted on the bed, his hands clasping and unclasping on a groan.

"He wanted to tell me something," Jake said, feeling oddly protective of the man he'd only ever felt contempt for in the past.

"It will have to wait." Olivia smoothed his father's forehead. "He really does need to rest."

"What if he—" Jake's head swam, and he couldn't bring himself to say the words. He felt so ill, he wasn't sure he could make it downstairs on his own, let alone drive back to Willow's house.

"Your dad is a stubborn man." Olivia laughed. "He's not going anywhere just yet. Come back tomorrow, all right?"

Jake stood there a moment, hoping she didn't notice him swaying on his feet. In the end, he decided not only was his father in no shape to share whatever he needed to say, Jake was in no condition to receive it. "I'll be back soon, okay?"

Walter's eyelids fluttered and closed in a fleeting expression of relief before his face went slack.

Alarmed, Jake asked, "Is he okay?"

"He's asleep." Olivia perched on the side of the bed. "Don't worry, Jake. I'll be here all night." She smiled at him. "You can go."

Jake nodded. Summoning his reserves, he showed himself out. He staggered at the bottom of the stairs and used the wall for support as he stumbled out the front door. His arm throbbed with every step with a pain unlike any he'd ever known. He gritted his teeth and hauled himself into his truck before collapsing into the driver's seat.

After a few slow breaths, he slid his phone from his pocket and dialed Willow's number. The call went straight to voice mail. Maybe it was just the macabre scene upstairs or the pain coloring his thoughts, but he suddenly had a bad feeling.

Why wasn't Willow picking up?

# Chapter 17

Willow clamped her trembling lips together to hold back a shriek. Goosebumps broke out on her arms as she looked at the screen of her back-up cam. What she saw didn't make any sense. Half of her wanted to crane her neck and look behind her to try to understand what she was seeing, and the other half thought that was possibly the worst idea ever.

She peered closer to the screen, and her stomach went into a freefall of horror. A figure stood about twenty feet behind the car, arms out like a gunslinger. *Skeletal* arms. The body was a complete skeleton, like one of those in an anatomy lab minus the metal pole. And this skeleton could move on its own. The skull had long dark hair, and the skeleton didn't look very tall—Willow knew it was a woman, the strix herself in what could only loosely be described as human form. What was worse was she wasn't *entirely* skeletal. Both hands were covered in flesh and the face—oh god, the face was terrible. Skin covered the front of the skull. She had lips and a nose, cheeks and brow, the face of what could be a young woman.

But when the strix opened her eyes, they were nothing but empty sockets, like twin black holes to hell. It was the scariest thing Willow had ever seen.

All of this took only a couple of seconds. Without thinking further, Willow gunned the engine. She waited for the satisfying smack of metal on bone, but in the back-up cam, there was a strange blurring, like the wavering of air over a hot road. The blur was gone in the blink of an eye, and an owl took silent wing to disappear from the camera's view. Willow glanced out her window and saw the owl flying low over the trees toward the house.

Connor. Alone and with a broken window, completely helpless and vulnerable.

Willow whipped the steering wheel around and put the car in drive, tearing down the road as branches thumped along the car. When she reached the parking lot of the raptor center, she skidded into the gravel. She corrected and gently goosed the accelerator. The car shot onto the highway.

Her shingle house came into view. A large figure loomed in the living room window, but she couldn't make out who—or what—it was. Willow's throat shut with terror. Connor was inside, all alone. The figure was too big to be the strix in her skeletal human form—too big to be Jake, for that matter, even though she wished it were him. Who the hell was standing there?

Willow screeched the car to a halt in the driveway and shoved open the driver's door to jump out. Freya's frenzied barking came from inside the house. A shape, lighter than the dark night, swept down from the ash tree. The red eyes of a demon glowed in the disc-shaped face of the owl-strix. It flew straight at Willow, sharp talons extended toward her face. Willow dove back into the car and grabbed up the hawthorn branches from the passenger seat.

In a moment of truth, she straightened back out of the car with one of the branches brandished high above her head. The strix wheeled and shrieked in a sound no bird and no human could ever make. The terrible screech was awful, worse than fingernails on a chalkboard. Willow almost dropped the armload of branches to clap her hands to her ears. The owl's wings just grazed the top of her head as it let out another scream. The sound made Willow's stomach heave in a wave of overpowering nausea, and she retched as she stumbled over the gravel and up the front porch.

Connor held open the front door, Freya barking at his side. "Hurry! It's coming back!"

Willow didn't bother to confirm this. She pushed Connor inside and shoved in after him, slamming and locking the door behind her. She dropped the branches to the floor at her feet with a clatter. Freya rushed forward to lick Willow's hand.

"The window," she gasped. She turned to look at it. When her brain registered what she saw, she started laughing uncontrollably.

The wooden Santa Claus from the garage was now pushed against the broken window, held snugly in place by the buffet table. The painted side faced the interior. Santa waved and smiled at the living room, his cheeks rosy and his nose like a cherry.

"How resourceful of you," she said once she'd regained control of her hysteria. It seemed she'd underestimated her brother.

"Why is that owl acting like that?" Connor's eyes were huge in his pale face. He moved closer to the window. "Whoa. That's a lot of owls."

"What?" Willow picked up a branch, once again brandishing it like a weapon. She stepped next to her brother to peer out. More shapes flew through the night. Other strix? Regular owls? Beside her, Freya growled. The owls landed in the trees surrounding the house.

"Let's get away from here." She tugged on Connor's sleeve and pulled him from the window. "I need to warn Jake." She took out her dead phone and rushed into the kitchen to plug it into the charger on the counter. It would be a few minutes before it could hold enough charge to bring up Jake's number. Hopefully, he hadn't started back yet.

Connor stepped into the kitchen doorway. "I don't like this."

"Me neither, but we're safe inside."

"I don't know about that." His tone was dark, and Willow's stomach clenched.

"What do you mean?"

Connor's expression was grim. "I saw The Bandage Man again right before you got here."

"Where?"

"I'll show you." Connor led her back into the living room and pointed to the fireplace. "Over there."

Willow stepped toward the river rock hearth. It was like moving into a chilly patch of fog. She shivered and turned in a circle. With a monster out there on the loose challenging her belief system, this was no time to doubt Connor about ghosts. "What did he do?"

"He just stood there looking at the window. Except he didn't have any eyes."

Willow shuddered, remembering the empty sockets of the strix-woman.

"What's going on, Willow? What's with the owl attacking you? And me seeing the Bandage Man?"

Willow studied her little brother. Only he wasn't so little these days. He was taller than her, and the shadow of a mustache was visible on his upper lip. He looked scared, but then so was she. But he also looked like what he was—a teenager on the cusp of adulthood. She wanted to protect him from unpleasantness forever, but he had a right to know what was happening here, didn't he?

He must have sensed her hesitation. "Just tell me."

"Okay, fine. This is going to sound crazy, okay? But when Jake cut the broken branch off The Old Tree, we think it released this—this monster called a strix. It can change shape between an owl and a woman. I think it was living in The Old Tree. Or it was suspended in it or something."

"Okay," he said slowly. "What does it want?"

"I don't know."

"How can it be defeated?"

"You make it sound like a boss in a video game." Connor rolled his eyes at her. "Okay. Um, you have to cut off the head or impale it through the heart, like a vampire or something. I don't know. This is all crazy. Strix are these creatures from Greek mythology, and I read how hawthorn can repel them. I brought some hawthorn branches back from the trees behind the raptor center, and it seems to have worked."

"Okay, we make some hawthorn stakes, and we kill it."

"No, *we* don't do anything. I do. You're getting the hell away from here. I'm sending you to stay with Grandpa and Bibi."

"Willow."

"Or Ethan, if you'd rather."

"I'm not leaving you."

"I'll have Jake."

"This is my home, too. I want to protect it."

"And it's my job to protect you."

Her phone chimed in the kitchen, indicating it had come back on. She ran in and snatched it off the counter, and dialed Jake.

On the third ring, he picked up. "Willow?" His voice was strained.

"Where are you?"

"In your driveway."

"Oh, no. Okay, stay in your truck. I'm coming for you." She unplugged the phone again to run to the front of the house. Connor stood at the window again, with Freya barking at his side.

"Willow," Jake said in her ear. "I'm—"

The phone died again, but it didn't matter. She could see the situation for herself. Jake stood in the driveway surrounded by a circle of around a dozen owls, all perched on the ground in perfect stillness about five feet from him in every direction, like numbers on a clock.

It was arguably one of the creepiest sights imaginable.

"Uhh," Connor said. "Are those owls all strix monsters?"

"I sure hope not." Willow snatched up a hawthorn branch and opened the front door. Connor picked up his own branch and followed, slamming the door before Freya could slip out. She whirled around and jabbed her finger in his face. "No. You stay here."

"I can help."

"No, Connor. Stay here. I'll be all right." With the hawthorn branch, she'd be all right.

Willow strode toward Jake. Twelve owl heads swiveled in her direction, some of them turning almost a hundred and eighty degrees to do so. Twelve pairs of glowing red eyes looked in her direction. As chilling as that sight was, Willow was more concerned by the great gray owl gliding through the night sky. Another odd blurring wavered through the darkness. The owl disappeared, and the skeletal woman now stood just beyond Jake's truck, staring at him from those empty sockets.

"Jake," Willow said in a soft voice. "Can you make a run for the house?" She figured he must be sick from being away from her property. "Do you feel up to it yet?"

"I feel better now I'm back. But they don't want me to move."

"What do you mean?"

Jake took a step toward her. The owl heads snapped back in his direction with warning hoots and screeches. One of them lifted into the air and beat its wings around Jake's head. He covered his face with his arms and backtracked to the center of the circle. The owls immediately settled back into their spots.

"That's what I mean." He slowly lowered his arms.

Willow's gaze flicked from Jake to the strix-woman. Jake seemed unaware of her presence. No need to alarm him further. The sound of the strix-woman's skeletal feet hitting the gravel was soft, but steady. It was like the owls held Jake there, waiting for her arrival. Vaguely, she was aware of Freya's frantic barking coming from the house.

She hefted the hawthorn branch onto her shoulder and stepped closer to the circle, within striking distance. When none of the owls moved, she swung the branch like a baseball bat. "Get out of here."

As several of them took flight and circled in her direction, Willow noticed they weren't the least bit bothered by the hawthorn. Hopefully that meant they weren't strixes, too. With a start, like cold water in the face, Willow recognized one of the owls as Rufus. Last she'd checked, there'd been nothing strix-like about the goofy avian. What was he doing here? How did he get out of his cage?

Before she could think more about it, a large barn owl headed straight for her face. She ducked, but right behind it sailed a great horned owl. Its talons connected with her head. Searing pain burned her scalp. Another owl swooped in behind that one, and a ripping pain shot through her right bicep. Willow used her branch not as a supernatural deterrent as she'd hoped, but a bludgeon to knock away another great horned owl. Feathers flew, and she winced, hoping she hadn't hurt the creature too much. As she swung wildly with her branch, a screech owl pulled up at the last moment, grazing her arm with its talons. She stood in a maelstrom of feathers, flapping wings, sharp beaks, and talons.

"Go, Jake! Run!" she yelled.

"Oh, shit!" Jake was staring at the strix-woman.

Which gave Willow an idea. She covered her head with her arms and crouched low, gripping the branch like a sword as the owls continued to swoop down on her. Even though they clawed and ripped at her flesh, pulled at her hair, and beat their wings around her, she focused her strength on getting closer to the strix.

The strix was too focused on Jake to notice Willow. The

skeletal woman was marching toward Jake. He fumbled with his keys, and the alarm on his truck went off, but it didn't slow the strix or the owls. Jake scrabbled at the truck door. Willow couldn't see past Rufus, who was beating his wings in her face.

Jake started shouting. Willow needed to buy him time to get into his truck. A spotted owl swooped down toward the strix—and Willow's throat constricted at the sight of that distinctive white splotch on the chest. Cynthia! The elderly owl shouldn't be able to fly, and yet here she was soaring through the air toward the strix. Whatever dark magic was allowing her favorite owl to do so, it provided the moment of distraction Willow needed. The strix lifted a skeletal hand toward the spotted owl. Willow sprang from her crouch and ran full speed toward the strix. The creature turned, and her jaw opened on a terrible scream to reveal a mouth full of fangs. The fangs were frightening, but not nearly as powerful as that scream. Willow staggered and almost fell.

A branch whistled over her head, chasing away another barn owl.

"Connor," she said, seeing her brother beside her. "Get back inside."

"Get her. I've got your back." He turned his back to hers and swung at the dive-bombing owls.

Willow didn't hesitate. She stepped within striking distance of the strix-woman and whipped the branch around in an arc. At the moment she should have connected with the strix, her branch met nothing by empty air. A great gray owl rose into the night sky, letting out one more terrible screech before disappearing.

At once, the owls fluttered to the ground, like puppets whose strings had been cut.

Some of the owls took flight immediately, while others appeared dazed for a few seconds before taking wing as well. In moments, they were all gone save one bird, leaving Willow, Jake, and Connor alone in the dark.

Connor stared at Willow, then Jake, and back to Willow. "What the actual f—"

"Connor!"

"—uck?" he said. He lifted his shoulders in a shrug, unimpressed by her glaring. "You always told me to save swearing for the right time and place. I thought this might be it."

"The boy has a point," Jake said.

Willow barked out a laugh. She glanced around, and noticed Rufus sitting in the driveway, his feathers fluffed up and wearing a dazed expression. She laughed again at the absurd sight of him, but as she surveyed the area, her laughter died. Her stomach clenched in alarm.

Her favorite owl was nowhere to be seen.

# Chapter 18

Jake watched Willow strip off her jacket, revealing a gash on her right arm. "What are you do—"

"Shh." Willow crept a few steps toward an owl still standing in the driveway. "Hey, Rufus, remember me, buddy?" she said in a soft, soothing voice.

She flung the jacket over the bird and scooped him up against her chest. "Open the door, open the door," she shouted.

Had Willow lost her mind? Jake stood there like an idiot for a couple of beats too long. Connor was already running toward the house. He yanked open the front door and Willow ran through. Jake followed after them both and struggled to make sense of Willow's actions. His brain was still in the grip of figuring out whether to go into fight or flight. Any thoughts more complicated than that were beyond him. He shut and locked the front door behind them.

Willow and Connor raced into the hallway with the owl, who'd started making despondent hooting noises. Freya chased after them, her claws scrabbling on the wood floors. The sound of a door opening—presumably the bathroom or laundry room—was followed by a *slam,* and a moment later, Willow, Connor, and Freya returned to the living room. Willow carried her jacket over her arm.

Jake stood with his hands on his hips, attempting to figure out why Santa was in the front window. He swiveled toward them. "Um, so why did you just catch one of the owls that was trying to *eat* us and bring it into the house?"

"He wasn't trying to eat us." Willow shoved her hair off her face. "That was one of my rescues. I think the strix was commanding those owls out there or something."

"Commanding them? Like an owl army?"

"Exactly. Didn't you notice how they fell to the ground after the strix left? It was like they were under her spell."

"A spell?" Jake shook his head at himself. All he was doing was repeating back Willow's words at her.

"Strix are sometimes considered to be witches. I think those other owls were under some sort of spell, like familiars under a compulsion to serve her."

"Sure." Jake felt his grasp on reality shift in an alarming lurch.

Her mouth tightened. "I just hope Cynthia is all right."

"Cynthia?" Jake asked.

"My first-ever rehab bird. She's old and alone out there, and she can't fly. At least, not normally," she added darkly.

"What are we going to do?" Connor stood at the window, peering out around the edge of the Santa.

"What's with the Christmas décor?" Jake asked.

Willow told him about the branch coming through the window.

"What do we *do?*" Connor repeated loudly. "That—that thing is going to come back, don't you think?"

"Almost definitely." Jake laughed a little, though why, he didn't know. "You two should get out of here. You can stay at my place."

"Why wouldn't you come with us?" Connor eyed him suspiciously, and Jake's brain finally kicked in. He needed to think, to act.

"I can't leave." He explained to Connor about his injured arm and what happened every time he got any distance from The Old Tree. Jake felt guilty, like it was his fault he was tied to this place. He guessed it was. If he'd never pulled that stupid prank at Toby's urging, none of them would be in this position. "You two can still leave." He turned to Willow. "Take Connor and get him somewhere safe."

"I'm not leaving." Willow's chin jutted up. "This is my home. I won't leave my animals. I need to find Cynthia. I need to check on the center and make sure no other birds got out." Willow started pulling on her jacket.

"You can't go to the raptor center right now," Jake said. "It's too dangerous."

"I have to check on my birds."

"No, Willow. He's right," Connor said. "Wait until morning. I don't want anything to happen to you. It's not safe out there. I wouldn't even want to walk to our car right now." He looked out the window and shuddered.

Willow froze with one arm halfway through her jacket sleeve and then withdrew it, hunching into a defeated pose. "Connor. What if the strix let out all our birds?"

"Are you going to somehow catch them all tonight?" Connor asked.

"Some of them can't fly. Like Cynthia. They'd be easy to capture."

"Easy?" Connor said. "Eas*ier* maybe, but we can't go running around in the dark trying to round them up if they got out—which you don't even know is true." He held up his hands to cut off his sister.

"And if some of them can't fly," Jake pointed out, "they'll still be nearby in the morning, and you can catch them then."

She pulled on her bottom lip as if thinking hard. "Cynthia

will probably be waiting at the center in the morning to be fed."

"Yes." Relief trickled into Jake's chest. "Any owls who got out will know where the gravy train is. Wait until daylight, and she'll be waiting for you there. The situation will be a lot safer when we can at least see. And maybe this thing is weaker in the day."

"We just wait here like sitting ducks all night?"

Jake tapped his fist on his thigh. "You're sure you won't take Connor away?"

Willow sighed and cradled her forehead in her hand to massage her temples. "No. I agree with both of you about it not being safe out there. It's like I sense her waiting for us, for any of us to do something stupid. I think Connor is right. Even going out to the car to make a run for it seems foolish right now."

Jake could sense it, too—a malevolence lurking outside the house. "In that case, I think it's best we hunker down here until morning."

Willow nodded a few times to herself. "Okay. It's not like we can call the cops or call in the strix exterminators, right? So, we make this place as safe as possible." She pointed at the pile of hawthorn branches. "I want a branch blocking every door and window in this house." She whirled around to the fireplace and bent to close the flue. "We need to secure every way inside."

"We need to see to those cuts of yours," Jake said.

"I'm fine," Willow grunted, straightening from the hearth.

Like hell she was. None of them were fine after what they'd just witnessed.

———

"That ought to do it." Jake put the last hawthorn branch across the windowsill of the guest room and returned to the hall. He'd had to snap branches into pieces to have enough, but he and Connor had placed the hawthorn across every entrance to the building while Willow had done her best to get Rufus comfortable in the downstairs bathroom.

"I hope that's enough to keep us safe." Willow looked at the pile of weapons they'd assembled in the hallway. A hawthorn branch for each of them, an axe, a couple of baseball bats, and two ping-pong paddles. Connor picked up his hawthorn branch and gave it a slow-motion test swing.

Willow kicked one of the paddles. "This is pathetic."

Jake silently agreed. "The hawthorn kept the strix away twice. We should be all right. Now, will you finally let me help you?"

Blood streaked Willow's left temple and jawline. Her hands were scratched and bloody, and a tear in her shirt revealed a deep gouge in her right bicep.

She sighed. "Fine. This isn't much of a plan. Put some hawthorn branches over the openings, and what? Go to sleep with our ping-pong paddles?" The scorn in her words was scorching.

"Until you can take Connor and leave, then yes." He brushed his hand over her shoulder, like he was wiping away some lint and not that he was desperate to touch her.

"For the last time, I'm not leaving you here alone, Jake. And I'm not leaving my birds."

Jake decided they could resume that argument in the morning. He bent and scooped up his share of their pitiful armament. "Connor, go to bed, man. You got school tomorrow, and you need some sleep for finals."

"We could all get eaten by an owl monster." Connor laughed. "You think I care about finals right now?"

"You should," Jake said. "I spent a lot of time helping you with that math. You better ace that test." He punched him in the shoulder. "Look, we're going to figure this all out, and you'll be glad you got good grades on your finals. For now, you need to get some sleep because it's late. I'll get your sister fixed up, okay?"

"Okay." Some color returned to Connor's pale face. Jake didn't miss the glare Willow shot at him. *Oops.* Stepped on some toes.

"First, I want you to pack some clothes," Willow said. "Tomorrow after school, you're going home to Grandpa and Bibi's house."

Connor groaned. "No, Willow. I wanna be here with you guys. I can help."

"Not happening." Willow's mouth set in a thin line.

"This is stupid. You're treating me like a child."

"Because you *are* a child."

"Right. What I should've said is you're treating me like a baby."

"It might be a good idea to stay with them, Connor," Jake said. "I mean, we don't know how personal this thing with the strix is. What if it goes after your grandparents? Who will protect them?" Connor's face took on a considering expression, while Willow's glare at Jake only intensified. He ignored her. "Your sister is going to be distracted by trying to protect you if you stay here. I'll be here to watch out for her, all right, man? *You* need to watch out for your grandparents."

"I guess."

"I'll call you if we need any back-up. I promise. And you'll call us if you need anything, okay?" Jake held out his hand and Connor reluctantly slapped his into it, and they shook.

Willow put her hands on her hips. "Connor, go pack and then get into bed." Her face softened, and she leaned up to kiss him on the cheek. "I love you, bro. I'll be right down the hall if you need me tonight."

"And I'll be right next door," Jake added. This earned him another glower from Willow.

Connor disappeared into his room, and Freya went with him. She really was a good dog. Willow shook her head at Jake, scooped up a hawthorn branch, and marched down the hallway. Jake followed her into her bedroom.

She turned to him. "What do you think you're doing?"

"What I said. I need to help you with those cuts."

She huffed out a breath and pushed her hair off her forehead. "I'm almost thirty years old. I don't need your help. I'm perfectly capable of doing it myself."

"You're perfectly capable of seeing the top of your own head?" He stepped closer and made a point of looking down at her hair. What he wanted to do was gather her in his arms and tuck her under his chin, but she looked pissed.

"Ever heard of a thing called mirrors?" She turned on her heel and strode into the master bathroom to demonstrate. Upon tipping her head down and parting her hair with her fingers, her face blanched.

"Yeah, it's a nasty cut," he said.

She stared at him in the mirror, keeping her back to him. "Connor and I have gotten along fine without you all these years." She unclenched her fists at her sides and took a deep breath that made her chest rise and fall.

"I know."

"I don't need you stepping in and trying to parent him for me." Another shaky breath escaped her. She began vigorously scrubbing her bloody hands in the sink, which had to hurt.

"Okay."

"And I sure as hell don't need you here to 'watch out for me.'" She did air quotes with her fingers, dripping water on the counter. "It's filling Connor's head with ideas women can't look out for themselves." She snatched the hand towel from the ring and dabbed at her hands. She ripped open a drawer so hard, it almost fell off its track and took out a box of Band-Aids and started applying them to her scratched fingers. "Last time I checked, you're here because *you* need *me* to let you stay on my property, so you don't get sick."

"That's true."

She turned to face him but seemed to have run out of things to say. She crossed her arms. "So, you're just agreeing with everything I say? Nice tactic."

"It's not a tactic. You were right about all of it."

"Then why did you completely overstep your bounds out there?" She lifted her head toward the hallway.

"You didn't play any sports in school, did you?" he asked.

"What does that have to do with anything? Like you did?"

He winced. "After I moved to Santa Cruz, I took up Ultimate Frisbee, and it just so happens I sort of ruled at it in both high school and college."

"Ultimate Frisbee? Wow. Super cool." She quirked one of her dark eyebrows at him. Her green eyes stood out beautifully in her pale face.

"Maybe not, but it's a *team* sport. Where each player needs the other as they work toward a common goal."

"Oh my God, are you explaining team sports to me? As a matter of fact, I was on the archery team in college."

"Oh." Jake cleared his throat. "I saw some sort of trophies in the closet. Why are you hiding them in there?" The silence stretched on uncomfortably, but Jake forced himself not to speak.

"My dad put them on display, but after he died, I hid them. I'm not a braggart, okay? That's more my mom's thing." Willow reddened. "She modeled when she was younger. She put up her photos all over the house. I thought it was cool when I was little, but that's weird, right?"

"You're not your mom, Willow. Just like I'm not my dad." Another long silence spun out between them. "Anyway, my point is, like it or not, you and I are a team. We have a common goal—defeat the strix and protect your brother."

"I don't need you on my team. Team Duncan has two members. Me"—she hiked her thumb at her chest—"and Connor." She pointed in the direction of his room.

"Wouldn't you agree working together betters our odds of achieving our common goal? That it would be smarter for the sake of Connor if you let me help?"

"And your idea of helping me is to manipulate Connor into thinking our grandparents need his protection? He's fourteen.

It's not his job to look after them. It's my job to look after him."

"It worked, didn't it? You're not standing in the hall fighting with Connor anymore."

"No, I'm standing in my bathroom fighting with *you.*"

Jake stepped closer. "You don't *have* to fight with me, you know." He took a risk and pressed his lips to her forehead on an uninjured patch of skin. She smelled good still, that scent of pine and fir he associated with her. When she didn't recoil in disgust or rage, he asked, "Surely you have room on your team for one more?"

"Don't try to parent Connor again, okay?" Her jaw was set in a stubborn line. "I don't need your help."

"Everybody needs help. At least sometimes. Is that so bad? Isn't that part of being human?" He gestured toward the plush bench in front of the bathroom mirror. "Would you please let me clean up that cut?" He held up his hands. "Even though I know—I know—you don't need me."

"Whatever." She reached into the nearby medicine cabinet and pulled out a small first aid kit. "Here." She lowered herself onto the bench and sat still while he did his best to clean the wound. It wasn't as deep as he'd feared, and the bleeding had slowed to no more than a thick ooze. There wasn't much more he could do about it.

"Can I see your arm?" he asked.

Willow stood up and pulled her shirt over her head to reveal a spaghetti strap tank top underneath. She shot him a challenging look, as if daring him to comment. He swallowed at the sight. The shirt was white, and she wore a thin bra. His gaze flicked to the shadow of her hard nipples, and in response, he felt himself harden. No matter the bizarre and frightening circumstances, his body seemed to shift into a high state of arousal at the slightest provocation from Willow. He forced himself to look at her bloody arm and winced when he saw how deep the cut in her bicep was. Crouching beside her, he tried to clean it as carefully as he could, but she still hissed.

His quads protested, and he straightened up for a minute. "Who knew an owl could inflict this kind of damage? This cut probably needs stitches."

"Not happening." She pulled open a drawer under the counter. "These will do just fine." She placed a box of butterfly bandages on the white tiles.

"Why do you even have these?"

Her mouth twitched. "Working at the raptor center can result in injury sometimes. Birds of prey can be dangerous."

"You ain't kidding." He started opening the packets of bandages with a rustle of plastic and paper. He crouched down beside her again and placed the first strip over the cut. It was difficult to be this close to all that warm skin and not want to touch her, even if he was administering first aid. "At least this was from a normal owl, right? So, it shouldn't get infected. Well, not in any weird way like my arm."

Her eyes widened. "Oh, no. I just remembered something."

"What?"

"Maureen. Remember earlier this evening? Elvis couldn't get a hold of her?"

"Maureen? She's the one who got scratched by the owl?"

"Not a normal owl, though. The strix, Jake. What if she's gotten sicker away from here?" Willow tapped her fingers over her mouth. "Only her injury didn't improve when she was here. It just kept getting worse."

"I wasn't hurt by the strix, it was the tree. Maybe she's just got an ordinary bacterial infection."

"I don't know, but now I'm really worried." Willow wiggled on the bench and fished her phone from her back pocket.

"You're calling her at midnight?"

"She's a night owl." Willow winced and gave him a half-smile.

Jake continued tending to her cut, but his mind was racing, thinking about his own wound. He didn't like that the purpose of it healing when he was here was obviously to keep him closer to The Old Tree. But why, exactly? Were the strix and the tree the same entity? It was all so confusing.

He finished placing the last Steri-Strip as Willow set her phone on the counter with a growl of frustration. "No answer."

"I'm sure she's fine," he said, wishing he believed it.

She blinked at him, as if she wanted to deny it, but found no point in doing so. Her face crumpled, but then she managed to rearrange her features into a brave expression. "Maureen is really tough. You're right, I'm sure." She dropped her chin to her chest. "I just wish I knew how to fix all of this."

Jake, still crouched at her side, took her hand in both of his. "Willow, I am so, so sorry all of this is happening. If I hadn't pulled that stupid—"

"Stop, okay? Apology accepted." She stood suddenly, and so did he. "You thought you were playing a funny trick on your sister. How could you know all this would happen? It wasn't like you were being malicious when you dressed up like The Bandage Man. But that reminds me—I just keep remembering one bad thing after another." She returned through the archway to the bedroom and paced at the foot of the bed. The only light in the room slanted in from the bathroom, and it was nice to be in the dimness. Jake sat in a squishy old armchair in the corner as she told him about Connor seeing the bandaged ghost twice.

"That's weird. How's that connected?" he said. Rex leaped up onto his lap, and he stroked his soft fur, allowing himself to be comforted by the cat's purring.

"I don't know. Do you know the real story of The Bandage Man?"

Jake shook his head, and shifted Rex, who was kneading his leg with his sharp claws.

"He was a man named Cyrus McClintock, and he was my great-great-grandfather."

"Really?"

"Yep. The story goes a woman in the logging camp got jealous when Cyrus proposed to his crew captain's daughter—

my great-great-grandmother, Emily. This other woman pushed him into the saw in the mill. He died a couple of days later from his injuries."

"Ew, that's awful. Wait, they never got married?"

"Sadly, no."

"So how was Emily your great-great—oh. Never mind."

Willow's lip twitched. "Yes, Jake, people had premarital sex even back then. Although she lied and said they'd gotten married in secret several months before."

"Why do you think Connor's seeing this ghost?"

"Maybe it's just his imagination."

"Yeah, because yours truly was an idiot and reminded his subconscious about The Bandage Man." He covered his face with his hands. "Ugh. I feel terrible about the whole thing with your dad and The Bandage Man on top of it all."

Willow gasped and stopped pacing to whirl around and face him. "*Your* dad. Oh shit. I forgot all about him." She clapped her hand over her mouth. "I'm sorry. I'm such a jerk."

"Hey, no you're not. Shape-shifting monsters can be a little distracting."

Willow drew closer to the chair. "How was he?"

"Not great." He summarized the visit in the most detached way he could. Willow stiffened when he got to the part about his father recognizing his wound, his desperate attempt to tell him how to survive it.

"Walter Bartlett knows about all of this?" Her voice rose. "You think he was trying to tell you how to stop the strix?"

Jake shrugged, suddenly exhausted. The image of his father's blue lips, his desperate struggle to communicate, was possibly as disturbing to him as the skeletal woman in the driveway. Maybe more so. "I'll need to get back as soon as I can tomorrow. In case—well, you know."

Willow was looking at him with a pitying expression. "You're sure he mentioned my dad?"

Jake shrugged again. "He used the name Mike. I assumed."

Willow clenched her fists in her eyes. "Years ago, I found my dad sitting under The Old Tree with a gun and a crossbow. He was muttering to himself, saying he told Walter it would happen again."

Jake sat up straighter, and Rex jumped onto the floor. "That's what my father said. He said Mike told him it would happen again. Something like that."

"How the hell were both our dads involved in this?"

"We'll see if I can talk to my dad tomorrow. But for now, can we—can we lay on the bed while we talk?" Jake waved his arm at the inviting queen. "I'll sleep in the guest room—if I can even sleep at all—but I'm so tired, I need to lay down."

"Um, yeah." Willow flicked off the bathroom light. He heard more than saw her toe off her shoes and cross to the right side of the bed. She lay down on top of the covers and patted the bed beside her with a soft thump. It was all the invitation he needed.

He climbed onto the left side and settled on his back, gazing up at the twin skylights above, and the cloudy night sky beyond. The full extent of his exhaustion hit him as his muscles relaxed. "This is the most comfortable bed I've ever felt."

She snorted. "It's an old mattress that belonged to my grandparents, but okay."

"I've been sleeping on a futon, Willow. A *futon*." He splayed his right hand out on the bedspread. "This is like a cloud in comparison. So, like, do you think this bed saw some old-people action?"

Willow's head made a rustling noise on her pillow as she turned to look at him with a wrinkled nose. "Are you asking me if my grandparents had sex on this mattress? What's wrong with you?"

Jake's face flushed with heat. "I'm sorry. Just trying to lighten the mood. Again. In the worst possible way."

"No kidding."

"I've killed the mood instead." He forced a chuckle.

"The mood of outright terror?"

Jake swallowed, the sound loud. "I still don't understand what I was looking at. A walking, living skeleton, except with a face and hands."

"It's like she's regenerating from eating people," Willow said in a near-whisper. "That guy in the ravine had his hands and face eaten, and that's all the strix had on her bones."

"She's going to need to eat a lot more people then."

"I already thought of that." She rubbed her hand over her forehead. "Which makes me want to be as far away from here as possible. I wish I could just jump in my car and keep driving until I hit the east coast. And then I'd get on a ship and keep sailing until I hit—what would I hit?"

"Depends which part of the coast you're leaving from." He squinted as he imagined a map of the world. "From Maine, you'd hit France. Further south from New York, could be Portugal. The Carolinas, Morocco. Or if it were Florida, maybe Mauritania." Willow stared at him open-mouthed. "What? I love maps."

"Oh-kay," she said slowly. "Anyway, the point is, my instinct is to get as far away from here as fast as possible. But this is my home. I can't leave my birds."

"And I can't leave."

"Right. You're stuck here with me." Her fingers slid across the bedspread until her pinky touched his hand.

"I don't mind," he whispered. Jake felt that electric jolt at her touch. As the fear was receding from his limbs, a new kind of energy filled him, and he turned his body toward her at the same time she turned to him.

# Chapter 19

Jake's eyes glimmered in the faint illumination from the skylight. It was too dark to see their color. Instead, Willow noticed his thick lashes as he blinked. She and Jake lay on their sides, facing one another. The only sound was his soft breathing, deep and steady. For a moment, she remembered her father's and her grandfather's—the slow and reassuring sounds large men make breathing. It shamed her how safe the sound made her feel and how grateful she was not to be alone in her bedroom.

He reached up and traced his fingers down the side of her face. "You're such a remarkable woman, Willow," he whispered. "I wish we'd been friends in school."

She surprised herself by saying, "Me too."

"Even though I'm a Bartlett?"

"Especially because you're a Bartlett. It would have pissed off your sister."

Jake laughed, and his fingers stroked her ear lobe, slid up to tuck her hair behind her ear. "You're smart and brave and strong." He scooted closer on the bed until their faces were inches apart. One of his feet reached out and nudged one of hers. "You have no idea how beautiful you are, do you?"

He closed the gap between their mouths, his lips meeting hers in the darkness. A slow, gentle kiss that made her sigh with the relief of it all. She was safe in her bed. Connor was safe. The strix was gone. Her wounds were bandaged. There was only this one single moment in which Jake was kissing her with quiet confidence. She sucked in a breath when his tongue slipped inside her mouth, sliding against her own.

It was like striking a spark to dry tinder, and all at once, they were back in the urgent place they'd been in the kitchen earlier—had that really been this evening?—and then Willow couldn't think anymore. His top hand roved along her side, grazing her breast before settling on her hip to pull her body even closer. She hooked her top leg over his. His hand tightened on her hip, squeezing with a desperation that was an echo of her own. Then his hand traced over her waist, down her stomach, and under her shirt.

His warm fingers splayed on her abdomen and slid back up over her waist and around to her back. He fumbled at the clasp of her bra until she took pity on him and wriggled up on her elbow to undo it. She struggled to free herself from her bra under her tank top, not yet ready to take off her shirt, and settled back on her side. Their bodies came together again like magnets, their hungry mouths connecting. She gave in and let herself kiss the scar at his jawline.

"Willow," he breathed as his hand ran up her stomach to her breast and cupped the weight of it. His thumb brushed over her already hard nipple, and she groaned.

In one smooth motion, he lay on his back and pulled her on top of him. Bracing her hands on his chest, she sat up for a moment and looked down at him. Now he had both hands free to roam over her breasts, her back, her waist. She could feel the hard length of him under her, the shock of it where it pressed at the seam of her jeans.

This was all happening too fast. She'd only known the adult Jake for a few days and hadn't really known the teenaged one. Still, her own hands trailed down to his waist and pushed up his T-shirt. Her fingers bumped over the muscles of his stomach but stopped short at the button on his jeans.

It had been so long since she'd been with anyone like this, and she was like a starving person who'd lost her appetite. That appetite was now whet to an overwhelming point, and tears sprang to her eyes as she realized it wasn't sex she'd been craving—it was connection, it was intimacy, it was being touched by someone who cared for her.

Was a crazy one-night stand going to help that need? Or would it make it a thousand times worse? She'd been fine until Jake showed up to rip back the curtain on her raw loneliness, an exposure worse than being naked. Could he feel it on her skin, a film of desolation?

"Hey, you okay?" Jake's voice was hoarse, a sound that belonged to the nighttime. "Come here." He laid out his left arm on the bed and used his right hand to scoop her sideways until she lay against him with her head on his chest and his arm curled around her. His fast breathing evened out after a bit, and he touched her face and wiped away a tear. "That was really fast. I kind of lost my head there. It's all the adrenaline from before. I'm not thinking straight."

"I just—I don't even really know you. It's not my style to go this fast." She sniffed. "You may have noticed I'm a little guarded."

"You? Guarded? Nope. Didn't notice." He chuckled, and the sound vibrated through his chest under her ear. "If it makes you feel better, I don't make a habit of going fast myself." He squirmed a little under her head. "Okay, this will sound insanely vain, okay? I realize that. But a lot of women find me, well, attractive."

"Really? Didn't notice."

That chuckle rumbled under her ear again, and she smiled.

"Anyway, I got burned in the past from women wanting to be with me for shallow reasons. I'm kind of over all of that. I ended a relationship a few months ago."

"Because she just liked you for your smoking hot bod?"

"Ha ha." He took a deep breath. "Maybe? All I know is I thought I loved her, and it turned out not only didn't she love me back, but she also didn't even really know me. She was as shallow as the rest of them. I really don't trust my judgment anymore. Everything she wanted was totally different than what I wanted. And it hit me—I'm getting old enough that I should be more intentional about relationships if there are things I want."

"What *do* you want? Like marriage and kids and all that?"

He shifted again on the bed and sighed. "I don't know. Maybe. I feel kind of jaded about it sometimes with my upbringing and the state of the world."

Her mouth twisted. "Believe me, I get that. My parents' marriage was ugly."

"How so?"

"My mom was a user—of drugs and alcohol *and* people. I'm sure a lot of addicts are, but probably only in pursuit of their addiction, but she really *used* people. When she'd used up all my dad and I had to offer, she left us. I was seven."

"That sucks."

"Not as much as her coming back again. My dad was stupid enough to think she'd changed. He always did love her. He couldn't see she was only back because she hoped for a windfall from the lawsuit."

Jake sighed, knowing how that story ended.

"I guess I should be grateful she did come back, or I wouldn't have Connor. She left again for the last time when he was a baby. At least she didn't hang around long enough to do him any real damage. Besides, you know, the damage of abandoning him." Willow hated the bitterness in her voice and chose to let it recede in the wash of memories of Connor as a chubby toddler on her hip as she'd studied for finals in her senior year of high school.

"You ever want your own kid?"

"Haven't really thought about it. Between Connor and my birds, I have enough to look after."

"Yeah. I'm not opposed to the idea of marriage and children—if it happens great, but I only want it with the right person. I guess *that's* the thing I want. The right person. I want to be with the right woman. Not just any woman."

Willow lifted her head up. "Like soulmates and all that cheesy stuff?"

He didn't answer for a while. His breathing changed several times like he was going to say something, but changed his mind. Finally, he spoke. His words came slowly. "I don't know if I believe in fate—that there's only one perfect person out there for each of us. I just know with every relationship I've had, there comes a point when I know she's not the right one for me."

"What if she never comes along?"

Again, he didn't answer for a while. "For now, I've decided I'd rather be with no one than the wrong one. Before I moved here, I decided to take a step back from dating to figure out how to—figure it out." He shifted his arm under her. "I'm really sorry. I shouldn't have let this get out of hand so fast." He ran his hand through his hair. "If you'd have let me, I probably would've slept with you and undone the work of trying to clear my head. It's just whenever I'm around you, I feel this electricity I've never felt with anyone before."

"That sounds like a line."

"I know. Totally does. But it is what it is. And all this weird stuff going on is intense. It's making me feel like I've known you longer than I have. I like you, Willow. I think I could like you a lot." His chest rose with a deep breath. "Wait, that's bullshit. I already do. But I don't want to mess up any possibilities with us by going too fast. Before I've had a chance to get my head on straight. I thought before, since you're a Duncan, and I'm a Bartlett, that it wasn't a possibility, but now I'm not so sure."

"What wasn't a possibility?" For some reason, Willow's heart beat in her chest like the frantic wings of a bird.

"You know. That you could be . . ." He eased his arm out from under her and made a show of looking at his watch, but Willow knew how that sentence was going to end. *That you could be the one.*

"Wow, it's late," he said. "I should turn in. We should try to get some rest." He sat up on the edge of the bed, taking his body heat with him.

Willow felt bereft—and confused. "Jake?"

"Mm?" His head swung in her direction.

"I don't care anymore. That you're a Bartlett, I mean. Okay?"

Even in the dark, she saw his cheeks move in a smile. "Good."

"I wouldn't mind if you wanted to sleep in here."

"Don't know if that's a good idea. Every time I'm near you, I want my hands all over you."

Willow swallowed hard at the pulse of heat that traveled through her body at those words. She was a foolish second away from telling him that was fine by her when the terrible scream of the strix came from above, an icepick through her eardrums.

Jake scrambled to his feet, and Willow did the same, glancing around for her hawthorn branch before gathering the courage to look upward. Something moved above the skylight, a quick flash of wings followed by a *thump!* as something fell onto the glass.

"What is that?" Jake's voice was hushed in the dark.

Whatever it was, the dark shape wasn't the strix. It was something far too small, and it didn't move. The strix had dropped something on the skylight. Willow had a sudden nasty feeling she didn't want to see what it was, but what choice did she have? "I'm going to turn on a light."

"Okay." Jake sounded like he felt the same reluctance. "Wait a sec." He came around the bed to stand next to her, positioned protectively. "Okay, go ahead."

Willow turned on her bedside lamp and tipped her head

back. "Oh, my God. What is that?" Blood splattered the skylight. In the center of the blood was something pink and bony, bits of flesh clinging to whatever it was. At first, she thought it was a rabbit, but as she stepped directly underneath it, a rush of horrified recognition hit her. "Is that—" She couldn't finish the sentence. It was too awful to consider, and saying it out loud would make it real.

Because it sure as hell wasn't a rabbit.

Jake stood staring up with a look of horror on his face that must twin her own. "I think it's time to call the cops."

Before she could do so, Willow's phone rang on the nightstand at the same time Connor burst through the door, Freya at his side.

"The Bandage Man is back." He was out of breath, his hair disheveled, his eyes large gleaming pools of terror. "I saw him in the hall."

Elvis's number popped up on Willow's phone screen, and she left Jake to deal with her brother.

"Elvis?"

He took a sobbing breath before speaking. "I found Maureen."

—

Willow risked opening the flue to start a fire since the entire house was chilled. She and Connor sat pressed together on the couch, staring into the flames, a blanket draped over their shoulders. She was still trembling—or maybe Connor was trembling against her; it was hard to tell. Jake hunched on the loveseat, dazed and exhausted. BiBi's regulator clock chimed three times and a moment later, blue and red lights swept over Santa and through the living room window. The lights quickly turned off.

A firetruck pulled into the driveway followed by a cop car and a van. Willow and Connor stood, and she opened the front door and found Officers Patterson and Ortiz standing on the porch with a female firefighter in a navy-blue uniform.

"Officer Patterson said you have an item up on your roof for us to retrieve?" the woman said.

*An item.* That was one way to put it. Willow appreciated the lack of introductions. She was too tired and devastated to care. She stepped onto the porch with the blanket wrapped around her and led the firefighter to the side of the house to point out the skylights. The woman nodded once and marched back toward the firetruck to jump in the driver's seat. Three people spilled out of the van and told her they were with the crime lab and asked if they could take a look around her property. Numb, she nodded in agreement. Was her property a crime scene? The crime hadn't been committed here.

Willow might have watched the trio sweep the ground with flashlights, watched the firetruck pull into position and the ladder extend toward the roof, if the two police officers hadn't called to her.

She turned from the crazy scene into the house, Patterson and Ortiz trailing her like her own Secret Service team. If only. She could do with a couple of bodyguards.

"I can make coffee," she said in a monotone as they entered the living room to stand in an awkward clump.

"That's all right," Patterson said at the same time Ortiz said, "Sure."

He nodded at his partner in some silent agreement that made Willow uneasy. "Uh, I'm good actually."

"Why don't you have a seat?" Patterson said. Her plain face looked almost remarkable in its extraordinary level of weariness.

It felt strange being told to sit in her own home, but Willow obeyed. Jake and Connor flanked her on the couch, with Freya settling at their feet. "Connor, you should probably go up to bed."

"I don't want to go upstairs alone." He sounded so young in that moment that Willow's heart squeezed in her chest.

"Why don't you go to my office? You can see the firetruck

from there." She regretted the words the instant they came out of her mouth, remembering the grisly item the firefighters would be collecting from their roof.

Connor didn't argue and slipped down the short hall into their dad's room. Willow straightened at the shock of thinking of it as her father's bedroom. It was her office, had been for years. Maybe it was just she wished her dad were here right now more than anything in the world.

Officer Ortiz took the loveseat and Patterson sat in the old armchair. She spoke first. "I'm sorry about your employee."

Willow's gaze went to the ceiling. "Thanks." What a stupid thing to say.

"Walk us through how a human foot ended up on your skylight," Officer Ortiz said. His eyes narrowed, and Willow decided she'd misjudged him as the more laid back of the two. His focus was razor sharp despite the late hour. "You mentioned an owl?" The skepticism in his words was so heavy, it was a wonder he had the strength to push them out.

"Um, yes. Like I said, we both saw an owl fly over the skylight and drop the—" Willow closed her eyes and swallowed. Maureen always wore hiking boots. She couldn't stop thinking about them. Jake put his hand on her knee. "The foot—her foot, I guess?"

Neither Ortiz nor Patterson looked ready to confirm this detail, despite the fact Elvis had been babbling about finding Maureen dead on her kitchen floor. *Her eyes,* he'd said. *They're ripped out. Something tore out her throat. She's so white, Willow. Like all her blood is gone. Fuck. There ain't any blood anywhere. And her feet are gone. Just ripped off her legs, and there's no blood.*

"An owl dropped someone's severed foot onto your skylight?" Ortiz leaned forward with his elbows on his knees. "And you believe an owl ate part of the victim from the car accident two days prior?"

"Uh, yes. Sir." The rarely used word sounded sarcastic from

her mouth, and she grimaced. "Here are the contents of the owl pellet dissection from earlier today." She leaned forward and picked up the plastic baggie with the poor man's finger bone, nail, and tooth, and handed it to Ortiz. For a brief moment, she allowed herself to slip into the comfort of her role as educator. "Owls aren't able to digest bones and hair. After swallowing their prey, they'll eventually regurgitate those undigested items in a pellet."

The policeman held it under the reading floor lamp and studied it carefully with a look of horrified fascination.

"When was the last time you spoke with Ms. Sullivan?" Patterson asked.

"This afternoon. It was right before the Scout class when I found that." Willow gestured toward Ortiz, who was still staring at the baggie. "It must have been about four. I told her to go see a doctor about an injury from an owl that scratched her neck and shoulder. The wounds looked infected. And she left."

"Wait, an injury from an owl?" Ortiz shot a look at Patterson. "Why's everything coming back to owls?"

*Maybe you should go to The Grumpy Owl and read their menu. Then you'll understand.* But Willow couldn't say that to the police. "We run a bird of prey rescue here with a lot of owls."

Ortiz held up the baggie. "Was this pellet from one of your owls? I don't understand how it would've gotten a chance to eat that guy—if forensics confirms that idea."

"The pellet came from an owl on the day of her rescue— which was the day after that accident. She'd just been brought in from someone's backyard and appeared to have been hit by a car herself."

"I see," he said in a way that said he didn't. "I think I gotta see me this man-eating owl of yours."

"Unfortunately, she escaped her enclosure. She's gone."

"That's mighty convenient."

"What do you mean?" Willow's voice came out sharp. Jake squeezed her knee, but whether in comfort or warning, she wasn't sure.

"It's just interesting you want us to believe an owl had something to do with the victim in the car accident right near your property and the dismemberment of your employee, and yet this mysterious man-eating owl isn't anywhere to be found."

Willow looked between the two cops. "You seriously don't think I have anything to do with either death? Maureen is my best employee—and a friend." She swallowed at the present tense. "And I never met that man from the car crash." Anger flared in her gut. How dare Ortiz sit in her house and hint she might be a murderer. "Why would I call you and tell you about the foot, about the pellet, if I had anything to do with it?"

"No one is accusing you of anything." Ortiz tucked the baggie in his jacket pocket. "I only said it was interesting."

Patterson intervened. "Miss Duncan, did Maureen have any conflicts in her life? Anyone who might want to hurt her?"

Willow blew out a shaky breath. "She has—had—an ex-husband who lives in Walla Walla, but she hardly ever mentioned him. They divorced years ago. I don't even remember his name."

Patterson continued her line of questioning, directing the inquiries around Maureen's personal life and whether it involved drugs, gambling, or anything else Willow knew of that might have made Maureen enemies. She asked for the names of employees in contact with Maureen. Ortiz took an even longer time grilling Jake, seeming to take great interest in what Jake was doing at Willow's house in the first place.

At last, Patterson stood up, and Ortiz followed suit.

"You have our number," he said. "In the meantime, don't leave town."

"I can't anyway," Willow said. "I've got my birds to take care of. It would be really hard to do alone, but I don't want to put my employees in danger. Do you think they should stop coming into work?" She was so tired, she was asking these two police officers how to run her own raptor center. The thought irritated her enough to pull herself together.

"I'd suggest you pare it down to a skeleton crew," Ortiz said without the faintest hint of irony at his word choice. "Until we have more information on this case."

"I'll help you," Jake murmured.

Finally, the officers left. The crime lab van and firetruck backed out of her driveway. Willow couldn't face going upstairs to her bedroom and staring up at that skylight.

Maureen was dead. How could that be?

The office door creaked open, and Connor appeared from the hallway. "They're gone?"

"They're gone," Jake said.

"I don't want to sleep in my room. Not after seeing him."

The Bandage Man. Why did Connor keep seeing him? What the hell did it have to do with the strix? Was The Bandage Man somehow the herald of the strix arriving, a warning she was coming? Something slippery slid through her thoughts and was gone before Willow could grasp it.

"You got any sleeping bags anywhere?" Jake asked. "I say we all sleep in the living room. Build up the fire again."

A few minutes later, the three of them—four when Freya piled in—lay nestled in sleeping bags on the living room floor in front of the fireplace, Connor between Willow and Jake. It might have been too warm if not for the chill coming through the cracked window. Santa could only do so much. He wasn't making an airtight seal.

The scent of woodsmoke hung in the air, a reminder of much happier times. Camping in the woods with her dad and Connor, camping on the beach with Hayley and their friends. Fires in that very fireplace when her father was still alive, when BiBi's mind was healthy and whole, when her grandfather's spine was straight, his steps strong. It smelled of her childhood.

This was her home, and even if she could leave, even if she had no wild animals relying on her for their care and she could pack up her car, she wouldn't do it. As if cementing the thought, Rufus hooted softly from the bathroom, a quintessential outdoor sound inside her house. Jake smiled at her over the top of Connor, a strained sort of smile, and she didn't blame him if the sound of an owl set him on edge.

Her brother quickly fell asleep. A little while later, Jake's breathing evened out. But Willow couldn't drift off. The initial shock and sorrow she'd experienced on the phone with Elvis was receding into something else, something much more useful.

Rage. Rage toward this monster that dared come into her life and hurt the people she cared about, threaten her birds, and her livelihood. She wouldn't stand for it. The time for reacting was over. A plan began to take shape in her mind, the steps she'd need to take in the morning if she wanted to protect what was hers. She went over and over it, like counting angry sheep.

# Chapter 20

Jake was walking through the forest, but he wasn't alone. Red eyes followed him from the nearby trees, and strange cries filled the darkness. A glance above showed nothing but the skeletal branches of trees and beyond that, the black, starless sky stretching into infinity, an expanse of unrelenting nothing that washed Jake in despair.

His steps made no noise on the needles of the forest floor, and he realized with a start that he was gliding. Something pulled him deeper into the trees, at once filling him with a dizzying mixture of dread and rapture.

Warmth spread across his left arm, and the silhouette of The Old Tree on his skin was no longer made of red lines, but an outline of blue fire licking across his flesh to illuminate the way by its ghastly light. He could now see the creatures all around, owls that he knew to be strix.

Something up ahead screamed—a warning or a welcome?

The fire in his arm began to burn, and Jake wanted no more of this. He tried to turn away, twisting his torso back, but still he was pulled along no matter how he fought, like a fish on a line. In the darkness, he glimpsed the form of a naked woman, stirring the deepest arousal in him even as he continued to fight to turn around. At last, he reached a small clearing surrounded by a circle of trees.

A large owl—the strix—stood on the ground before him, her back to him and her wings spread out as if shielding something. Her head swiveled around and faced him, and when her glowing red eyes locked on him, his arm sang with the burning of it. She took to the air on silent wings and revealed what she'd been hiding.

Jake gasped and would have staggered back if not for the invisible force holding him up and guiding him forward.

He was looking at himself on the ground. He lay pale and motionless, his chest torn open. Jake shook his head in horror, desperate to get away from this macabre scene, but still he glided closer and closer until he was gazing down at his own form.

There, in the center of his bloody chest where his heart should be, rested an ivory-colored egg, perfectly smooth and oval. The egg grew and grew, absorbing Jake's body inside itself like some horrifying time-lapse film of decomposition. His flesh stripped away from his bones to disappear within the egg, followed by his bloody skeleton until nothing remained. The egg sat there a moment, and then it trembled slightly. A small fissure appeared on its surface. Then another and another until blue light glowed through the seams. His arm answered that blue light with a searing pain.

*Crack!* The sound was louder than the loudest thunder, sensed not through Jake's ears, but by the vibration in his bones. The egg split apart with a blue bolt of lightning that reached skyward. In its wake lay a woman curled in the fetal position. Great wings sprouted from her shoulder blades and curled around her body to cover her nakedness. At once, the trunk of a tree heaved from the broken pieces of eggshell, engulfing the woman within its hollow. The tree speared upward, expanded outward, as branches unfurled, and blue flames danced along the leaves. Along the ground, snaking roots of blue light shimmered and disappeared as they dug deeper into the soil.

The blue light danced up and down the tree trunk and along every branch like St. Elmo's fire. So beautiful, Jake couldn't stop watching until it finally slowed, sparked a few times, and winked out. In the dark silence, the tree stood as a tall black imprint on the night sky, both sentinel and fortress for what lay inside. And Jake knew, oh he knew with a terrible knowledge, that the strix was resting within the hollow of that tree, waiting for the time to awaken.

The scream of the strix came again—

Jake awoke with a gasp on the living room floor. Freya was licking his face, and his phone was ringing somewhere. Only a nightmare. It felt real, though. Real enough. He rubbed his knuckles over his heaving chest and felt the phantom pain of it ripped open. What if it *was* real? A glimpse of things to come.

Freya kept licking him, and while her doggie concern was touching, he pushed her away and wiped the dog spit from his cheek. The phone kept ringing. Where the hell was his phone? He sat up and spotted it on the coffee table. Olivia's number lit up the screen. The hospice nurse. His already pounding heart ratcheted into overdrive as he snatched it up. The sick feeling of dread followed him out of his nightmare.

"Yes?" he said.

"Good morning, Jake. Your dad's doing a little better this morning."

His father was still alive. Relief flooded his limbs, rendering them weak. He had the distinct and uncomfortable idea that he wasn't just glad because he needed information from his dad about the strix. Hope was an ugly thing sometimes. Even now, with his father about to die at any moment, he couldn't stop himself from hoping for something more from the man.

"He's real insistent he sees you as soon as possible," Olivia said. "Any chance that could happen?"

He glanced at the clock on the mantle. Already after nine. He couldn't believe he slept through Willow and Connor getting up. It was like that nightmare had trapped him in his sleep. *Time to shake it off.* "Yeah, of course. I can be there in half an hour."

He hung up and hurried into the bathroom. A feather rested on the floor. The owl. Willow had gotten up and even dealt with removing an owl from her bathroom while he'd slept. Equal parts guilt and unease burned in his gut like black coffee. He needed to help with the raptor center, to fix those railings, and help Willow come up with a plan for how to defeat this strix.

To do that, he needed to speak with his father. Jake drew a deep breath. He'd faced his fears last night, and he'd keep on doing it.

He was beginning to suspect that, for Willow, he'd do just about anything.

Jake brushed his teeth, pulled on a fresh T-shirt and a blue flannel, and shot a quick text to Willow.

Going to see Walter. Back as soon as I can.

—

Jake groaned, clutching the steering wheel in a death grip as he guided Eduardo the truck back into Willow's driveway. He said he'd be back soon, but this was ridiculous.

It's getting worse, his brain told him.

"No shit," he muttered back at himself.

He'd gotten maybe a quarter of a mile down the highway when he'd been overtaken by a wave of sick dizziness that made driving impossible. After sitting on the side of the road for several minutes, gazing into the deep forest on either side, he caught his breath and gathered enough strength to turn around and head back to Willow's.

He rolled up the sleeve of his flannel shirt and watched as the red lines of the tree on his forearm faded away, taking with it the dizziness, nausea, and weakness. It pissed him off. The strix, the tree, whatever the hell it was, was keeping him on a shorter leash.

Within a few moments, he felt back to normal. That in itself made him feel a little ill. He got out of the truck and slammed the door with a curse.

If he were mad about this situation, he could only imagine how Willow was going to react when he told her what she'd need to do.

—

"Okay," she said at once.

"Okay?"

"Yep. We have a huge problem here, and your dad might have answers. I'll do it. I just need to finish feeding these guys."

Jake smiled at the owlet Willow was feeding. It was just the two of them in the hut—plus the three owlets in a box. The air was close and warm and smelled of birds and bleach. The baby owls made funny little noises, and the industrial fridge and freezer in the corner hummed conversationally to each other.

"You won't believe this," Willow said, "but I found Cynthia in her mews this morning. I don't know how she got back in, but she was sitting right there as if nothing had happened."

"I *wish* nothing had happened." Jake ran his hand through his hair. "Maybe last night was just a bad dream, right?"

Willow didn't respond. She seemed absorbed in the task of feeding the owlets using a puppet on her hand she inserted through a hole in the box. He wasn't a bird expert, but he figured it had something to do with making sure they didn't imprint on her. He hadn't really seen her in her element before, and he found he liked it. Her entire focus and energy had already moved back from him to the birds. Even though it was only her and Elvis working at the raptor center, and the visitor building was closed, she still wore the olive-green uniform shirt with jeans. Her dark hair was up in a messy bun, revealing the owl in flight on her neck.

On impulse, Jake moved close behind her and kissed that

tattoo. She shivered and turned toward him with a startled frown. He suspected she'd forgotten he was there.

"Sorry." Their eyes locked, and he swallowed, trying to read the expression in hers.

"I'm not," she said quietly, maybe even shyly. She gave him a quick peck on the cheek and returned to her work.

"Connor okay this morning?"

"Not really, but I'm glad he's got the distraction of school. He's agreed to go to our grandparents, so that's good. I think that's because of you. So, thanks."

Jake nodded. "How can I help?"

"Elvis and I have it handled for now. Hayley will be in later, too, with Tyler. The other employees know about Maureen's death, and I've told them not to come in for the next few days while the investigation is ongoing. Of course I told Hayley some of it. Not sure she really believes it yet. And Elvis--I told him everything we know."

"Did he think you were crazy?"

Willow shook her head. "He saw the owl—the strix—when it first came in." She shuddered. "He knew something was wrong with that owl. Something evil." Sadness crossed her face like a shadow. "I think it's easier for him to wrap his head around the strix being real than Maureen being dead." After a long silence, Willow used her arm to swipe at her eyes and sniffed. "Anyway, I need you to keep working on those railings so we can open Branching Out on time." Her jaw set in that way that was fast becoming familiar, and he barely resisted kissing that, too. "Because we're going to fix this."

"You got it. Whatever you need, let me know." He considered sharing his nightmare with her. "I, uh . . ." He trailed off, deciding against it. She had enough to deal with. "I brought Toby in the loop, too. At least, a bare bones"—he winced at this fitting expression—"explanation of what's going on. And he *does* think I'm crazy. He's still working on the wiring today."

Willow lifted her head toward a corner of the hut. "I collected more hawthorn this morning. Make sure he has a few branches nearby."

"Will do."

"But don't take any from that pile." She used her chin to point to the farthest one. "Those are for the arrows."

"Arrows?"

She turned away from the owlets to fix him with a granite gaze. "I'm sick of reacting. It's time to *act*."

A slow smile spread across his face. "Hell, yeah."

"I'll come find you when I get back from your dad's," she said. "And we'll make a plan for us."

For a wild, nonsensical moment, Jake's heart leaped when he imagined she meant a plan for *us*. A plan for Jake and Willow.

You barely know her, he reminded himself. You came to Cedar Beach to contend with your father's impending death, to sort out your head, and build a new life with your priorities straight, not fall into another relationship before you've figured yourself out.

But his heart was in an argumentative mood.

You *do* know Willow—the parts that matter, his heart said. You see this woman, so strong and independent, so brave and selfless, yet vulnerable and alone.

And you're falling in love with her.

# Chapter 21

Willow stood in the driveway of the Bartlett house—or mansion, more like—and craned her neck to try to guess which window was Walter's.

"How the hell do I do this, Dad?" she muttered, wishing as much as ever he was standing beside her now.

Of course, that would probably mean this encounter would end in a fistfight. The thought coaxed a small smile and gave her enough courage to approach the house and knock on the front door. A woman with bright blue hair opened it.

"You must be Willow," she said. "Jake told us to expect you. I'm Olivia."

The nurse led Willow through the cluttered rooms, dim due to the surrounding trees blocking out the light. She tried not to gawk at the staggering luxury of the house, at the sweeping grand staircase. They passed by the living room, open to the second floor, where gorgeous built-in shelves flanked a massive fireplace with a river rock chimney stretching up to the high ceiling. In the kitchen, she noted the Viking appliances. Even the staircase they took, small and narrow, left Willow impressed, seeing as it was a second set of stairs, like for servants.

Or a hospice nurse.

The thought sobered her. This house might be far grander than anything she could imagine living in, but that didn't stop its owner from dying all the same. A bedroom door stood open at the end of the hallway, and Willow's steps slowed until she fell behind Olivia.

"Walter?" Olivia stuck her head inside the bedroom. "Willow is here to see you."

If he replied, it was too faint for Willow to catch, though she heard the soft *whoosh* of oxygen. The air hung thick with the cloying scent of eucalyptus and menthol, causing her stomach to turn. Willow wanted to leave, and at the same time, she wanted to see for herself. See that this man she'd made a monster in her mind was only mortal after all. Walter Bartlett had ruined her father's life, and she would see when his own was ending.

Willow straightened her spine as she crossed the last few feet and stepped into the stuffy, warm bedroom.

"I'll be just down the hall if you need me." Olivia slipped from the room, a fact Willow barely registered in the face of meeting her father's nemesis.

"Willow—Duncan," he gasped. He sounded grim, but maybe that was the only way he sounded these days.

She stared at his small form on the bed with an odd mixture of disgust, pity, and disappointment. It reminded her of the time a carnival came to Cedar Beach when she'd been a young girl. Her grandfather took her on the haunted house ride, much to Bibi's dismay. Willow pressed herself against Grandpa and hid her face for most of it, terrified of the dark, the moaning, the pop-up ghosts, and the creepy music. Then the ride broke, the music turned off, and the lights came on with blinding brightness. The cheap carnival ride seemed hardly more than flaking paint and plywood, the ghosts no better than sheets on wires.

Willow's fear had morphed into disillusionment.

That's how she felt now. Walter Bartlett, the man who stalked her memories as the one who'd destroyed her dad and his dignity, who'd spawned a bully for a daughter, and exploited the people in town with low wages and long hours that would make Scrooge blush—this mythological figure in her life was no more than a frail, dying man who looked, to her intense discomfort, scared.

"It's—happening—again." His words were no more than the faintest stirring of sound waves, a tiny ripple through the air from his bluish mouth to her ear. He patted the bed with his thin hand and Willow drew closer.

"You told Jake my dad said it would happen again? You both knew about the strix?"

A strange noise, like the pop of wet bubbles, came from Walter. It took her a minute to realize he was laughing. When he stopped, he said nothing for a few long cycles of oxygen and patted the bed again. "Sit."

Willow swallowed hard, but she sat and didn't hide her study of him. Echoes of Jake remained in the shape of his jaw and the slope of his brow, and while his hair was white, it shared the same thick wave as his son's. His blue eyes didn't match the startling turquoise hue of Jake's, but they held a certain mesmerizing power of their own, and she found she couldn't look away.

"I'm—sorry."

A surge of anger heated her face. Walter Bartlett was dying and now he wanted her forgiveness? She sensed under that thick, tight cover of her anger lay a well of sadness for her father—and worse, sorrow for herself. Sorrow for the little girl abandoned by her mother to be raised by a damaged father, who had to pinch every penny to scrape by. For the teenage girl bullied and humiliated every day at school. For the young woman shouldering the burden of raising a brother at the expense of her own youth.

"So—sorry." Walter's frail fingers grasped for hers, and in her shock, she didn't respond in time to pull them away. He squeezed her hand and when she looked at his face, he was crying.

A crack in her anger allowed some of that sadness to spill up, and she was shocked again. That sorrow hurt, but for a split second, it was a sweet sadness that washed away a little of her bitterness.

She couldn't forgive so quickly and easily as that, but she squeezed his hand back for what it was worth.

"You'll—have—to—kill—" He broke into a coughing fit that went on so long that Willow headed toward the hall, ready to call Olivia. Before she could, Walter waved his hand back and forth in a frantic gesture. Willow rushed back to his side. "Mom," he gasped before the spasms of fresh coughing overtook him.

Was he delusional? Oh God, was this man dying right now with visions of his mother? His entire face took on the dusky hue of his lips.

"Olivia!" Willow shouted. Muffled footsteps on the thick carpet rushed down the hall toward them.

Suddenly, Walter grabbed her hand with the strength of a hawk closing its talons. His chest heaved, and his lips moved. She bent and leaned her ear toward him. "Save—Jake." He dropped her hand and pointed under the bed. When she didn't immediately react, he pointed more forcefully, even as the coughing overtook him again.

Willow crouched down just as Olivia bustled to the side of the bed. Willow peered underneath and saw a small cardboard box. She slid it out and straightened to find Olivia pulling Walter into a sitting position.

"I think you should go," Olivia said gently.

Willow nodded and held up the box at Walter with a questioning raise of her eyebrows. It was hard to tell if he was nodding back as his body shook. Then she saw him struggle to raise his right hand and, despite the horrible circumstances, she smiled back at him.

Walter Bartlett was giving her a thumbs-up.

—

Willow sat in her Subaru on the steep driveway of the Bartlett house and stared out the windshield, not really seeing the view in front of her. So many emotions swirled through her, but the prevailing feeling was stunned.

Walter Bartlett's lawyer must've thought the man was insane. The box contained a few transcribed pages of a confidential statement Walter had given his attorney regarding the lawsuit with Willow's father. After reading the statement, it was clear none of Walter's version of events would be part of his lawyers' strategy in court or that any of his statements would ever be included. Willow fingered the pages and read them a second time, trying to glean any more meaning from it.

*Owens: In your own words, can you summarize the events that led to Michael Duncan's injury?*

*Bartlett: I want to remind you of client confidentiality. What I say now doesn't leave this room.*

*Owens: [coughs] Then I need to remind you that I can't knowingly allow you to provide false testimony, and I can't lie to the court. Be mindful of that when you share.*

*Bartlett: Trust me, when you hear this, [laughs] you won't want to repeat this to anyone within a hundred yards of a courthouse. I'm only telling you this because I need you to understand what happened up there. All right?*

*Owens: I just want to hear the truth.*

*Bartlett: Fine. Mike got hurt because he wanted to save a monster.*

*Owens: [pause] The monster you referred to earlier?*

*Bartlett: Yeah. The day of the accident, Mike returned to work after his lunch break—and the woman followed him to the site.*

*Owens: Who was the woman?*

*Bartlett: The—the [expletive] woman. Only she wasn't a woman.*

*Owens: Ah, yes. That woman. You maintain she was a shapeshifter? Who changed into an owl you claim ate people?*

*Bartlett: I don't claim. She did. Don't [expletive] look at me like that. I swear it's true. I'd swear it in court on the biggest stack of Bibles you got if they wouldn't put me in the nuthouse. Look at me, Owens. I'm a businessman. A millionaire many times over. I'm a very smart man. Do I look like some kind of fruitcake that believes in ghosts and werewolves and [expletive]? Like I clutch crystals to my chest and call up my psychic? I'm not bull[expletive] you here. You [expletive] stop looking at me like that if you really want to know the truth, all right? You think there aren't other lawyers out there hungry for Bartlett money? You look at me like that again and I [expletive] walk out of here and find one of them. Is that clear?*

*Owens: Absolutely. Please continue, Mr. Bartlett.*

*Bartlett: [expletive] lawyers. I was up there checking on the site, confirming with one of my supervisors on a timeline for a shipment. I like to keep track of these things myself. I'd finished my conversation, and the supervisor left. The only person there at that point was me and the driver of the truck, which was loaded up and ready to go.*

*Owens: The truck loaded with lumber?*

*Bartlett: With logs. Mike returned from his lunch—after a couple beers, mind you—and walked onto the site and up to the driver's side of the truck to speak with the driver. He seemed unaware the woman had followed behind him.*

*Owens: Where was the woman in relation to the truck?*

*Bartlett: Standing right beside it. [pause] I saw my chance.*

*Owens: [coughs] Chance?*

*Bartlett: To kill the monster. Mike didn't have to do anything at all. Just stay the [expletive] out of the way. I had it under control. The logs were held in place by two vertical bunks at each end of the truck bed as well as chains. One of the chains broke, and well, the very top log was higher than the vertical bunk, and it swung down—*

*Owens: The chain broke?*

*Bartlett: That's right. That's what I said.*

*Owens: All by itself?*

*Bartlett: Chains break. What can I say? You sound like you don't believe me.*

*Owens: I want to make sure I understand that my client wasn't personally responsible for the injuries to the plaintiff. Or I'd have to withdraw representation.*

*Bartlett: Didn't you hear me? The chain broke. [pauses] The log swung down on one end, and Mike saw the woman was about to get hit. He shoved her out of the way and was struck himself. [laughs] Did you know Mike told me later that getting crushed wouldn't have killed her, anyway. He didn't think in the moment, only reacted to save her, and it wasn't even necessary. And now he's suing me.*

*Owens: Who is this woman?*

*Bartlett: You're not listening to me. She's not a woman.*

*Owens: Okay. This monster who looks like a woman. Does she have a name she goes by?*

*Bartlett: I—uh. [pause] Even I have limits. I won't do that to [inaudible 1:34] It doesn't matter. She's not a woman.*

*Owens: Do you know where this—this, uh, monster masquerading as a woman is?*

*Bartlett: Look. I don't know where she is.*

*Owens: You sure about that?*

*Bartlett: It doesn't matter. [mumbling] He knows how to kill her. Mike knows. He went to Greece to learn about them, and I know he found out. The hawthorn isn't enough. It only keeps them away. But it won't kill them. [inaudible mumbling 1:58] He has the info, but he won't tell me. He just scribbles in those little books. If I could find them, I'd know how to finish this once and for all. But Mike [laughs] that son of a bitch says he wants to do it himself. He says he can do it on his own. Says it's his fault he woke up the monster, but we both know that isn't true. How the [expletive] could anyone know cutting into a tree would unleash a monster? Mike was only doing his job—for Bartlett Timber, no less—and he won't even let me help. He's going to need all the help he can get to kill it.*

*Owens: Mr. Bartlett, I must warn you that it almost sounds as though you and Mike are discussing a possible murder?*

*Bartlett: I'm trying to save Mike. Trying to save a lot of people here. I was looking out for Mike. And now he's suing me for it. Do you see how that's unfair to me, Owens? You see that, right? Mike knows it, too. He told me as much. The injury was his fault, but I still offered him some money. [sighs] He got greedy and wanted more. So, get this [expletive] lawsuit off my back. I forgot to tell you Mike was messing with the chains, okay? I hate to say it, I really do, but he was using incorrect procedures for adjusting those chains after he'd been drinking at lunch. You got that? I personally witnessed it myself. I'll attest to Mike Duncan being sloppy and careless. Nobody was responsible for Mike Duncan's accident except Mike Duncan. You hear me?*

*Owens: Loud and clear.*

Willow shoved the papers back in the box on the passenger seat and reversed out of the drive. She pushed the car hard down the highway until the trees on either side were no more than a green blur. Other than a couple trips to Baja to go fishing, she hadn't thought her father had ever traveled out of the country, but he'd gone to Greece? When? How had she never heard of this trip? Did Grandpa and BiBi know? And if Walter Bartlett was right, and that woman was a strix, why had her dad thrown himself in front of it? Some stupid chivalrous reflex? She could imagine it. Strix were supposed to shapeshift into beautiful women. Perhaps his protective instincts, always so strong in her father, had kicked in. Just like Walter said. He'd reacted in the moment without thinking.

How much money had Walter offered her dad? *Was* her dad

greedy, or was Walter being stingy? Walter had been responsible for the accident, that much was clear from his statement. But for some reason, Willow felt less inclined to be angry at Walter for it than before. He'd been trying to destroy a strix, like she herself was trying to do now. It sounded like he'd been trying to help her father as well, but he was too stubborn to accept it. Which sounded just like her dad.

Everything about Walter's statement left her unsettled about never knowing the truth about what really happened surrounding the accident that changed her dad's life forever for the worse.

One thing Willow knew, however. She knew where those little books were that Walter referenced. And if what he said was right, they might hold the key to knowing how to destroy the strix.

# Chapter 22

Jake shut off the power saw and wiped his forehead with the back of his arm, knocking his ear muffs off. The silence hung heavy in the forest, and the base of his skull prickled. He glanced around for Toby before remembering he'd gone into town to grab something at the hardware store. He wondered how Willow was faring with Walter, but that wasn't enough to explain the uneasiness unfurling in his chest like a small dragon spreading its wings.

It wasn't a noise that tipped him off. Some sixth sense had him glancing up into the tree. An owl perched on the railing of the tree house deck. He thought maybe it was a barn owl. Weren't those the light-colored ones? The bird stared down at him from liquid black eyes set in a white disc-shaped face. Jake didn't know much about owls, but everyone knew they were nocturnal. Was this normal behavior to have one sitting here in the open in the late morning?

His forearm throbbed—not with pain exactly—more like a pulsing thrum. If that weren't enough of an answer whether or not this owl's behavior was normal, another owl glided silently over his head. The tiniest disturbance of air tickled the small hairs on the back of his neck as the owl soared up and landed lightly beside the first one.

It was a different kind of owl, but Jake's ability to identify them ran out at either barn owl or great-horned, and this was neither. His mind flashed back to the night before as he'd huddled helplessly on the gravel of Willow's driveway. The stack of hawthorn branches was within reach, but that hadn't worked on ordinary owls last night.

Ordinary owls, maybe, but certainly not ordinary *acting*. He picked up one of the branches, anyway, feeling better for the heft in his hands. A third owl swooped down from a nearby tree to alight on the deck railing.

It was like a terrifying version of the owlery in Harry Potter. In a matter of moments, owls filled the air to land on the deck railing until at least a dozen perched there. Jake looked up at their staring eyes, some black like a shark's and some yellow, and all of them fixed on him. They were as still as the wooden owl statues used to scare away pigeons, except the feathers ruffling in the breeze indicated these were real birds.

Jake turned and ran toward Willow's house, and all the owls took flight so quietly, it was like watching a film with the sound turned off. As the first owl struck him in the back of the head, he changed course and launched himself up the staircase to the nearest tree house. His feet stumbled on the steps, and his hand slipped on the new double railing he'd installed just this morning, but he kept his focus on the door at the top. He didn't slow even when another set of talons sunk into his shoulder with a searing pain. Soft feathers brushed his face as the attacking owl flew off again. He swatted at them with his branch and launched himself through the door and into the tree house, slamming it behind him. A few soft *thunks* followed as the owls flew into the door.

He winced and hoped none of them were injuring themselves

as another thumped into the window. If what Willow had guessed was true, these owls didn't *want* to behave this way and were being compelled. He rushed forward and drew the curtains across, then spun and pulled the curtains across the opposite window. Jake lowered himself to the couch, ashamed his hands shook, and allowed himself a few breaths. He touched the back of his head, and his fingers came away with a little blood. Pulling down the sleeve of his T-shirt, he saw two deep scratches on his shoulder, but nothing a little ointment wouldn't fix.

He needed to warn Willow. He pulled his phone from his pocket to text her, only to have her beat him to it.

*Meet me at the sawmill.*

His thumbs flew across the screen to explain the situation when he heard Toby shouting outside.

"Jake? Where are you? Brought you a sandwich, man."

He crept toward the window. Feeling stupid, he pulled the curtain back an inch and peeked outside. Toby stood in the clearing in the center of the tree houses, holding a white paper bag and looking around.

There were no owls anywhere. If it weren't for the very real scratches on his head and shoulder, Jake might have wondered if he were losing his mind. Would the owls return if he came out?

It took no small amount of courage to open the tree house door. No Hitchcockian swarm of birds descended on him.

"Jake?" Toby shouted again.

"Right here." Jake swallowed hard and started down the stairs, bracing himself with every step for the return of the owls, but he reached the ground without incident.

"What were you doing up there?" Toby held out the bag with the sandwich and eyed the branch Jake clutched.

"You wouldn't believe me if I told you." Jake erased the text he'd started to Willow and typed something new.

*On my way.*

—

Jake rushed through the trees toward the pond and the old sawmill, using the hawthorn branch as a walking stick. An owl would surely swoop down on him at any moment, but he reached the building without seeing a single bird of any kind. Willow waited in front of the sawmill. It was constructed of vertical pieces of rough-cut lumber and looked like a narrower version of a barn, with a steeply pitched corrugated metal roof.

Willow spun a keyring over her finger. "There you are." Relief flooded her voice.

Quickly, he told her what happened at the tree houses, while she shared about his father's statement to his lawyer, including the thought that her dad's old notebooks might be stored in the museum and contain information for defeating the strix. Jake's heart sank at the news his father was the one responsible for hurting Willow's dad.

"But my dad was the one who put himself in danger," Willow said. "It was *his* fault, really. Anyway, neither of us is responsible for what our fathers did or didn't do. It was never fair of me to feel hostility toward you for who your dad is. I'm sorry." She reached out and took his hand in hers. "You're Jake Bartlett, but you're your own person. One I really like. It's ridiculous to let your last name stop either of us from pursuing anything." She shrugged in a vulnerable way that had him stepping closer. "I mean, if that's what you want."

An unexpected lightness filled him as he shed the heavy weight he'd been carrying ever since he'd met his father. Willow was right. He *wasn't* responsible for his dad or his actions. Jake always felt guilty for his father's behavior—guilty enough he'd done something crazy for Willow, which he finally realized wasn't his place to do. Willow would be so furious if she ever knew, but he didn't regret it for a second, given how he felt toward her now. He cupped her face in his hands and studied her mix of strong and soft features. He hadn't given himself time to figure out what he wanted from a relationship, but suddenly he found he didn't need to.

He wanted Willow.

"I like you quite a lot, too," he said at last. He pressed his lips to her soft ones and rested his forehead against hers. For a few moments, they stood like that, breathing each other's air.

Finally, Willow pulled her face away. She was smiling, but it didn't reach her eyes. "You ready to go inside? Hopefully get some answers?"

Jake ran his hands down her upper arms. "You're trembling."

She licked her lips and looked away. "I haven't been in here since my dad died. I—I hate the whole Bandage Man thing, and this is where it happened."

Jake's jaw tightened as he thought once more what an ass he'd been pulling that prank.

Willow must've noticed. "No, you didn't know before, okay?" It was kind of weird, in a good way, how quickly she was getting the hang of reading him. She sighed. "It's not just the Bandage Man. My dad loved creating this museum. He put so much of himself into it, and I've left it closed up all this time. I dread going in there with all those memories and my guilt."

Jake opened his mouth to reassure her that her dad wouldn't have minded her leaving the museum shut, but who was he to say? Maybe he would've. This seemed like something Willow had to work out for herself. "Well, you're not going in there alone, okay?"

She nodded and reached for the doorknob. "Ready?"

He picked up the hawthorn branch he'd leaned against the building and followed her inside the large, dark space. It smelled like dust and old wood. Over that, he caught a whiff of something metallic, like rusty metal.

Willow flipped a light switch, but nothing happened when she clicked it up and down a few times. "Power's out," she said unnecessarily. "Probably a tripped circuit breaker. My house does it all the time." She pulled out her phone to use as a flashlight.

Jake thought he heard another click, but not from the light switch. The sound came from the back of the mill. As his eyes slowly adapted to the dimness, he could make out the blocky shapes of old mill equipment. Willow's light reflected off glass display cases along the walls and passed over the toothed curve of the circular saw blade on the far side of the room.

*That* blade.

Something stirred in the shadows pooling around it, a slight disturbance in the darkness. He glanced at Willow, but if she'd noticed, she gave no sign. She stood frozen to the spot, her face a pale oval in the dark, and looked around the space. He moved farther into the museum, around a plexiglass cube full of dollar bills and change donations, and toward the saw.

"Wait." Willow put her hand on his arm. "My dad's office was back here—is back here." Her voice caught, and she pointed her light at a short hallway to their left.

"You go." Jake's fingers tightened on the branch. "I thought I saw something move over there." He gestured toward the saw.

Willow's eyes gleamed in the darkness. "Let's check it out together."

"No, let me," he whispered. "You need to get the books, remember?" A sudden urgency overtook him. If her dad really had written how to stop a strix, then it was critical she get those books.

No matter what might lie waiting in the darkness.

Willow gave a single nod, her gaze sliding toward the menacing saw blade. "Be careful," she whispered back and continued down the hall past a restroom and disappeared through a doorway at the end.

Jake took out his phone in his left hand and hefted up the branch like a baseball bat in his right as he crept toward the saw blade. The metallic smell grew stronger the closer he got to the blade. What was it? For a second, he convinced himself the saw blade itself was giving off that funny metallic scent. It stirred some primitive fear in him as a terrible suspicion took hold.

Before he could investigate further, something white flashed to his left, like a nightlight blinking on and off again. A cold breeze ruffled his hair, and Jake whirled from side to side, trying to figure out where the air current had come from. Goosebumps broke out on his arms, both from fear and the cold. The hairs on the back of his neck stood up as a light pressure ran from his shoulder down to his wrist. Jake jerked away with a yelp.

Something brushed past him. He stood listening to his own breathing in the dark, heart pounding in his chest, when a flash of movement caught his attention. There and gone again in the far-left corner of the museum. Was someone prowling around?

"Hello?" Jake forced himself toward where he'd spotted the movement. The temperature dropped a few degrees with every step he took until he stopped, shivering, in front of a glass display case.

He held up his phone light and saw his own reflection in the glass. And someone else's. Jake gasped and whirled around, but there was nothing there. Yet he'd seen him in the glass. The Bandage Man. Wrapped in bloody bandages, stained black in the dark, the afterimage of him seared to the inside of Jake's eyelids. The man's face had been covered, except for the eyes, but where the eyes should have been were only black hollows. He'd been pointing at the case. Jake was more terrified than he'd ever been in his life, but he moved closer to the display.

How could this be real? Wasn't the strix enough without adding in a ghost? Poor Connor. He'd been seeing this horror as well. Jake drew a breath of cold air and held his phone up to the glass, bracing to see The Bandage Man's reflection again.

Nothing. Jake peered closer. An old newspaper page plastered the back of the cabinet, featuring a black-and-white photograph of a man labeled Cyrus McClintock. *Who Really Killed the Bandage Man?* He quickly scanned the article, struggling to take in much meaning in his heightened state of fear. It felt like someone breathing icy breaths on the back of his neck. Still, he managed to learn some people thought Cyrus tripped and fell into the saw blade, while others swore a woman shoved him, only to disappear out the back of the sawmill, never to be seen again. Three men claimed to have seen her, all of them commenting that she'd been uncommonly beautiful.

Jake's stomach clenched at the possibility, and he couldn't wait to pose his theory to Willow. It would certainly explain why the ghost of the Bandage Man was appearing now. Was this what Jake was supposed to find out? He glanced at the bottom shelf in the cabinet where rolls of bandage rested, along with photographs of other men with horrifying injuries from logging and milling.

That's how he noticed the cupboard of the cabinet was ajar and remembered the odd *click* he'd heard entering the building. He knew in his gut something important lay in this cupboard. Jake squatted down and opened the cupboard door to see a stack of black moleskin notebooks. He pulled the top one out and opened it to the first page.

*Michael Duncan* scrawled across it in tight, neat handwriting.

He flipped through the pages of sketches and notes about various fish in Oregon. The sketches were really good. Willow's dad had even colored them with pencils. This couldn't be what the Bandage Man wanted to draw his attention to, though. Jake pulled out the next book and the next, riffling through their pages. It wasn't until the fourth that he flipped the book open to a page that read, *Life Cycle of the Strix.*

Bingo. Something rustled above Jake. He straightened to his feet, shoving the notebook in the back pocket of his jeans, and looked up to where the noise had come from. A gleaming pair of red eyes stared back at him from the face of a great-horned owl. Time to go. Jake weaved his way through the displays back toward the entrance and couldn't stop from glancing once more at the saw blade. He also couldn't stop himself imagining Willow's great-great-grandfather going into that spinning nightmare and surviving for two days after.

He sucked in a breath when he realized what he was looking at. From this angle, he could see a large, dark puddle on the floor. Jake quickened his pace, heedless of the owl that now flew through the rafters above him to shadow his path.

He cast his phone light over the scene and gave a startled shout upon seeing the bloody mess of viscera. Was it human? He didn't care to examine it further, and his arm faltered to lower the phone to his side.

His stomach turned ominously.

"Jake?" Willow whispered from the front of the mill. "Are you all right? I heard you yell."

"Yeah," he called, no longer worried about making noise. "Stay back." He retched and covered his mouth with his hand.

"What?"

Jake fought a losing battle with his stomach, dimly aware Willow was making her way toward him. He roused himself and turned to face her. "No, Willow. You don't want to see this."

Too late.

"Oh, my god." Her phone light painted the scene in vivid pinks and reds. "Is that—is that a heart?"

Worse, it was half a heart. Like something had eaten it. Jake's stomach heaved again, and above them, the great-horned owl let out a mournful hoot.

# Chapter 23

From her front door, Willow watched the police car drive off with Officers Patterson and Ortiz. A patrol car remained at the end of her driveway, and the mobile forensics lab was parked over at the sawmill, still humming with activity and currently crisscrossed in yellow tape.

The viscera had indeed been human, and all too easy to connect to the eviscerated man who'd been discovered earlier that day in the farthest reaches of Spalding State Park, about four miles from Willow's property. He appeared to be itinerant, and no identification had been made yet. This kind of excitement hardly happened anywhere, let alone in a quaint tourist town like Cedar Beach. To make another gruesome find, and again so far from the actual murder scene, must have made the local police feel a little out of their depth.

Willow sure as hell did.

White news vans lined the road across from her house, waiting like vultures at a fresh kill. The officers had tried to convince Willow to leave, citing the extreme danger of living in the epicenter of what everyone was calling a serial killer spree, but if anything might have tempted her to go stay somewhere else, it was the news vans.

Not that she could abandon her birds. It's not like she could pack up a couple dozen birds of prey and leave home. The transportation logistics would be bad enough, but where would she take them?

She, Jake, Connor, Hayley, and Elvis were the only ones to really know what they were up against. Plus Toby, although he was understandably confused after Jake's vague warning about a dangerous creature running loose.

Take care of the strix, too. The strix had come from a tree on Willow's property, and she felt responsible for stopping the monster. If she only knew how.

The police car's taillights disappeared from view, and she shut and locked the door and turned to face Jake on the couch. "I thought they'd never go away." She dropped her head with a heavy sigh. "I'm so glad Connor's at our grandparents'." At least he'd been spared the ordeal of the police questioning, not to mention the fact that Officers Patterson and Ortiz viewed her and Jake with growing suspicion. She lifted her face and realized something. "The window. It's covered with plywood."

Jake cleared his throat. "Didn't take long. Thought that took priority over the railings. I got most of another tree house done today before those owls came along."

"Thanks." It came out a grunt brought on by the uncomfortable feeling she and Jake were becoming a team. She swore long and creatively. "What a day. And after all that, I didn't even find my dad's notebooks."

"About that." Jake shifted on the couch to prop himself on one hip and withdrew something from his back pocket. He tossed it onto the coffee table with a grin.

At once, Willow recognized the black moleskin notebooks her dad had loved to scribble in. A regular Jane Goodall—mostly of the rainbow trout world. "How?"

Willow listened in stunned silence as Jake described seeing the ghost of The Bandage Man by the display cabinet, which led to his theory and subsequent discovery of her father's notebooks. "You think The Bandage Man—my great-great-grandfather—was killed by the strix?" If it were true, it made sense why they were seeing the ghost now, when the strix was here. It didn't explain why she'd seen him as a teenager, though.

"I think your great-great-grandfather might be trying to—"

"Protect us," Willow finished. She blew out a long breath of consideration. Perhaps Cyrus McClintock appeared when she was younger when her manipulative mother returned because he'd been looking out for Willow then, too. It felt oddly comforting to think she had a guardian angel of sorts. Even if he was The Bandage Man. Of course, if The Bandage Man wasn't evil, then he hadn't been the cause of her father's accident. If it had even been an accident.

*Stop it. Some things you can never know.*

She picked up the notebook and sank onto the couch next to Jake. He leaned in close as she flipped through each page, his body warmth counteracting the growing chill from her father's words and sketches of large owls and women with wings, of cross-sections of trees showing strix tucked inside—in owl and human form. *Always female,* her father had scribbled on one page. Her eyes raced over the notes explaining how new strix were born from a hatched egg that grew a strix-tree. She also read if they failed to feed for some time and became weak, strix returned to their trees to hibernate.

*It can take many, many years for a dormant strix to absorb enough nutrients to regain their strength. They will awaken, however, if their tree is disturbed or chopped down. In a ravenous state, they must quickly feed on human flesh and blood until they can fully attain their human form again. Depending on the size and strength of the strix owl, it can accomplish full regeneration within three to ten human victims. From that point on, they will only feed on the blood of humans.* Her father underlined something twice. *Vampires are real then!*

Her father's handwriting appeared distressed when he'd written the following: *Destroying the tree doesn't work. It will only regrow in a matter of minutes by absorbing nutrients from other trees and plants in a huge radius. Must destroy strix. Strix are nearly immortal.*

"Nearly," Jake said. "How are they not?"

"That *is* the pertinent question here, isn't it?" She turned another page. "Oh my God, look at this, Jake."

*The strix tree itself is also dangerous. Any splinter from its wood results in the victim being marked for future use—either as food or a mate—and the strix doesn't need to worry about the victim escaping. Extreme illness befalls anyone who strays too far from the strix tree. It's a convenient way for the strix to keep a mate or food source nearby to use at her leisure.*

Jake traced his finger down his forearm, but the outline of the tree wasn't visible when he was so close to the Old Tree. "It's got me right where it wants me," he said grimly.

Willow squeezed his hand. "Don't worry, we're going to kill it." She started to read the next page only for Jake to interrupt her with a gasp as he bolted upright on the couch beside her. "That's what I dreamed." He tapped his finger on a paragraph and told Willow about his dream of seeing his chest open with a strix egg laid inside.

*The strix takes on the form of a woman to mate with a human victim for the purpose of reproduction. Dimitris told me they can lay eggs as an owl or give birth to a child while in the form of a woman. He even showed me an egg in our travels outside Athens, which he'd removed from the chest of an unfortunate man. We destroyed it together. The human children of the strix can become strix themselves if ever fed human blood. Dimitris theorized that many human strix children become guardians of the forest, a way for the strix to safeguard their kind.*

"Come on, Dad," Willow muttered. "Where's the part about

how to kill the fuckers?"

She and Jake shared a stunned look, reading how their fathers had first discovered a strix when Willow's dad brought down a tree. An owl had flown out of it and attacked a man on the work site. Several days later, the man had been found dead and partially eaten at his house. Walter funded Willow's dad to travel to Greece and learn all he could about the strix from this Dimitris. Walter also put her dad in charge of checking for the telltale signs of a strix tree—bloody sap—before any logging was done in an area and paid him extra for the service.

"It sounds like they worked together a lot." Willow flipped through pages and pages of her dad's journal entries about his work with Walter and their discovery of several strix in the area.

On the very last page, they found the information they needed.

*I couldn't do it. God help me, but I couldn't. I starved her for weeks and let her return to her tree. With any luck, she won't appear again in my lifetime. But if she does, I know how to destroy her and any of her kind. A weapon made with the wood of the strix tree is the only thing that will kill one.*

Willow barely finished reading the sentence before she was on her feet and out the door.

"Wait." Jake followed her onto the front porch and around the side of the house.

The stack of wood from the Old Tree's limb was bundled against the wall of the house in several neat piles. The bloody sap oozed from the cut ends, and by the time Willow and Jake had each brought in a pile and laid it by the fireplace, their arms were covered in it.

"Time to make some arrows," Willow said. "My dad taught me how to make wood arrows since I was ten. Now I know why." The archery lessons, the arrow-making. It had all been in preparation for this.

And for the first time, she felt hopeful.

———

Willow and Jake were halfway to her father's workshop when the first owl sailed through the night above their heads. This time, they were prepared. She and Jake wore hard hats and several layers of clothing, including scarves, to protect the back of their necks. A barn owl swooped down, and its talons bounced harmlessly off Jake's yellow hard hat. But as more and more owls flew toward them, Willow didn't feel quite so confident their wardrobe choices would keep them safe. She and Jake broke into a run, holding their arms over their heads to protect themselves from the onslaught. It was awkward for Willow with her recurve bow gripped in one hand and a hawthorn branch in the other. Jake carried a heavy rucksack filled with wood from the Old Tree.

They reached the workshop, and Willow threw open the door and rushed inside. Jake slipped in behind her and slammed and locked the door to the sound of birds thumping against it. It was a metal shed, and Willow had never been more grateful for the fact it was windowless. Immediately, soft thuds and scratching came from overhead as the owls alighted on the roof. She and Jake were both breathing heavily when she turned on the light of the long, narrow workshop. This was a space where her dad had been happiest, working on his projects to make cupboards and shelving for their house. Willow smiled, having used it often herself since his death. The smell of fresh-cut wood hung heavy.

Jake moved deeper into the room and whistled in admiration at the power tools. He turned toward her with that sexy grin of his. "How can I help?"

Her heart flip-flopped in her chest, but whether it was excitement for finally having a way to kill the strix, or Jake's grin, she didn't know.

He strode back over to her and, okay, maybe she knew. He grabbed her face with his warm hands and kissed her hard. "We're going to do this, Willow. We're going to kill the strix."

His use of the word *we* should've bothered her. Instead, warmth spread through Willow's limbs, dissolving her discomfort with the realization that Jake was right. They *were* a team now. They needed each other to get through this, and maybe that was okay.

—

An hour later, Willow was finishing up her first arrow made from the wood of the strix-tree when Jake spoke.

"You must have other arrows?"

"Loads of them at the archery range," she said, glancing up at the ceiling where the scrabbling noises continued on the metal roof.

"So why don't we just make arrowheads from the strix tree wood and attach them to your existing arrows?"

"That's—that's brilliant." Willow chose to swallow her annoyance and be grateful instead. She stood on her tiptoes and kissed him on the cheek. "Great idea. We'll just wire-wrap them to my recurve arrows. Obviously, they'll fly differently, but we can practice at the range."

"We?" Jake laughed. "I've never used a bow in my life."

"There's a first time for everything, right?"

Like considering space in her life for a man. Attempting to forgive Walter Bartlett. Allowing herself to be part of a team. She'd opened a tree house hotel called Branching Out, and she herself was doing just that.

She and Jake fell into a rhythm of shaping and notching the arrowheads with a couple of handheld rotary saws. They finished their dozenth arrowhead, and Jake turned off his saw a moment after Willow finished hers. It took Willow a second to register what was wrong. Jake put his hand on her arm, noticing it as well.

"Do you hear that?" he asked.

She nodded, knowing he meant there was nothing to hear in the silence. The constant scrabbling of owls on the roof had stopped. "They're gone." Jake sighed in obvious relief, but Willow didn't feel any.

"Why?"

As if in answer, something crashed onto the workshop roof with enough force to bow the metal ceiling inward. Willow fisted her hands. The windowless box of a shed they stood in no longer felt safe.

It felt like a trap.

There was a rolling door at one end of the workshop, but her dad had used it so infrequently that he'd blocked it with a workbench and piles of lumber—not exactly a quick exit point. That left only the door they'd come in earlier. Without windows, they had no way of seeing what might be waiting for them outside. Footsteps moved across the roof. Each step bent the metal down, only for it to snap back with a startling *pop*.

"It's her," Jake whispered and rubbed his forearm with a grimace.

Willow turned to the door, their only exit, and tried to come up with a plan. Jake was rubbing his arm some more.

"Does it hurt?" Willow asked.

He shook his head and held out his left arm for her to see. The outline of the Old Tree glowed in sharp relief on his skin, the lines vivid in a sickly blue-white.

"I think she came for me," he said.

"Well, I won't let her have you." Willow picked up her bow resting against the wall between two workbenches.

His mouth tugged up in an almost-smile. "I hope you're as good a shot as those trophies suggest, because we only have one arrow ready." He gestured to her finished arrow, lying next to the pile of arrowheads that would be useless until attached to shafts.

Willow ignored the footsteps on the roof and focused on the door. "There's only one way out of here. You know what that means?" Jake shot her a confused look. "Only one way in." She picked up the single arrow and notched it in her bowstring. "Use that piece of plywood as a shield and open the door." There wasn't time to question the wisdom of this plan.

To Jake's credit, he didn't question her either. He picked up the plywood and crept toward the door. Willow planted her feet and squared off perpendicular to the doorway, hearing her father's voice in her head as if he stood beside her. *Stable and steady, now you're ready. That's it, Willie-Boo.*

As Jake pulled open the door, Willow pulled back on her bow. The tension in her body mirrored the tension in her bow, but her arm was solid. The door opened onto a rectangle of darkness. The footsteps on the roof ceased. Jake backed up against a workbench across from Willow, and they waited. She fought the urge to hold her breath.

Time spun out long enough that her shoulder and arm muscles ached. Willow let her bow drop for a moment, and her muscles cried out in relief.

"Hello?" said a woman's voice that was also not. There was no other way to describe it. It sounded hoarse and unused, like how a mummy might sound if awoken after thousands of years. Something about the quality of it sent a shiver of paralyzing dread through Willow's core. There was a multi-tonal aspect to the voice that her human ears could barely catch. Willow immediately raised her bow again.

"Is somebody there?" the voice called. It rose and fell at the wrong places like the soundtrack of a horror film.

Jake shifted across from her, but she didn't dare take her eyes off the open doorway. Footsteps approached, a soft sound over pine needles. Willow's breaths became ragged, and she concentrated on evening them out.

"I know you're in there." The singsong voice was chilling with its mistimed cadence.

A moment later, a silhouette stepped into the darkness of the doorway, a black shape of a woman that was so human that Willow's arm faltered and dipped. "Come out, my darlings." Willow gasped when she realized she'd taken a step toward the creature. "That's right. I don't want to hurt you."

Willow's thoughts thrashed and spun as if caught in cobwebs. Maybe it was possible the strix really meant them no harm? She took a few more steps toward the door, the bow limp in her left hand, the arrow in a loose grip in her right. If she could only see the creature, she would know if she were evil, wouldn't she? Willow was vaguely aware Jake stepped closer to the doorway. That seemed bad, and yet she wasn't exactly sure why.

The figure of the woman stepped to the side, out of sight, and Willow lifted her right hand in entreaty as if to say, *No*. Willow needed to see her for herself. It was desperately important she see her.

"I'll bring you such happiness," the strix said. Her voice coiled and writhed in a seductive dance of vibration in Willow's skull.

Words tickled in the back of Willow's mind. *Striges. Strega*. Words for witch. Was that what the strix was? A witch enchanting her.

"I'm right here," sang the voice with all the worst notes.

Willow and Jake stepped in unison now, their footfalls stirring up sawdust. Jake reached the door first. He reached out his arm, and light pulsed around and around the outline of the tree on his skin like blood flows through veins.

"I'm here," Jake said. He moved through the doorway, and a terrible scream split open the night like a knife slicing through the very fabric of existence to expose a gap into something Willow knew she never, ever wanted to see.

The spell, or whatever it was, broke for them both with that scream, and Jake turned toward Willow with a look of terror on his face. Before he could move, a large, dark shape flew through the air behind him, snatched Jake up, and carried him away.

Willow's brain processed what she'd seen—the shape of a woman with feathered wings—at the same time her bow arm came up and her right hand pulled back the arrow. The strix struggled with the weight of Jake but still managed to fly him above the workshop roof. Willow didn't even take the time to debate whether or not she should risk Jake falling.

Letting the strix carry him off would be far worse than falling from that height, of that she was certain. Even accidentally shooting Jake would be better than the strix escaping with him into the night.

The strix held Jake in her arms and began to fly into the forest. Willow took aim at the center of the creature's back. With any luck, the arrow would go through to her heart. With a whistling *snap,* the arrow shot through the darkness and found its target. The strix screamed, a different noise than before, full of pain and rage instead of triumph, and dropped Jake onto the top of the workshop. Willow watched helplessly as Jake rolled down the pitched roof, while behind him, the strix flapped and struggled to gain altitude.

Jake grunted and caught himself on the edge of the roof. This was followed by a strangled gasp of pain. He let himself fall to the ground and managed to land on both feet in a deep crouch. Willow ran toward Jake but kept her gaze on the night sky. The strix flapped its demonic wings, wobbling and dipping. Even in the darkness, Willow could see the dark stain of blood spilling over the gray wings of the strix. Jake straightened beside Willow with a groan and pulled her against him, and together they watched the monster's erratic flight through the air as her form grew smaller and melted into the darkness.

"You saved me," Jake said, and Willow let herself collapse against him.

# Chapter 24

Jake pressed Willow closer to him and hissed at the pain from his wrenched fingers.

She pulled away. "You all right?"

He grunted. "I will be."

"Let's get back to the house. We don't know if she'll be back."

Every crack of twig underfoot and every sough of wind through the branches scraped Jake's nerves raw. He'd never been more thankful to see anything in his life than the light spilling from Willow's kitchen window.

As he and Willow stumbled up the porch steps, she grabbed his arm. "Look."

Jake felt the release even before he looked down. The outline of the tree had disappeared. "It's gone." At the sight of his unblemished skin, he felt boneless with relief. It was over. "She's really gone."

Willow stared at his arm for a long moment. "Let's go to the archery range. Get those arrows."

"Don't you think this means she died?"

"You want to take that chance?"

He gazed into the darkness, remembering the way those talons had dug into his flesh. "No."

They set off and hurried through the task of retrieving the arrows. His heart rate started to slow as they approached Willow's house once more—until he saw the patrol car idling in the driveway. Two police officers stood on the front porch.

"Heard some sort of screaming," one of the cops said, his eyes narrowed in suspicion.

In the end, Willow convinced them it was only the eagle owl screeching at the raptor center.

As soon as the cops left, Willow set upon the task of attaching the arrowheads with a wordless fervor. Jake joined her on the sofa and found he didn't care for conversation either. Both of them seemed to be processing the horror in their own heads. He was grateful for the mindless work of the arrows. It kept at bay the memory of that sinister, hypnotic voice, the feel of his terrifying flight through the trees. At last, completely spent, he and Willow fell asleep on the couch.

Images of blood and guts and a man's half-eaten heart haunted Jake's sleep, but he didn't dream again of the tree or moving through the forest against his will. When he woke in the morning, he found Willow asleep against his chest and Freya draped over their feet. He could've stayed there for hours, but Willow wasn't a woman to sit still. She instantly stirred and was out the door to tend to her birds with no more than a granola bar and a shouted instruction for him to keep working on the tree house railings, which he did so, despite his aches and pains from last night's ordeal.

When he took a trip to the hardware store, he expected the tree to reappear on his arm and the sickness to return, but he returned to Willow's unscathed from his errand. Could everything really be all right? He remembered a Dickinson poem his mother loved. *"Hope" is the thing with feathers that perches in the soul.*

The image made him shudder.

By early evening, Jake's body was heavy with exhaustion and something else unexpected—the settling weight of happiness. As much as he tried to guard against hope, he couldn't help believing the strix was gone, that he would finish Willow's tree houses in time for her grand opening, that he and Willow were on the cusp of something he didn't dare put into words considering their short time together.

So, it was a shock when Willow found him cleaning up supplies under one of the tree houses on her way back from the raptor center and told him he needed to return to his place that evening.

"What? Why?" he asked stupidly.

Willow wiped her hand over her sweaty forehead. "Because Connor is coming back from our grandparents. I don't want him thinking you've moved in." She wouldn't meet his eye, and he sensed this had nothing to do with her brother and everything to do with Willow.

"Okay," he said slowly. The last thing he wanted was to spook her. Maybe she needed time to sort out everything in her head. Shit, he certainly did. "Can I make you dinner first?"

"I think it's better if you get going." She gazed at her shoes. "I want to get Connor home and explain everything."

"Sure." Jake suddenly knew how the strix felt last night. Willow's words were an arrow piercing his heart. He finished pulling a tarp over a stack of lumber and turned to catch her looking at him with a stricken expression. In three steps, he was in front of her, reaching for her hand. "Willow." How could he explain what he was feeling without scaring her?

She flashed a fake smile and slipped her hand from his. "It's all good, Jake. I just need . . ." Her smile faded as she clearly didn't know how to finish.

"Some space." He nodded. "Sure. I'll be back in the morning." He hiked his thumb over his shoulder toward the tree houses. "I'll have the railings done in time for your opening."

"That's great." Willow glanced toward her house, as if hoping to escape there.

Jake rubbed his hands down the front of his jeans. "Well, you have my number if you need anything, okay?"

"Yep." She turned, her ponytail swinging, and took a few steps before spinning back to wave in an awkward farewell. "See you tomorrow."

"Yep," Jake echoed back, wondering what the hell just happened.

—

For the next two days, Jake was lucky to see Willow briefly in the mornings and evenings, and that was only to confirm neither of them had seen any sign of the strix. She rebuffed every attempt he made to speak to her and said she was busy dealing with the cops swarming her property and phasing in employees again at the raptor center. At least Connor was talking to him. He gleefully reported the A- he got on his math final and asked when Jake could take him surfing.

But Jake was too busy for surfing. He worked from dawn to dusk on the railings and used his lunch breaks to fix little things around Willow's house. A missing bit of baseboard, the jammed pocket door to the laundry room, a broken light fixture in the hallway. The next day, he found a note stuck to his lunch box with an envelope of cash.

*Thanks for the repairs.*

He left the cash and ripped up the note in an uncharacteristic fit of temper. They'd spent several intense days together, and he'd thought they'd agreed to see what might happen between them. Now she'd barely look at him, let alone speak to him. Jake couldn't figure it out, but by Thursday night, he was preoccupied with something else.

His father was dying. When Jake joined his sister at their father's bedside, Walter had enough strength to grab Jake's healed arm and sag back against his bed in relief.

"She's gone," he whispered, and Lindsay shot Jake a confused look.

And those were the last words Walter spoke. He slipped into a coma and died a few hours later. If Jake hoped for some resolution from his father, some heart-to-heart, or a moment of forgiveness, it hadn't come. He was surprised to feel a profound sadness at his father's passing for what had never been and would now never be.

His throat constricted every time he thought of Willow and how that felt the same.

———

The next day marked the opening of Willow's hotel. That morning, his chest tight with grief, Jake pulled his truck into the gravel parking lot and got out.

Toby walked toward him, shaking his head. "What are you doing here, man? Your dad just died."

"And?" Jake crossed his arms and sniffed.

"And you're not working today."

"Hotel opens tonight."

"Yep, and I got a crew in to wrap up all your hard work. I'm stopping by really quick to get them up to speed and then heading to Lindsay's. She shouldn't be alone today." Toby raised his eyebrows at him in unmistakable judgment.

Jake didn't want to explain that being around his sister made him uncomfortable. They'd had completely different relationships with their father, in that she'd had one, and he hadn't. Their kinds of grief were completely different; it made him feel at turns angry and useless around her.

Toby studied him and heaved out a sigh. "You shouldn't be alone, either."

Footsteps crunched over the gravel behind Jake. "He won't be," Willow said. He turned and took in her denim shorts, a purple windbreaker, and flip-flops, Freya leashed at her side. She and her dog strode off toward the house. "Come on," Willow called over her shoulder.

Jake hurried after her. "Don't you have to work at the raptor center?"

"Called in some volunteers so I could take the day off." She stopped and gave him a somber look, and Freya rushed forward to lick his hand. "I'm sorry about your dad."

"Are you?" Jake shot back, shocked at his flash of anger. "Last I checked, you thought he was a bastard."

"He *was* a bastard." For a bit, there was only the crunch of gravel as they walked. "But maybe I didn't understand everything about him."

"I didn't either. Now I never will."

"Well, I *am* sorry. For your pain."

"I don't know if pain is the word," Jake said. "Regret, I guess? I didn't know him that well, and what I did know wasn't . . ."

"Great?"

"Yeah."

"I get it. Same with my mom." They reached Willow's driveway, and she opened the back door of her Subaru. Freya bounded in with a joyous bark.

He and Willow climbed into the car. "Where are we going?" he asked.

"There are two places I want to be when I need to clear my head." She jammed her key into the ignition. "The forest, around my birds. Or the beach."

They didn't say much as Willow guided the car down the ribbon of highway. After a while, the ocean came into view. It was a rare and beautiful day, the sky a cheerful baby blue and the water a deep lapis. Jake cracked the window and copied Freya in the back seat, sniffing the salty air.

A few minutes later, Willow parked and climbed out carrying a green plastic ball launcher fitted with a tennis ball. Jake zipped up his hoodie in the stiff wind and stumbled down the sandy hill beside Willow. The beach was mostly empty at this early hour. Freya barked continuously, eyeing the launcher and then

Willow as if to say, *Throw the ball, already!*

Willow handed the launcher to Jake. He whipped it back as hard as he could, and the ball flew down the beach toward the shore. Freya took off like a streaking black bullet and splashed into the water to retrieve the ball.

Despite the fact his father had died, and Jake had no idea what was going on with him and Willow or what he was doing in Cedar Beach, a smile spread across his face. Freya raced back along the sand and dropped the ball at his feet. For a while, he let the sound of the waves soothe him, punctuated by Freya's barks of encouragement any time he hesitated to throw the ball again. Willow planted her butt in the sand and locked her hands around her knees.

At last, Freya returned with the ball, shook cold sea water over them both, and plopped down into the sand to pant. Jake stroked her damp head. The smell of wet dog was grounding in a moment when he felt adrift. He opened and shut his mouth several times, but it was Willow who spoke first.

"I'm sorry." The wind carried the soft words away. "For not thanking you more for all the work you did around the house. I wanted to apologize for—ignoring you, I guess."

Jake's hand froze on Freya. "Is it because I'm a Bartlett? Because that's never going to change."

"No." Willow waved an impatient hand. Several waves crashed onto the beach before she spoke again. "I got scared. Everything was moving too fast. Maybe we only feel something for each other because we shared this extreme ordeal."

Jake glanced at her, but she stared at the water. He followed his instincts. "Maybe so." From the corner of his eye, he saw her head whip in his direction. "We lived through something horrible. Might not even be over. Do we really need to open ourselves up to more hurt?" Jake didn't look at her, so he'd be able to say what was needed. "People can get hurt when feelings are strong. I feel pretty strongly about you, Willow. But I don't want to cause you any more trauma than what's already happened in your life." He let himself look at her, and the open vulnerability on her face cut him to the quick. "I just want you to be happy. If you think you'll be happy on your own, I respect that." He took a chance and ran his finger down her cheek. "But if you choose to see where this is headed, I promise I'll work hard to make you happier than you'd ever be alone."

She caught his hand in hers. "Will you be my date?" She shook her head, flustered. "I mean, there's a fundraiser for the raptor center that Hayley's been planning for months. At the Cliff House. It's semi-formal. You'll need to wear a suit." She sounded embarrassed at this admission, like she'd said it would be a nudist event. "It's next Saturday at—"

"Yes."

"Yes?"

"Yes."

"I didn't even say the time. Maybe you're busy."

He squeezed her hand. "There's nothing I could be doing that could be more compelling than seeing you."

Willow's mouth twisted into a sardonic smile. "Don't you know you're not supposed to make yourself so available? Play a little hard to get."

He met her gaze. "I don't play games, Willow. And I won't play with your heart. Ever."

She blinked a few times and cleared her throat. "Then it's a date." She nudged his shoulder with hers. "I hope it's not inappropriate asking you on a date when your dad just died. I never know what to say. At any time. But especially after something like that. I just—I know how I felt with my dad. There really wasn't anything anyone could say. Sometimes it's nice to have a distraction."

Jake's throat tightened, and he patted Freya's sandy side. "Yeah."

They sat on the beach until his limbs felt frozen, and his face wind-scoured. Willow drove most of the conversation and only deviated once to the matter of the strix to announce she'd made two dozen more arrowheads and collected more hawthorn for her house and the tree houses. There was no mention of the reason for this, and they didn't dwell on it.

Instead, Willow shared family anecdotes. Like the time her family was picnicking, and her grandfather warned Willow to mind her paper plate in the wind just when his own flew up to cover his face in baked beans. Or when Willow visited Hayley in town with baby Connor, and they were flirting with two boys at the pizza place only for Willow to stand up and discover Connor's diaper had leaked all over Willow's lap. They talked about her pets, well-loved and gone. Of childhood hopes and dreams and fears. Willow told him all about Cynthia—that spotted owl she learned so much from and loved best of all.

When they were both weary of the wind, they stood and brushed sand from their backsides. Jake found the aching hollow in his chest wasn't quite as painful. He'd be dealing with the fall-out and complicated mess of feelings over his father's death for weeks and months to come, but he could get through this day thanks to Willow. As they made their way back to the car, Jake recognized what this time had been.

Willow's true apology. Sharing about herself was something he knew didn't come naturally. By giving him this glimpse of herself, she'd given him the gift of her trust. Of herself.

"Thank you," he said, climbing into the car. His face stung from the sudden windless warmth.

"It was nothing."

"It was you," he said. "And you're really something."

She stared at the ocean a moment before looking his way. "I think you're really something, too, Jake Bartlett."

# Chapter 25

Willow zipped up her cobalt dress with the giddiness of a schoolgirl. She was excited about the fundraiser, but other emotions swirled inside her like a storm. With every passing day, she felt less afraid the strix was coming back and more terrified about her growing feelings for Jake.

She could barely admit those feelings to herself, let alone to him, and yet that's what she'd dared herself to do tonight. She owed him that much, to be brave and make the first move after how she'd treated him in the days after they'd faced down the strix.

Jake Bartlett was a good man, a solid man, the kind of man she'd be a fool to let slip away. He'd designed her tree houses, understood her vision, and made it come true. He'd righted his wrong with the railings, fixed a dozen niggling jobs around her house, and started on other areas of her property this past week. He'd pitched in at the raptor center, tutored her brother in math and taken him surfing, and charmed BiBi and Grandpa when he'd met them two days ago for lunch at their condo.

He'd accompanied Willow to Maureen's funeral. At the wake afterward, he'd won over Elvis as well. The next day, Willow attended—to her bemused amazement—Walter Bartlett's funeral and met Jake's mom, who was crazy about him. So was his sister, despite the rocky start to their sibling relationship all those years ago. Hayley loved Jake. Willow's staff loved him. And Willow—she swallowed a lump in her throat, unable to even think it. So how was she going to say it?

She and Jake had gone to the Grumpy Owl twice this past week, but tonight would be their first real date. The kind with dinner and implications. Jake spent every day at her place, but he'd slept every night in his studio. She sensed he was giving her the space he himself didn't need, which showed how much he understood her and respected the situation with Connor. Tonight, though, Connor was spending the night at Ethan's. When she'd told Jake they'd have the place to themselves, his eyes had lit up with understanding—and something she was pretty sure was outright lust.

Willow examined herself in the mirror. The uneven flirty hemline skimmed mid-thigh, the cinched waist highlighted her curves, and the dress's neckline approached plunging. Underneath, she wore sheer cobalt panties and a matching lacy bra. Strappy silver heels and dangling silver earrings completed the picture. Her hair fell in dark waves past her shoulders. She took a shaky breath and smoothed her hand down her stomach. Everything was planned to the smallest detail—not that it helped her nerves at all.

She tottered down the stairs, gripping the banister like her life depended on it, which it did in these heels, and plastered on a huge smile at Jake and Connor in the living room.

"Wow, Jake," Connor said. "Maybe I shouldn't let you go out with my sister dressed like that."

Willow laughed, and her heart constricted to see her little brother standing like Jake, their arms crossed in identical manly postures. Connor definitely wasn't a little kid anymore.

She shifted her focus to Jake, and the nerves beat a tattoo in her belly. He wore a dark gray suit, fitted snugly to his lean body. His sun-streaked hair fell into those amazing eyes of his, and they darkened at the sight of her. He looked nervous too, but he shoved his hands in his pockets in a cocky posture and grinned.

A car honked outside, and Connor scooped up his backpack and pillow. "Good luck at the fundraiser tonight." He started out the door but hurried back to hug Willow and whisper in her ear. "It's good to see you happy."

Connor was gone before she could respond, but her squeezing heart warmed with gratitude for her brother's maturity and kindness.

Jake brushed his hand down her arm, eliciting a shiver. "Willow, you look so beautiful." He reached up and ran his thumb over her bottom lip. "I love seeing that smile. I've seen a lot of it lately. Can't seem to wipe off my own either." Sticking out his elbow, he gave a little bow. "Shall we?"

—

The Cliff House restaurant overlooked the ocean, twinkling in the evening summer sun. Willow and Jake stepped inside, where strings of white lights and gold bird baubles crisscrossed the room from corner to corner. Iridescent paper cutouts of raptors hung suspended from the ceiling. The table centerpieces were hurricane lamps with nests inside holding egg candles.

At this early hour, the restaurant was empty, with the exception of some white-shirted catering staff and the swing band warming up on a small stage. Behind the band, a slideshow played scenes from the Tree Top Raptor Center. Jake exclaimed when a slide appeared of him feeding an osprey nestling a few days ago.

Willow swallowed hard at the overwhelming feeling when she gazed up into his handsome features. She tugged on his hand and lifted her head toward the slideshow. "I just wanted to say thank you. For everything you've done. For me, for Connor, for the birds. You—I—" She faltered, unsure how to continue.

Fortunately, Jake solved that problem by kissing her. Desire stirred in Willow's belly. Her fingers slid through Jake's thick hair, and she pulled him closer, her mouth greedy. His soft lips tasted of spearmint, and he smelled of sawdust. She could kiss him all night, except she needed more than kisses. Far more.

And tonight, she would have it.

The first jeers and whistles didn't penetrate her fog of lust.

"Hey, Boss," Elvis called. "Get a room already."

That nickname finally got through, and Willow pulled away from Jake, tumbling down to earth with an unpleasant jolt. *Boss.* Poor Maureen. She turned to Elvis and saw most of her staff had been watching her and Jake make out like a couple of teenagers. Her face flamed with heat, but she lifted her chin an inch. "Hey, everyone."

"Let's get this party started," Hayley cried.

———

Willow's heart pounded as she stood at the podium and gave her speech. But as much as she hated public speaking, those nerves were nothing compared to her speech for Jake. The hundred and fifty attendees clapped and cheered exuberantly. That was probably more to do with Hayley's family donation of several kegs of beer rather than her eloquent oration. Hopefully, all that beer would translate into more reckless bids for the silent auction.

People shook her hand as she came off the stage. It was clear some only wanted to ask questions about the grisly murders associated with her property. By the time Willow extricated herself from yet another conversation in this vein, she'd lost sight of both Jake and Hayley. Had they gone outside? Willow wouldn't mind some fresh air herself.

"Willow!" A red-faced Toby stepped into her path. Lindsay, pink-cheeked herself, entwined her arm through his. "You taking good care of my boy, Jakey?"

"Jakey?" Lindsay snorted. "He'd hate that."

"Then don't tell him I said that." Toby's words came slurred, and he put a finger to his lips. "Shhh." He patted Willow on the arm. "Seriously, take good care of Jake, all right? He's a good guy. Like really good."

"And you're, like, really drunk." Willow craned her neck to try to spot Jake.

"You making a lot of moolah for your raptor place?" Toby flung his hand in the direction of the auction tables. "I bid on a spa package for Lindsay."

"How sweet," Lindsay said.

"Oops." Toby hiccupped. "That was s'possed to be a secret. I'm terrible with secrets. That's why I hate Jakey's making me keep that secret about Willow."

Willow crossed her arms. "What secret?" Toby shook his head, and she forced a smile. "C'mon, you can tell me."

"Fine, if you really want to know."

"I really want to know."

"Jake subs—substi—subsidized!—your tree houses. That's it. Subsidized."

Willow's heart beat hard enough to bruise her ribs. "What do you mean, Toby?"

"I shouldna said anything."

"No, you shouldn't have," Lindsay agreed.

"Jake subsidized my tree houses?" Willow said. Toby mimed zipping his mouth shut and throwing away an invisible key. Willow turned her attention to Lindsay. "What's he talking about?"

Lindsay looked completely sober now—and completely uncomfortable. "Look, Willow. Jake always felt terrible about how our dad treated yours." Her eyes filled, and Willow was keenly aware this woman's father had died a week ago. "When Toby called Jake in as the architect on your project, Jake said he'd only accept if Toby let him pay some money toward your build. You weren't supposed to find out."

"How much money?"

"Wait, you seriously didn't know?" Toby asked. "You really believed that bid?"

Willow bristled as humiliation welled up in her like a thick, dark liquid. She gritted her teeth. "How much did Jake pay?"

Toby's eyes shifted between Lindsay, who gave a resigned shrug, and back to Willow. He blew out a long sigh. "Half."

"*Half?*" A nearby couple glanced in her direction, and she lowered her voice. "Jake paid for *half* of Branching Out?"

Toby nodded, miserable. "You can't say anything to him, 'kay? He'll kill me."

Lindsay rolled her eyes. "Sure, Toby. Willow won't say a word." She shook her head in disgust. "We'd better head home." She touched Willow's arm. "Don't be mad, okay? Try to understand Jake wanted to do a good thing. He's a wonderful person."

"I know that." Willow's words came out indignantly. How was she supposed to figure out this mess? And where the hell was Jake? She glanced around the crowded room and spotted him and Hayley coming through a side door from the parking lot. They appeared rattled, and Hayley and Jake rushed over.

"What's wrong?" Willow asked. Hayley and Jake exchanged a glance, and her irritation with Jake doubled to see him in on something with her best friend.

Hayley pulled Willow to a corner away from the crowd. "Sweetie, it was your mom."

"What?" Willow lowered herself onto a chair. "My mother was here?"

"She was pretty intoxicated," Jake said, his face grim. "Hayley asked her to leave before she made a scene, but she wasn't taking no for an answer."

"Jake helped me escort her out," Hayley added. "We put her in a taxi."

"She's—she's—" Willow almost finished with *alive?* But that much was obvious already. "What did she want?"

"To see you." Hayley sounded concerned.

"Why?" Willow asked.

Hayley looked helplessly at Jake. "Money, maybe? She said it was really important she speak with you."

Willow's heart thundered in her chest. "How did she look?" What she really meant was, did her mother look like someone who'd encountered some terrible health problem that precluded her from visiting the two children she'd abandoned? Twice, in Willow's case.

Hayley frowned. "Same as before. Drunk."

Willow tried and failed to think of a time she'd seen her mother sober. She only held a handful of fuzzy memories of her mom when Willow was a small child. A walk in the woods near the house, her mother making her a peanut butter and honey sandwich, the time Willow skinned her knee and her mother tended to it. When Willow was a teenager, her mom spent little time at the house, hardly making eye contact with Willow, as if too ashamed to look at her own daughter. For the most part, her dad would meet her mom at the cabin she rented in the woods.

Which had suited Willow fine.

"Did she say where she's staying?"

"We didn't have much of a conversation," Jake said gently. "I hope it's all right, but I told her to stay away from you."

Willow shot to her feet. "Would you stop trying to take care of me, Jake? You're impossible, you know that?"

"Whoa, what the hell, Willow?"

"Half?" Her voice came dangerously close to a screech. "You paid for *half* the construction?"

Jake looked like she'd slapped him, his face stunned before it fell in resignation. "Toby."

"Yeah, Toby. He told me. I'm going to pay you back, Jake. Every damn penny."

Hayley backed away. "Why don't you two head off? Sounds like you have a lot to discuss. I'll wrap up here."

Willow didn't argue with her friend. She strode out the side door and into the chilly night. Jake hurried after. To her horror, Willow was crying. She swiped at her cheeks, grateful she wasn't the type to wear mascara.

"Willow." Jake's voice was pleading.

"I'm going to pay you back," she repeated, disgusted at the tremor in her words.

"How?"

They'd reached Jake's truck, and she whirled on him. "I don't know, okay? I can barely pay my remortgage as it is, and now I find out that was only *half* the cost?"

"You weren't supposed to find out." Jake held his hands up in a begging gesture. "I don't want you paying me back, okay?"

"I feel like an idiot." She angrily brushed away more tears. "How could I be so stupid to believe Toby's price? Do you know how foolish I feel holding all this anger at your dad when I never really knew the truth of what happened with the accident? That I still don't and never will? And you did it out of some misplaced guilt? How do you even have that kind of money?"

"Wow, okay, hang on. That's a lot there. First, you're not an idiot, Willow Duncan. You're an incredibly smart and capable woman. If anyone was an idiot, I was. You're right, okay?" He took a step closer. "That money—it was given to me by Walter. I didn't want anything to do with it. As far as I was concerned, it was money won by his unethical treatment of employees and his disregard for the environment. That's all still true. But I helped you out of guilt for what happened to your family, and that *was* misplaced. I'm not responsible for my dad's choices." He let out a long breath. "That's huge for me to realize. And you're not responsible for your dad's. Whatever happened that day when your dad got hurt—that's all done and over between two men who are dead now. We need to let it go for our sake. For our relationship."

She snorted. "Our relationship."

"Yes. Our relationship. Because I don't regret helping you

for a second. I'd do it again in a heartbeat, now I know you. I took that money and did some good with it." He stroked his hand down her arm. "I helped the woman I love."

Willow's tears returned. "No, Jake!"

"No?"

"*I* was going to say it first. I had it all planned for tonight."

His mouth quirked. "You were going to say what first?"

"That I love you!"

"You love me?"

"How could I not? You're the kindest, most generous, decent, and amazing man I've ever met." Even to her own ears, she heard the anger in her words.

"You forgot smart, good-looking, athletic."

She laughed, some of the anger dissolving.

"You're shivering." Jake took her into his arms, and she melted against the warmth of his body. "Willow, you're the most brave, incredible woman I've ever met. You're beautiful, and your heart is so good even when you don't see it yourself."

"I love you, Jake."

"I'll pretend you said it first, okay?"

She laughed again, and so did he, the sound rumbling through his chest under her ear.

"Now, God, woman, can I finally take you home and bed you?" She nodded. "If you insist on paying me back, let it be in sexual favors, okay?"

She pulled away and glared at him. "I *am* paying you back, Jake. It might take a while, but I'll do it."

"Oh yeah, you will."

Willow rolled her eyes, but she couldn't stop smiling. "I mean it. The money. I'm paying it back."

"Whatever makes you happy, Willow."

# Chapter 26

Mothra-sized butterflies flapped in Willow's stomach as Jake pulled his truck behind her car in the drive. They got out, and Jake took her hand. She shoved aside all thoughts of money, her mother, and all the recent strange events and focused solely on what was about to happen. She started toward the front door, but Jake pulled her back.

"What are you doing?" she asked.

"I thought I made that clear. I'm taking you to bed."

She ignored the pleasant zing of nervous anticipation and pointed to her upstairs window. "The bed is up there."

"Come on." He tugged her toward the back of the house to the gravel path.

"Where are we going?" She kept her voice low, mindful of the guests in the tree houses at ten p.m. "I'm wearing outrageous heels in case you hadn't noticed."

"Oh, I noticed. For once, Willow, can you try not to control everything?"

"I had everything planned."

"I'm sure you did." He chuckled and snugged her against his side as they walked.

Willow gasped when she realized he was leading her to her favorite tree house where yellow lights flickered in the windows. "That house is booked for Brett Somebody-or-other."

"Brett Kajatel." Jake hiked his thumb at his chest. "You're looking at him."

Willow narrowed her eyes. "Is that an anagram?"

"Wow, yeah. How did you realize so fast?"

"I love word scrambles. You seem really pleased with yourself there, Tom Riddle."

He snorted. "I may have booked the other houses, too. We have the whole place to ourselves."

"What? You're crazy."

"Crazy about you. I thought it would be fitting for this night to happen where it all started—over a shared vision of tree houses. I wanted them for us alone. You're not the only one who can plan things."

"Well, you clearly didn't plan on how I'd get up that spiraling staircase in these shoes." She bent down to unstrap her sandal. "And you're not going to pay the nightly fee for the tree houses because—"

She shrieked as Jake scooped her into his arms and started up the stairs.

"Jake." She slapped his arm. "Put me down. This is ridiculous." The drop over the side of the railings was terrifying, even if they were regulation height now, though she'd never admit she was scared. She looked instead at the rough bark of the tree trunk.

He laughed. "This is what they call a romantic gesture."

"You're being a caveman." She clutched his neck.

"Admit it. It's kind of fun."

"I'll do no such thing. How are you not out of breath?"

"You're not that heavy. Plus, I'm super fit."

Willow rolled her eyes, but once again, Jake had her

laughing.

They reached the top of the stairs, and he set her back on her feet. She immediately missed the close contact with him. As Jake reached for the doorknob, Willow blurted, "I'm so nervous!"

Jake turned to her. "Why? You're one of the most confident women I've ever met." He pushed the door open.

"This is different—this isn't just sex. It's—oh, wow."

Every available surface twinkled with battery-operated candles. The interior of the tree house was made up of odd angles fitted around the tree trunk, making niches for the kitchenette there, the couch here, and the double bed in one corner.

Jake might be in good shape, but he sure was breathing hard now. When Willow turned to face him, he was staring at her. "I had a plan of my own. A fire." He pointed to the wood burning stove laid with wood and kindling. "Champagne." He pointed to the silver bucket with a green bottle on the kitchen counter. "But I find I don't care about any of it now."

His eyes of his shimmered in the candlelight, and suddenly his mouth was on hers, his hands in her hair. The kiss deepened, and Willow moaned, which Jake echoed with one of his own. Already, she felt him hard against her stomach through the thin fabric of her dress. His tongue flicked over hers and in an instant—"I'm not nervous anymore," she breathed into his mouth. "I want you, Jake Bartlett." She wanted—needed—his skin on hers, but he was covered in so much clothing.

She slid her hands under the jacket of his suit and swept it off his shoulders as he tugged at his tie. He kicked off his shoes while Willow reached for his white shirt, unbuttoning in a frantic line that wasn't fast enough. She started to tug at the fabric, but Jake stopped her and stepped back with a laugh.

"Hey, this isn't some movie where you get to rip off my shirt. It's a nice one, okay?" He stood there with a sexy smirk, his eyes on hers, and continued unbuttoning, including the cuffs, with slow deliberateness. He shed the shirt and stood in his dress pants and a white undershirt, clinging to the muscles of his chest. Light danced over his golden skin, over the definition of every lean muscle in his arms. Slowly, he pulled his undershirt free from the waistband of his pants and slid it up to reveal, inch by inch, that gorgeous six-pack stomach that took her breath away that first time in the guest room. He crossed his arms and peeled it off his torso, tossing the shirt in a corner.

"Wow," she breathed. She wanted to kiss him, lick him, bite him. She wanted *him*.

"Your turn." He made a twirling gesture.

Obediently, she offered her back and the zipper of her dress.

———

Jake wanted Willow so badly it hurt, but he forced himself to slow down as he unzipped her dress. He turned her around, and his breath caught as she slithered out of the dress to let it puddle on the floor. She stepped out of it and stood before him in a sheer blue bra and panties and those high, high heels. Her dark nipples peeked through the fabric of her bra. His body was demanding he take her now—take her in those shoes—but he swallowed and drew a deep breath.

Willow was right. This wasn't just sex. This was about showing her his feelings, and his throat constricted with the magnitude of them.

"I love you," he said.

"I love you."

In the distance, thunder rolled, his hazy brain able to think for a second that a storm would be romantic. Then they clung together again, and he groaned at the feel of her soft skin under his hands. He tried to kiss her gently, to communicate his love, but his mouth devoured hers. His hands caressed her back, sliding up and down her smooth skin before undoing the clasp of her bra.

Her breasts spilled into his hands, and his thumbs circled her taut nipples until she groaned.

"Jake," she gasped into his mouth. She writhed against his

body. "Jake."

"Yes?"

"I need to take off my shoes. They're killing me."

He laughed, grateful for the pause, allowing him to see better what his hands had been enjoying. She undid the straps of her heels and stepped out of them, dropping her height by several inches.

They returned to their kisses with a new hunger, and her hands tugged against his belt. In moments, he was kicking his pants away even as Willow tugged down his boxers. The moment her hand found him, he gasped. He remembered the first time he'd brushed against her, the electric current that leaped through his body.

Only now it was concentrated there. Her hand, so light, danced up and down the length of him. Before he lost full control, he caught her wrist in his hand and stepped back. He dropped to his knees in front of her, and her eyes widened.

—

Jake's breath was hot and damp through her sheer underwear, and with the first flick of his tongue, her legs began to tremble. After a minute of this delectable torture, Jake growled and yanked her panties down. When his mouth returned to her, she wondered if she'd simply crumple to the floor. Her legs shook harder.

Fast, it was happening so fast.

But just as the first wave threatened to crash over her, Jake was pushing her back onto the bed, pulling her from the brink, from the release she so desperately craved. Frustrated, she pulled him toward her, her fingers gripping his back.

"Wait, Willow." He produced a condom from the pocket of his pants on the floor and slipped it on. He settled himself over her, propped on his elbows, to gaze down at her. She arched her back, bringing her hips up to meet him, poised at her center. "Stop." He looked down at her with a grin. "I want to enjoy this moment."

"You'll enjoy the next ones more," she said, "if you'd stop thwarting me."

He chuckled. "Oh, I know I will." He brushed the hair from her face with a tenderness that made her stop writhing long enough to notice the ache in her heart. How could a man be so full of lustful need—and also so sweet at the same time? "But I wanted to tell you I love you again."

"I love you, too." She gasped out the last word as he eased inside her. Slowly, he began to rock against her, keeping her teetering on the edge. He kissed her forehead, her nose, her mouth. She felt the restraint in the tautness of his body, his breathing ragged. She forced herself to match his pace and traced her fingers down his back to make him shiver. A clap of thunder made them both jump, and then laugh, and the sensation wasn't at all unpleasant with him inside her.

"God, Willow, you're so sexy," he groaned into her ear, and at last he quickened his rhythm. The sound of rain lashing the windows mixed with the sound of his body pounding against her.

Another rumble of thunder, and she wasn't sure if it was outside or inside her body as she rode the building wave. It rolled through her like the rising sound, and she cried out. Jake shuddered against her, riding the wave of his own pleasure with a shout of release.

They lay on their backs, panting and smiling, and stared up at the wood ceiling while they listened to the rain and thunder.

---

It was only half past midnight, and they'd already made love three times. Jake crouched naked by the woodstove, feeding a piece of wood into the bright flames. Willow lay on her belly on the bed, the most satisfied and content she'd felt since—maybe ever. Jake shut the door to the stove and straightened to give her a full view of his naked body. The firelight danced along every hard plane of him.

When he noticed her staring, his arousal grew, and she laughed. "No. We're not going again."

He gave a sheepish shrug. "He gets greedy. What can I say? Although I can't promise this kind of performance every night." Jake walked into the tiny kitchen area, now giving Willow a pleasant view of him from the back and poured two glasses of champagne. He strode to the bed, and she sat up and took the glass.

He settled beside her and wrapped an arm around her shoulders. The crisp, cold bubbles exploded on her tongue with the first sip. She leaned over to kiss that scar on his jaw. "How did you get that?"

"Fell off my friend's motorcycle. It wasn't even moving. We were just hanging out in his garage, and I was sitting on it and lost my balance." He laughed, the sound intoxicating to her. "Caught it on the edge of a toolbox."

"Fake motorcycle accident. Fake shark attack."

His eyes met hers. "Nothing fake about what we just did."

"It was—it was incredible," she said.

"We *are* pretty amazing at sex." Jake clinked his glass against hers.

"Turns out it's different when you actually love someone. I thought I kind of loved some guys before." A few of their faces flashed by in her mind. "But I think I was wrong."

Jake stilled, and the smile on his face changed. "Yeah. I know what you mean."

"Can I confess something?" She looked into his blue eyes, soft and kind in the flickering firelight. "That terrifies me."

He pressed his forehead to hers and kissed her. "It exhilarates me." His mouth curved against hers. "I've met someone who's such a straight shooter. I know for sure she loves me for me."

On the nightstand, Willow's phone vibrated. They broke apart and shared a concerned look before she snatched it up. "Hello?"

"It's Stacy." Ethan's mom sounded panicked, making Willow panic herself. "Are you okay?"

"What? I'm fine. What's wrong?"

"So, you're all right?"

"Of course, I'm all right. What are you talking about?" Her heart lodged in her throat, threatening to cut off her words. "Is Connor okay?"

Jake got off the bed and started searching for their clothes.

"Um, I'm not sure. This woman—Selene—showed up at our house. Said she's your mom—and Connor's mom."

"What?" Jake handed Willow her underwear, and she wriggled into them. "What happened?"

"She said there was an emergency. You'd been in an accident, and she needed to take Connor to the hospital to see you. I told her we'd be happy to drive Connor, but she insisted."

"Please, Stacy. Please tell me Connor didn't go with her." Willow snatched her dress from Jake's outstretched hand and yanked it over her head, juggling the phone to pull it down. "Jake saw my mom earlier this evening. She'd been drinking."

Jake squeezed her arm and hurried to pull on his pants.

"Connor said it was fine, that it was his mom. But he seemed—off. In a daze or something. Brandon and I didn't even have time to react, and they were both out the door. I'm so sorry, but Brandon and I stood there for a minute, totally confused, and when we opened the door to follow them, they were gone. Should we call the police?"

"I will. Did you hear a car? Did she drive off? Did she seem really drunk?" Willow didn't care she was blasting Stacy with questions.

"I didn't see or hear a car. She didn't seem drunk, but it was really weird. She was just wearing a dress, and she was barefoot. Her foot was bleeding, so I couldn't help noticing. She made some nasty comment about me being rude for staring at her missing toe. Which, to be honest, I hadn't even noticed yet."

*Missing toe.* Something horrible, some yet unnamed, but

always present knowledge, swam to the surface of Willow's brain. Her vision darkened at the edges, and she staggered, catching herself on Jake's arm. "I'm sorry. Can you repeat that?"

"She was barefoot and—"

"No, the other part."

Stacy sounded confused. "The part where she didn't like me staring at her missing toe?"

Willow's stomach roiled, and she gripped the phone. "Thanks, Stacy. I gotta go."

"I'm so sorry, Willow. I didn't know what to do. Please let me know when you find Connor and let me know if I can do—"

Willow dropped the phone and rushed into the little bathroom and slammed the door, barely making it in time to throw up the contents of the fundraiser dinner.

*I couldn't do it. God help me, but I couldn't.* Her father's words in his notebook came back to her. It made sense now why her father couldn't kill the strix, why he'd risked his life to save hers.

A knock came at the door. "Willow? What's going on?"

Willow flushed the toilet and rinsed her mouth. How could she even say the words? But she opened the door and looked Jake in the eye.

"It's my mother."

"I gathered that from your half of the conversation. Is Connor okay?"

"She took him. The strix took him."

"Wait, I'm confused," he said. "Your mother took him or the strix?"

"My mother *is* the strix."

# Chapter 27

Jake shook his head in denial as Willow explained about the missing toe. "A coincidence, Willow."

"No. Don't you see? It all makes sense. My dad wrote they could have human children. He couldn't kill her." Willow was so pale, and her eyes so huge that the whites showed all around. "He starved her, put her back in the strix tree. She didn't abandon us." Willow laughed, an odd sound devoid of amusement. "She isn't a monstrous mother. She's literally a monster. *I'm* half-monster."

Before he could respond to this outrageous claim, Willow was marching across the tree house and throwing open the door. "Willow? What are you doing?"

Her dress was already plastered to her body in the downpour. "She's got my brother, Jake. My mother—the strix—has taken Connor. We have to find him."

"What do you think she wants with him?" Jake followed her outside and down the spiral staircase.

"I don't know. Do you want to find out?"

"Willow, stop for a second. Let's think, okay? Where might she take him?" *Where* she might have taken Connor was much easier to wonder than *why*.

"I don't know. I don't know, Jake." She rushed along the gravel path barefoot, her feet and ankles picking up mud on her determined course toward the house. Suddenly, she turned toward him. "His phone. If he has his phone with him, I can see where she took him." She hunched over the phone in her hand. A few seconds later, she lifted her head in triumph. "It looks like he's moving along Pacific Avenue."

Willow broke into a run, and Jake chased after her, only stopping when he realized she was heading toward her driveway. His truck was parked behind Willow's, and he patted his pocket with relief to find his keys still there.

His relief evaporated when he rounded the house to catch Willow and saw what she stared at in horror. Dozens upon dozens of red-eyed owls, like in his nightmare, perched everywhere he looked. They scrabbled with their talons to find purchase on the roof of his truck cab. They lined the bed. Owls of all shapes and sizes covered Willow's car. Red eyes gleamed in the trees near Willow's house, and as he drew his gaze upward, he saw them perched on her roofline. Rain pelted them, soaking their feathers and rendering them even more horrifying as they appeared skeletal.

Willow pressed herself against the side of the house and grabbed his hand. "They can't fly very well in the rain. I say we make a run for your truck."

"Don't you think we need to arm ourselves? You're just running off half-cocked, Willow."

"You're not in charge here." Jake felt his face sag with disappointment until Willow sighed. "Neither of us is in charge, okay? We're a team. You're right, we need weapons. Come on." She slipped into the side door of the attached garage, leading him into the crowded dark space. The rain on the roof was deafening, and inside the house, Freya was barking her head off.

"Why isn't the light coming on? There's a motion-detector light in here." Willow swore as she bumped into something.

Jake didn't know how it was possible, but even being drenched, the hairs on the back of his neck rose. He grabbed her arm. "Willow."

"Something's wrong," she hissed back.

An overwhelming sense of evil, like walking into an electrical field, buzzed through his brain and set his teeth on edge, making him nauseous, just like the day he'd entered the trunk of the Old Tree. "Let's get out of here," he whispered.

Freya's barks dropped to a deep and vicious growl just as something rustled in the darkness to his right. Willow shoved at him, turning him in the direction of the side door. He bumped and smashed his way back toward it, Willow's hands on his back until they burst back into the rainy night and slammed the door.

"Go, go, go." Willow shoved him some more around the side of the house, away from the driveway. Behind them, the sound of owls flapping through the rain filled the night. It was eerie enough to have watched owls fly so silently in the past, but this sound filled him with dread, an unnatural wet noise of struggling birds that defied description.

He and Willow pounded up the porch steps and into the kitchen, where Freya greeted them with desperate full-body wags. To his relief, he didn't sense that evil feeling in the house. Jake grabbed the bundle of hawthorn branches by the back door and snatched up one of the stakes he'd crafted weeks ago from the wood of the Old Tree, feeling like some sort of vampire hunter. Willow pounded upstairs, Freya at her heels, and he knew she was going to her bedroom where she kept her bow and quiver of Old Tree wood-tipped arrows. Less than a minute later, she returned to the kitchen and had changed her clothes to jeans, a sweatshirt, and tennis shoes. She screeched to a stop, almost falling on the wet, muddy tiles of the kitchen floor. On the back porch, owls clumsily crashed and landed and crash-landed with awful splats into the windows, the back door, and the porch itself. Freya resumed her barking.

"The front?" Jake suggested.

Willow gave a curt nod and clipped Freya's leash to her collar. "I'm not leaving her here alone."

"Of course not."

They hurried through the living room to the front door, and Willow pulled it open. Jake pushed Willow behind him with a protective instinct he immediately regretted because she hip-checked him out of the way with an irritated grunt. "I couldn't find Rex anywhere. I just hope he stays hidden."

He might've laughed if the situation weren't so serious. Willow peeked outside, Freya growling beside her with her head held low. "Mostly clear," she whispered. "A few owls on our cars, but nothing we can't handle."

Jake hefted up a hawthorn branch and fixed her with his most menacing glare. "I'm going first. You stay behind me."

He expected a fight, but she reached up and stroked his cheek with a smile. Before the moment could get too tender, she said, "Keep your pretty face safe, okay? Don't want you uglying it up again like last time you protected me."

Jake snorted. "Ready?"

"Let's go get Connor."

They dashed into the rain, and the owls on the vehicles struggled into the air. At first, Jake had no trouble batting them away with winces and apologies—after all, these were ordinary owls under the thrall of the strix. Except that owls, when soaking wet, no longer looked ordinary. They looked more like evil gargoyles. He'd never seen anything quite so disturbing as those bedraggled, shrunken forms of wet owls, their eyes appearing even larger than normal in their furious faces. His initial ease at batting them away soon became a numbers game as more and more owls swooped down from the surrounding trees.

Talons caught him in the back of the neck, and he felt warm blood trickle down into his jacket. Freya yelped, and Jake swung too late at a retreating owl. A cut bled on Willow's cheek.

"Go!" she shouted over the rain.

They ran until he reached the passenger side of the truck, and he shoved in Willow and Freya. He hurried around to the driver's side and took a blow to his shoulder from a great horned owl. Jake slid behind the wheel and started the engine. The rain pattered on the roof, and Freya shoved her head between them from the backseat of the cab, panting loudly.

He reversed down the drive and pulled onto the highway with a squeal of tires. About two houses down the road, a searing pain gripped his left arm. Sudden dizziness made him swerve off the road onto the grassy shoulder with a teeth-jarring bump that made Willow shriek. Jake ripped open his door and retched.

"Jake. Oh my God, Jake. Are you okay?" Her voice seemed to come from the end of a long tunnel, and he tumbled headfirst onto the ground, his truck engine still running.

A moment later, he felt the heat of Willow's body crouched beside him. Her hand, however, was icy as she shoved up the sleeve of his jacket and gasped. His head felt like a lead balloon as he turned it on his wet-noodle neck to see what had upset her.

The Old Tree's outline shone with that sickly blue light on his skin, each pulse of light making his head pulse in time as it gleamed in the falling rain. "Go on without me." He was relieved he wasn't so far gone as not to realize that sounded like a cheesy line in a bad war movie.

"Would you get up?" Willow sounded impatient as she tugged at his good arm. With a lot of assistance, Jake managed to get back to his feet and allowed Willow to deposit him on the passenger seat.

In seconds, they were pulling into Willow's driveway, but instead of continuing along it, Willow whipped the wheel to the right and drove between the trees toward the front porch.

"Hey, don't hurt Eduardo," he said, his strength returning rapidly with every inch of proximity he gained with the Old Tree.

She spun the truck at the last moment to bring the passenger side flush with the porch and brought the vehicle to a juddering stop. She handed him her house key. "I don't want to leave you, Jake, but I have to get—"

"Connor," he finished. "Go get Connor." He grabbed her hand off the steering wheel and squeezed it hard. Swearing, he pulled her against him for a desperate kiss. "I hate not being able to help you with this."

"I'll be all right, Jake. I have a feeling I have to face her myself. This is between her and me."

"Now who sounds like a cheesy movie?"

"What?"

"Never mind." He stumbled out of the truck and took the hawthorn branch and stake with him, turning back to Willow. "Be careful. I can't stand the thought of anything happening to you when I just found you."

"You be careful too." She glanced at her phone. "Connor's stopped moving. He's at the—at the Grumpy Owl." Her voice sounded puzzled.

Knowing time was wasting, Jake slammed the door. "I love you," he shouted, and she tore off into the night.

Owls still perched in the trees and the roof and Willow's car, and though they stared down at him, none of them made a move. Jake took a shuddering breath and turned to unlock the front door.

As he slipped into the house, that electric current of evil crackled through the air, and he knew he'd made a big mistake.

# Chapter 28

"Come on, Eduardo." Willow gripped the steering wheel like a Formula One driver and finessed the truck around every curve and bend of the highway, going faster on this stretch than she ever had. The rain, at least, was easing up. "Hang on, Connor. I'm coming."

As hard as she tried, Willow couldn't stop thinking about the car accident victim with his hands and face eaten off, or Maureen's foot landing on her skylight, or the gruesome pile of half-consumed organs from that poor man. She would *not* connect those thoughts and images with her little brother. He would be all right. She pushed the images from her mind.

Unfortunately, her brain rewarded her with a barrage of images of her mother. A haunting melody in a language she didn't know sung at her bedside when she was sick. The terrible lasagna her mom made when Willow was fifteen, and the way her dad laughed when her mother dumped the entire thing, pan included, into the trash. The way her mom stared at Willow the last time she'd seen her right before walking out the door. How

Willow's heart had cracked in two when her mother left, even as she'd felt relief to see her go. The echoes of her mother's face in Willow's every time she looked in the mirror, how she detested the resemblance even as she hoped she could be half as beautiful as her. As Selene.

Could she really kill her own mother?

Willow ground her back teeth together. Yes. For Connor. She would do anything to save him.

The streetlights of Pacific Avenue came into view below, blurred softly by the falling drizzle. Willow eased off the accelerator a bit, and the engine stopped its concerning whine to zip down the street. The Grumpy Owl's lights were off at this late hour, but the shape of the eponymous bird on its façade was unmistakable. She pulled the truck into the parking lot going too fast and lurched over the driveway.

Willow scrambled out of the truck, Freya bounding out after her, and hoisted the quiver of arrows over her shoulder. She managed to snag her dog's leash before she got away. The parking lot was empty. She crept around behind the brewery and found nothing but deep shadows. Freya walked beside her, slinking in a way Willow had never seen her do before. Heart pounding in her throat, she completed the circuit around the building to reach the entrance.

A gust of wind rattled the front door, which stood ajar. She snuck into the brewery and heard voices to her right, at the back where the copper of the brewing equipment glinted in the light from a single bulb in the hallway leading to the office.

Hayley and Connor. Freya jerked the leash free from Willow's grasp to disappear into the maze of equipment.

"Hello?" Willow plucked an arrow out of her quiver and readied it in her bow. She felt ridiculous and terrified all at once and wished she'd brought a stake as well.

"Willow?" Hayley appeared from around the curved edge of a large copper vat. Her pale face hovered in the darkness. Willow heard relief—and alarm—in her friend's voice. Hayley glanced at the bow with its notched arrow and back to Willow's face. "You need to see this."

Willow rushed toward her friend, who backed up to reveal what was around the back of the vat. Connor kneeled on the far side of a woman lying on the floor in the middle of a pile of blankets and held her limp hand. Freya curled against the woman on her other side. The woman's face was so covered in blood, it took Willow a moment to realize it was her mother.

The strix. What she'd mistaken as a pile of blankets was, in fact, two large, feathered wings. Willow's heart stuttered in her chest at the unbelievable sight. Her mother wore a knee-length black dress. Blood flowed freely from a huge gash across her chest as well as from her foot where a toe was missing. Something nagged in the back of Willow's mind. The worst injuries were to her chest, but her scalp wounds were bleeding onto her face. "Connor. Get away from her. Freya."

Both Connor and her dog ignored her command. Connor tipped his face up, tears streaming down his cheeks. "She's dying. But she said we can't call an ambulance. They can't see her like this."

"What should I do?" Hayley grabbed Willow's arm. "I heard a horrible scream and came outside to find Connor half-carrying your mom down the street. I let them into the brewery, and he keeps insisting we can't call 9-1-1." Her fingers tightened on Willow's arm. "Because she has wings, Willow. *Wings*. What's happening?"

"She got stuck changing forms," Connor said, rubbing her hand.

"Connor, get away from her." Willow put every ounce of authority she could into her words. "She has you under some kind of spell." It must work on dogs, too, for Freya to be snuggled against her like this.

He shook his head. "No. She did at first, so I'd go with her and leave Ethan's, but it was only to keep me safe."

"Connor, get away from her now. You don't understand."

"No, Willow, it's *you* who doesn't understand." Connor used a clean bar rag to wipe the blood from their mother's face, and her dark eyes fluttered open for a moment. "Everything about our mom you had wrong. Her abandoning us. Her drinking. All of it. Hayley, can you find something to cover her?" His voice broke.

Hayley hurried away and returned with a tablecloth, which Connor used to cover their mother.

Willow shook her head. Their mother had bewitched him. It was the only explanation. She looked warily at her mom before stepping over her and Freya to reach Connor. "Come on, buddy." She stooped and pulled on his arm. "It's been a scary night and you're scared, but I'm going to get you out of here."

Connor stood and shook her off. "Stop treating me like a baby, Willow, and listen to me. For once, can you realize I'm not a little kid? You always act like I need you to take care of me, but it's *you* who needs to take care of me. *You're* the one who's scared. Scared of me growing up and leaving you alone. But I *am* growing up. And I need you to listen to me now as your almost grown-up brother and not a little kid, okay? Our mom is dying, and you need to hear this."

His words slapped her in the face, shocking her in their brutal truth. She dropped her hand from his arm and nodded, staring at the stubble on his jawline. She looked at the still form of their mother on the floor. Their mother who had *wings*. Her gaze swept over her mother, who let out a moan, and the niggling in the back of her mind came to the forefront at the sight of her mother's foot sticking out from beneath the tablecloth.

Curtis had said the owl's missing talon had been an old injury. Her mother's foot was bleeding from a fresh one. And with a bolt of realization, Willow saw it was the wrong foot and even the wrong toe. She shook her head in confusion and met her brother's eyes.

"Okay, Connor. I'm listening."

# Chapter 29

The most beautiful woman Jake had ever seen stood in the middle of the living room. He had enough time to notice the flickering taper candles scattered over the buffet table before the first punch of lust hit him. He shut and locked the front door and stepped toward her. He'd known, ever since the Old Tree's splinters had worked their way into his flesh, this was how it would all end. Somehow, he'd known.

The outline of the Old Tree danced with light on his arm, alive and pulsing.

For a second, his vision split, showing him both the shimmering vision of beauty before him and the sight of his mangled body, his chest ripped out and an egg lying in its cavity where his heart should be. Then the vision snapped back into one, and it was only her again.

Dark, lustrous waves fell over her bare shoulders and brushed the thin straps of a cream satin nightgown skimming the top of her feet. His mind noticed, and quickly discarded, that one of her toes was missing. He returned his gaze to her face, to the twin pools of yellow eyes that threatened to drown him in his own need. The nightgown clung to her body's curves, which he longed to touch.

*You can touch me.* Her mouth—that full-lipped mouth—hadn't moved. The words had merely swum to the surface of his thoughts.

Oh, how he wanted to touch her. The first flicker of lust roared into an inferno of need, and his hand drifted up to grip her hip, the stake clattering to the floor between them. Equal parts desire and revulsion writhed through him, something ancient and reptilian slithering through dark waters.

*That's right. Take me now.*

Jake yanked her against him and cupped her jaw with his other hand like he had when kissing Willow. The Old Tree blazed with light on his arm, claiming him as hers.

Willow.

Something scratched in the back of his mind, the small and furtive warning of a tiny animal in danger. Think of Willow.

But this *was* Willow. And he needed her, needed to take her right now. He looked into her yellow—no, green—eyes and stroked his thumb down her jaw. She cocked her head, and the gesture was so bird-like, Jake's thumb stilled.

"Willow?"

*Yes. Take me. Do what you will with me. I am yours completely. I'm nothing without you.*

That didn't sound like Willow. His Willow wasn't nothing without him. She was everything. The memories crashed through his mind. Willow joking with her brother, Willow feeding baby owlets, Willow speaking in front of a group of donors, Willow swinging a hammer to fix a broken sign, Willow fixing him with that steady, stubborn look from those gorgeous green eyes of hers.

These were not Willow's eyes, and he broke their locked gazes.

He dropped his hand and tried to step back, but the woman

wrapped her hands around his neck and brought her mouth up to his. His lust, like a piece of paper caught on fire, had burned up in seconds to leave nothing but ash in its wake, while his love for Willow washed his mind clean. He pushed the strix away and reached down for the stake. As his fingers closed around it, the woman before him shifted and juddered with a sound of snapping bone and ripping meat, and by the time he straightened, a monster stood in her place.

The Old Tree burning on his skin winked into darkness and disappeared. In that moment, Jake felt the shift within him. He'd been marked as the mate of the strix, but his love for Willow had saved him from that fate.

Now, like so many others, Jake was nothing more than food.

He looked up into a pair of yellow eyes, as pale and cold and unfeeling as chips of citrine gemstones and understood there was much he and Willow didn't know about the strix. For instance, there was an owl form. A woman form.

And this one.

# Chapter 30

"Read it, Connor," came a feeble voice, and Willow gasped at her mother's voice. Connor took out a small leather-bound book from the pocket of his hoodie. He looked down at their mom, who gave one slow nod and nodded back. He cleared his throat and read in a clear and steady voice.

Connor spoke only for a short time, a few minutes at most as their mother lay at their feet, but those minutes flew in the face of everything Willow had believed to be true. And yet. And yet, her memories, their father's notebook, her instincts told her what Connor read to her from their mother's journal was the bigger truth.

"'Many years ago, a strix named Acantha arrived in the New World, having found passage on a ship. She had hunted her way through the woods of North America, settling at last on the lush forests of Oregon, rapidly filling with fresh victims pouring in for the riches promised by the logging industry. Too rapidly. These rapacious men with their machines felled the trees the strix relied on to sustain their own. She knew she must do her part to bolster their numbers, to thin those of the humans, and she set her sights upon a man with whom she would mate. Cyrus McClintock.

He loved another, though, and when he rejected her advances, she became enraged and pushed him into the spinning silver blade at the mill. The young doctor who fruitlessly tended to his grievous injuries became her willing victim instead.

That man was my father, and I was born into a tree in the forest. My mother taught me our ways, and I feasted and fed on the humans that drew me to them time and again. But it wasn't their flesh and blood that attracted me the most. In the end, it was their bright souls, lights in the darkness of a world where monsters such as my mother and I could exist. I tried to live among them and follow their ways. I learned to speak out loud like they did, and not just with my mind into theirs. I learned their knowledge. I basked in that light, but my hunger overtook me. Nightly, my mother and I quarreled as she struggled to understand why I saw my victims as anything more than a source of sustenance. Yet humans were more than food to her, too, for she delighted in their slaughter whether she hungered or not.

At last, unable to bear it any longer, I knew I must stop my mother and me in the only way I knew. We fought a terrible battle, and I ripped one of her talons away. She escaped into her tree, and her injuries were such that she fell into a state of hibernation. I returned to my own tree and the large amounts of blood I spilled meant that I, too, slipped away into slumber.

Until the day Michael woke me with one of those machines my mother despised when he came to destroy my tree. I killed a man, a worker from the timber company, and was able to shift into human form again. The insatiable hunger returned once more, and I showed up on the doorstep of Michael ready to devour him, too. But his soul was too bright. I found I couldn't do so. I refused to enchant him, and in time we fell in love. I became pregnant with a human child. A girl who could become strix too if she fed on human blood.

Enduring the pregnancy without human sustenance almost killed me, and after the birth of Willow, I chose a man to kill and eat. He was a horrible man, and I do not regret it, but it woke the hunger within me yet again. The only way I could keep it at bay was to consume the human poison of drugs and alcohol. Michael and I knew this was no way to raise a child, with either an intoxicated mother, or one who sought only to murder. I begged him to kill me.

He wouldn't do it, nor had I the courage to do the task myself. Instead, he starved me, even when I begged for food, begged for his own blood, and when I was finally weakened enough, he placed me back into my tree. But I had deceived Michael, overstating my weakness because I couldn't stay away from my daughter, my precious Willow. I had enough strength to change back into an owl and remained in that form, feeding only on rodents, watching Willow from a distance.

As I saw Willow grow and change into a young woman, it all became too much. The knowledge of the time I'd lost with her brought me to my lowest point, and I once again gave into temptation. Not the temptation to devour a human, but the temptation to reveal myself to Willow once more, to look at her from a mother's eyes. The photos of myself I left around the house were insufficient to remind her she had a mother. So, I killed and returned again in human form. This time, it was Michael who would pay the price. Michael was injured in a misguided attempt to save me from being crushed by a log.

For some time, I struggled with what to do. In the end, I decided I would sacrifice another human if it meant I could be with Michael in his hour of need, if just for a little while. I returned to him again, and we created Connor. I deluded myself for a short time into believing I could control my urges, my basest desires, that alcohol would be enough to stave off my truest self. But it was all a lie.

I would always be a monster. I will flee to the forest once

more, and there I will remain. I will live upon the love I hold most dear. For Michael. For Willow. For Connor."

"Only she didn't stay there long," Connor said, shutting the book. "She told me you rescued her when she was hit by a car, and she's been keeping watch over us every day. Until Jake woke up our grandmother in the Old Tree."

"Our *grandmother?*" Willow glanced at Hayley, whose mouth hung open in the same way Willow was sure hers did. "Wait. I rescued our mother?"

"And she rescued *me*," Connor continued, as if Willow hadn't asked a question. "Our grandmother was coming for me at Ethan's, but Mom got there first. She wanted to take me home to you, to protect us both, but on our way, our grandmother tried to attack me. Mom saved me, and this is what happened." He waved his hand to encompass their mother.

How had he so quickly shifted to calling her *Mom?*

Connor crouched beside her. "I read it for Willow. Now what do we do? How do we save you?"

"You don't save me," their mother whispered. "You find the monster and kill her before she kills anyone else. With a weapon—" She gasped for air.

"Made from the wood of her tree," Willow finished, numb.

Their mom lifted her hand and stroked Connor's cheek. "I love you." She gestured to Willow, who found herself dropping the bow and arrows and kneeling beside Connor at their mother's side.

It was no compulsion or enchantment that made Willow do so, but the deep yearning borne of a lifetime without a mother. Her mom's hand was cool on her cheek as she reached up to stroke Willow's as well. "I love you, Willow." She gasped in another breath. "Always."

Her hand fell back to the floor, limp, and began to shrink and recede. Willow watched in horrified awe as her mother's body began to morph before them, her limbs and wings shrinking, her skin rippling as feathers swept over it, her face compressing into a small, round shape with the large, liquid-black eyes of a beautiful spotted owl, which now lay deathly still upon the floor.

Cynthia. *Her* owl. The very first owl Willow had ever rescued had been her mother.

All of it was too much to take in at once. Emotions swirled in a hurricane that threatened to overtake her. Her mother had loved her, had murdered people, had sacrificed everything to be with her, had saved her brother, and had looked out for them both for years.

And now she was dead. Willow traced her fingers down the smooth, silken feathers of the owl's unmoving chest, and they came away covered in blood. For an anguished moment, she felt the keen double loss of her mother and the owl she'd loved most. Beside her, Connor heaved silent, racking sobs that tore her heart.

There was no time to process the swirling hurricane of feelings, because in its center, Willow found the focus she needed with one pressing thought. "Jake."

Her mother was dead, but they might still have time to save Jake.

# Chapter 31

A *demon*. She looked like a demon. Her face defied description, no longer human, with gleaming yellow eyes staring at him from above a curved beak that could tear him to pieces. The satin nightgown had torn away to leave her form, still vaguely human in shape, covered in feathers. Sharp talons protruded from where fingers and toes should be, and large wings unfurled from her back.

The monster let out an unearthly screech that pierced Jake's ears.

*Selene is gone. She's dead,* hissed the voice in his mind.

Jake started for the front door, the stake gripped in his hand, but her wing blocked him, sweeping over the candles on the buffet table in the process. One of the curtains caught fire with shocking speed. He pivoted and launched himself over the loveseat toward the kitchen. He didn't dare look behind him as he heard the strix knocking furniture over in pursuit.

As soon as he ripped open the back door and sprinted for the trees, he realized his mistake. The forest was no place to flee from a strix. His best chance at fighting her had been in the confines of the house, not out in the open in her natural element with room for her to fly. He screamed as talons sank deep into his shoulders, and his feet lifted from the ground.

*This shouldn't be possible.* His mind couldn't comprehend the true horror of his situation and instead focused on the aerodynamic impossibility of this creature flying him through the trees. He brought up one of his hands, the other still holding firm to the madrone stake, to cover his face from the slapping branches. The movement made him cry out from the pain of the talons digging into his shoulders. Peeking through his fingers, he glimpsed glowing red eyes in the trees around him.

His nightmare had come true. The Old Tree loomed ahead of him, the evil rolling off it in waves, and suddenly, the strix released him from her clutches to send him sprawling onto the deck of the tree house. He rolled like a pill bug in a tight ball until he landed against the sliding door with a jarring *thud*. The strix landed beside him. Wasting no time, he launched himself up at her chest with the stake held high above him.

It was no use.

Her taloned foot smashed down onto his arm, pinning it to the deck. The stake went spinning across the wooden boards and fell off the edge of the decking, and Jake's hopes sank with it. Except he heard an immediate soft *thump,* as if the stake had only fallen a few inches. Before he could react, the strix smashed her other foot into the center of his chest, one of her talons poised at his throat where his pulse thundered. She stared down at him in the unblinking manner of owls in a moment that stretched for an eternity.

"What?" he growled. "What do you want? Just eat me and get it over with."

*You will not be for me.*

Jake jerked his head to the side, scanning the surrounding trees for the red eyes boring into him from every direction.

*No, not them. For* her. *Selene is dead, but there is still hope for my granddaughter. She will drink your blood and join me. Willow will be a true strix as she was always meant to be.*

"No." Jake struggled to push the word out of his constricting throat. "She'll never do that."

*You would deny her immortality? Beauty beyond compare? Power?*

"She doesn't want any of that. And she's already beautiful."

*She will not grow old. She will not die. Surely you would wish this for the woman you love? Your death will not be in vain. Part of you will live inside her too, forever.*

Jake looked up into those citrine eyes, latched onto his face with unwavering focus. A warm, buzzy feeling fizzed through Jake's veins, as if his very blood longed to move through Willow's veins instead. Yes. It was a wonderful idea. Nothing had ever held such an appeal to him before. Willow would live forever, and he would live inside her, exactly where he wanted to be. He would cut a vein open for her now.

*Soon. She will be here soon.*

# Chapter 32

Willow got to her feet, swiping at the tears streaming down her face, and picked up her bow and arrows. There wasn't time for this. "Take care of Connor," she said to Hayley.

"Where are you going?" Hayley asked.

"I have to save Jake."

"I'm coming with you."

"No, I need you to stay here and keep Connor safe."

Connor was busy wrapping the spotted owl—their mother—in the tablecloth, but as he stood with the unthinkably light bundle in his arms, his face was defiant and angry. "Willow. We're coming with you. You still aren't learning. I'm not a little kid. You can't keep doing everything alone."

Willow's teeth gnashed together, and a muscle twitched in her jaw. Then she looked at her brother, holding their dead mother, and saw the determined expression on her best friend's face and let out a long breath. "You're right. Let's go."

The three of them rushed into the night. The rain had stopped, and they piled into Jake's truck. Freya lay in the back seat next to the wrapped body of the owl and whined. As soon as Willow made it onto the highway, she pushed the truck as fast as she dared.

*Mind that curve, Willy-boo.* Her hands jerked on the steering wheel to hear her father's voice so clearly beside her. She slowed fractionally and shot out the other side of the bend in the road.

She saw the flickering light of the fire before she rounded the curve and saw flames leaping through the front window of her house. She swerved into the drive and slammed on the brakes, and the front bumper thunked into the tree at the end of the driveway.

"Sorry, Eduardo," she muttered.

The truck doors flew open, and she and Hayley spilled out into the smoke-scented night. Connor reached into the back of the truck for their mother's body.

"Leave her," Willow said. "We'll come back for her later. Keep Freya in there, too."

Her dog barked frantically when they locked her in, and Willow's heart cracked a little more. "It's for your own good, Freya." She looked at the house. "Oh God. Rex." *Please let her cat be okay.*

"Go," Hayley said. "I'll call 9-1-1 and deal with this." She gestured at Willow's house, at Freya barking in the truck.

Willow grabbed her friend by the shoulders. "It's just a house, Hayley. Remember that, okay?"

"Go." Hayley had her phone out and gave Willow a little shove.

Willow raced around the back of the burning house, Connor running alongside her. Willow knew exactly where she would find her grandmother, the monster called Acantha. Her footsteps pounded on the wet gravel, and her bow and quiver slammed against her side as she wound along the path to The Old Tree.

It wasn't hard to see in the darkness. The entire tree pulsed with a weird black light. The cleft in the base of the trunk glistened with a ghastly purple-black. "Stay back," she said. "Stay out of sight until I need you, okay?"

Connor looked uncomfortable, but he nodded, melting into the darkness to hide behind some trees. She spared a glance at the billowing cloud of dark smoke building over her house in the distance, at the dancing orange flames consuming the house her grandfather had built. Then Willow stepped into the clearing.

A soft hooting came from above, and her gaze traveled up to the deck of the tree house where something crouched over Jake. The creature's head slowly turned around almost a hundred and eighty degrees to look at Willow. The pale-yellow eyes of a great gray owl gleamed at her from the face of a—a what? Willow was at a loss, but she had a feeling she was finally seeing Acantha in her true strix form. Not entirely human, not entirely owl, but wholly monster.

Those eyes looked deeply into hers. Willow looked at the cleft of the tree and was overcome with the desire to crawl inside it.

*You must first drink of his blood,* came the odd, soothing voice in her mind. *Drink, then you may sleep in my tree until you will be like me, dearest. The strix you were meant to be.*

Jake's blood. That was what she wanted more than anything. Willow took lurching steps to the base of the winding staircase.

*That's right. Come here and drink deeply.*

"Willow!" Connor darted out and pulled Willow back under the cover of the overhanging deck. "What are you doing?" He jerked her around to face him, and the spell was broken.

Willow sucked in a breath and shuddered with horror at what she'd been about to do. "Thank you," she whispered, glancing up in the direction of the strix, out of sight on the deck above their heads. "Oh my God, Connor, you saved me."

Connor gave her arm a little shake. "Don't look into her eyes, okay?"

Willow suddenly knew what she needed to do. She needed to listen to her brother. She shrugged off her bow and quiver and handed them to Connor.

"What are you doing?"

*Come, Willow. He is waiting for you.*

"You're right. You're not a little kid," Willow said. "I need you to kill her when I distract her." She pointed straight up. "I'm going to let Acantha think she's won."

Connor pulled her into a quick, hard hug before stepping back and notching an arrow. Willow felt a lump in her throat, remembering the first time she and her dad took him to the archery range. Dad would be proud to see his son now, so fearless.

Willow concentrated on slowing the pounding of her heart. Was she doing the right thing going up to meet the strix unarmed? What if she fell under her spell again and hurt Jake? No, she had to trust Connor wouldn't let that happen. She forced her movements to take on a dreamy floating quality as she spiraled around the staircase.

*Yes, Willow. Come to me.*

Willow unfocused her eyes and trailed her hand along the double railings Jake had made. She concentrated on her love for him, for this unexpected man who'd come so unexpectedly into her life. Jake Bartlett. *I love Jake,* she thought with every step until she found herself cresting the top. It wasn't her plan to fall in love, but she had. It wasn't her plan to need a man, but she needed Jake like she needed air.

It wasn't her plan to forgive Walter Bartlett, but she somehow did. It wasn't her plan to make room in her heart for her mother, but she was there inside her all the same, even after death.

And it wasn't her plan to have her baby brother—no, her brother—be the one to kill the strix.

But sometimes, plans change.

Willow felt the slightest vibration of Connor's steps farther down the staircase as she crested the top stair. She stepped onto the deck to face Acantha.

*Come, drink of him.*

Willow looked at a point just to the right of Acantha's

terrible face and shuffled forward to where Jake lay pinned to the deck like a butterfly on a board. Blood seeped from his shoulders. Willow examined herself for any bloodthirsty urges and was relieved to find none. She crawled to Jake on her hands and knees. He lay limp and submissive under the enchantment, though Acantha clearly wasn't taking any chances. She stood with her wings stretched over the scene. Her talons were inches from Willow's face when Willow dipped her head, pretending to lap at his wounded shoulder in a gesture that revolted her.

The vibrations moved through her hands on the deck boards, stronger now. Connor must be nearly at the top. She shifted her mouth to Jake's ear and breathed into it. "I love you, Jake."

The effect was instantaneous. He sucked in a breath like someone who'd surfaced from a deep dive and shoved Acantha's taloned foot from his chest.

The strix reared back to strike when a glowing figure appeared behind Jake. Willow gasped and, for a moment, they all stared at the bandaged figure standing on the deck.

*But you're dead, Cyrus.*

Acantha screeched with surprise as an arrow sprouted through her wing. Instantly, it began to smoke. As she whirled, Jake rolled onto his stomach and army-crawled to the edge of the deck, where he reached over for something Willow couldn't see. Connor struggled to pull another arrow from the quiver on his back.

Acantha screeched again and flapped her wings. They couldn't let her take flight. Willow tackled the monster's legs, those scaly, horrible legs, and held on even as the strix jabbed for her with that razor beak, cutting Willow's arm.

"Gotcha!" Jake sprang to his feet with a stake clutched in his hand. He charged Acantha and stabbed her in the back.

The strix spun with another eardrum-piercing shriek in what proved to be a fatal error. As she spun, she presented her feathered chest to Connor, and this time, when he let the arrow fly, it found its target dead center.

Willow felt the tremor through her hands and let go at once to move back. The strix screamed once more, and then her body exploded into flames that seared Willow's skin. Jake hooked his arm around her waist and pushed Connor toward the stairs.

"Time to go," he said. "Go, go, go."

Within seconds, the entire tree was ablaze. She and Jake and Connor were spiraling around a column of fire, burning with a blistering heat. Their feet reached the soft damp earth below, and they kept running.

Sirens sounded in the distance as they moved from the inferno of The Old Tree behind them and Willow's burning house before them. Willow snuck a look over her shoulder and saw the white figure of the Bandage Man standing beneath the burning Old Tree. She saw him flicker once, twice, and then fade away. Jake's arms were around both of them as he ushered them toward the gravel parking lot. A minute later, a fire engine roared into the lot, lights flashing.

"She's dead," Willow said to Connor. "You killed her." Despite her house burning, despite the Old Tree and its tree house burning, Willow couldn't stop herself from smiling. "It's over. The strix is dead."

But Jake only frowned at her.

"What is it?"

"Your eyebrows." Jake ran his fingers across her forehead. "They're gone. They're just—poof!—gone."

For some reason, the three of them found this hysterical so that when the first firefighter reached them, he found them laughing like lunatics.

# Chapter 33

*Eighteen months later*

"You ready?" Jake shouted to Willow and Connor.

She and Connor called back in the affirmative, and Freya barked once, which made Rex meow in his carrier at their feet.

"Three. Two. One." Jake flipped the switch, and Willow squealed in delight.

God, she was the kind of woman who squealed now, ever so occasionally, and it was all Jake Bartlett's fault. "It's incredible." She launched herself into Jake's arms, still mindful of his shoulder injuries that pained him, though much less now. His shoulders had recovered, their various cuts and bruises disappeared, and Willow's eyebrows grew back—as did Rex's charred tail, which got burned when he'd escaped the fire to her nearest neighbor's house.

Eventually, even their souls started to heal from the trauma and loss they'd endured together—and they were stronger for it. Willow had even mostly conquered her fear she might one day be compelled to drink human blood and become a strix, but Jake still liked to tease her that it was a good thing she was vegetarian.

Jake might have unshakable trust Willow wasn't a killer, but the Cedar Beach Police Department still viewed her with suspicion. The "Tree Top Murders and Arson" were marked as a cold case. Authorities hypothesized that the killer returned to Willow's property to destroy evidence with a fire. Whether the charred bones found at the tree house site were those of the murderer caught out by their own uncontrollable inferno or another victim remained unclear. The DNA was contaminated with that of an owl and matched nothing in any database. The killings ended, and there was no evidence to implicate either Willow or Jake in the bizarre events.

That didn't stop the crazy conspiracy theories sprouting up. They only added to the popularity of the tree house hotel. And none of the conspiracy theories were as crazy as the truth of what had happened.

It was behind them now, Willow reminded herself, gazing at the wondrous scene before her and refusing to think of the acres and acres of forest beyond.

Twinkling Christmas lights outlined the structure. The old Santa cut-out stood in the front yard, waving for all it was worth.

"It's beyond my wildest dreams," she said.

Where her old house had been, a new one now stood. An almost carbon-neutral, eighteen-hundred-square-foot tree house perched on a platform ten feet from the ground, constructed between and around several trees. Two trees grew straight out of the roof of the second story. Jake had designed the house and seen to every detail. Every wish of Willow's—both voiced and not even fully formed—had sprung to life in this house.

Willow and Connor had spent the past few months crowded into an old RV lent to her by Hayley's parents. It allowed Willow to live on site with her temporary home parked near the raptor center. Connor escaped as often as he could to Ethan's house, and Willow spent many evenings with Jake in his studio. While they might miss the heavenly scent of waffle cones, she and Jake were ecstatic to be moving into the new house.

Their house. She picked up Rex's carrier, and together, she, Jake, Connor, and Freya climbed the short staircase to the entrance. In the dying rays of the sunset, Willow's engagement ring sparkled as she reached for the doorknob and opened the door.

She let Rex out of his carrier, and he and Freya bounded through the house. Jake was like a little boy as he led them from room to room. First was the living room with the river rock they'd salvaged from Willow's destroyed home. Grandpa himself had helped set the first stone into the hearth with Jake. BiBi created a framed shadowbox with the collection of feathers from Willow's favorite birds—including several from her mother. It now hung over the mantle.

She followed Jake into the kitchen. A tree grew through the corner, cupboards on either side of its trunk. Jake opened the pantry with a flourish to show her the food he'd already stocked. He picked up a container of white rice. "So you can make me that fried rice that made me fall in love with you."

Willow snorted and slapped him on the arm. "You're going to be doing most of the cooking, Jake."

"That's fine, as long as you make that fried rice now and again."

Connor, unable to wait, pounded up the stairs to the second floor. Willow took advantage of the privacy to sneak a kiss. She shrieked when Jake deepened the kiss and dipped her.

Upstairs, Connor shouted, "This is awesome."

"Shall we, future Mrs. Bartlett?" Jake offered his elbow.

"I don't know if I can be a Bartlett," Willow said, for the umpteenth time in an ongoing discussion.

"Yeah, Lindsay said you didn't deserve the name. Better not

take it."

Willow laughed. "Nice try with the reverse psychology." To her utter amazement, she was excited to have Lindsay as a sister-in-law. Willow wouldn't tell Jake yet, but she was tempted to take his name. Lindsay had whipped Toby into shape, and Willow wouldn't be surprised if an engagement announcement was in the works soon for those two as well.

"Come upstairs," Connor shouted.

Jake started to lead her away, but she pulled him to the sink to gaze out the window at the small purple jacaranda tree they'd planted in the backyard. They'd buried her mother at the base of its trunk, where she could still keep watch over Willow and Connor.

And Jake.

Jake stood at her side and squeezed her shoulder. "You never really had your mom, and I didn't ever have my dad. Not really. But we sure miss them, anyway."

Willow stirred at the mention of Walter Bartlett. In his will, he'd left a charitable trust to the Tree Top Raptor Center that meant she wouldn't have to worry about her birds again. Strangely, she did miss Walter—or at least the chance to speak with him once more. She wished she could thank him for his gift, tell him that she understood more, if not everything, that had transpired between him and her father. That she forgave him and was grateful he'd never told the lawyer who her mother was.

And she was slowly paying Jake back for her tree houses.

The Old Tree and its house were gone, and Elvis, now taking on more and more of Maureen's role, helped Willow create the Maureen Sullivan Memorial Garden blooming in the center of the clearing. The other tree houses remained and were booked out months in advance. Beyond the tree houses, the light caught on the corrugated roof of the old logging museum. Willow knew her father would be pleased she'd reopened it. Tyler—whose man-bun belied a surprisingly mature man who turned out to be perfect for her best friend—now ran the museum. Willow still avoided looking at that silver blade, though she hadn't seen the Bandage Man since that night, and neither had Connor.

"Ready?" Jake smiled down at her, and she nodded, following him upstairs.

They found Connor exclaiming over the new kiteboard propped in the corner, a source of far more excitement for him than his new bedroom.

"Early Christmas present." Jake grinned when Connor threw his arms around him.

"Thanks, man."

The bedroom would only be Connor's for another couple of years, and then he'd be off to college. She was okay with that. More than okay. Connor was growing up, and it filled her with happiness to see it.

They left Connor to gaze in adoration at his board and went back into the hall. Jake waggled his eyebrows at Willow. "Wanna see our room?"

"Do I ever. Maybe I can give you an early Christmas present tonight, too. Connor's going out with his friends later."

"Oh, really?" Jake paused in front of a third bedroom and opened the door to a space sparsely furnished as a guest room, with a beautiful tree painted on one wall. "Bibi did that for us. Know what I think?"

"What?"

"She wants us to add another branch to the family tree. This would make an amazing nursery."

Willow burst out laughing. "Whoa, dude. One step at a time."

He pulled her into another hug. "All right, all right. One step at a time. As long as you promise I get to take them all with you."

"I promise." Willow smiled against Jake's mouth as he pressed it to hers.

# Acknowledgements

First off, thanks to Literary Wanderlust and Susan Brooks for always wanting to read what I write and being my editor on this one. Thanks for the super fun cover.

Thank you, as always to Amy Wilson and Amanda Nay, for being such great critique partners and friends. A long overdue thank you to so many people at Rocky Mountain Fiction Writers. Some of you I haven't seen in years, some I just saw last week, and some I'm forgetting to list because there are so many great writers in this organization. All of you have cheered me on in my writing journey in one way or another. Sue Hinkin (who introduced me to Susan), Andrea Catalano, Mindy McIntyre, Kathy Reynolds, Liesa Malik, Michelle Winkler, Kevin Wolf, Lawdon, Rachel Dempsey, ZJ Czupor, Kathy House, Nikki Baird, Wendy Spurlin, Val Moses, Laurence MacNaughton, Mary Ann Kersten (we miss you!), Chris Devlin, Mark Stevens, Martha Husain, John Turley and many more.

Although he's a stranger to me, I have to give a shout-out to Ken Shults, a photographer who captures the most amazing photos of great gray owls that inspired me throughout writing this book. I hope I didn't malign these animals too much, because great gray owls are truly majestic, awe-inspiring birds, and I don't think one has ever eaten any humans—that we know of.

Thank you to my current and former library co-workers (both public and school) for all the fun conversations about books. Librarians are the kindest and coolest people I've ever met.

I'm so grateful for Danielle Greenleaf, who reads my books with a sharp gleam in her eye and an attention to detail for anything Scout-related. Any mistakes are mine. Thank you also to friends like Kathy Dannen, Kristina Brown, and Sonya Gruszczynski who always buy my books and read them with such enthusiasm.

Thank you to my British (and Irish) family who are excited for my books: Dave and Jenny Meredith, Matthew and Caroline Meredith, Lucy and Tim Chaloner, Niamh Plunkett, and Max Chaloner.

To my family, I can't believe how blessed I am to have you all. I got the world's best husband, so it's no surprise he gave me the world's best kids. Jon, I love you more than words can ever say, and your tireless support of my writing means more than you'll ever know. Isabelle, Zoe, and Luke, this mom couldn't be prouder of my own little nestlings taking flight into all your adventures. I love you!

And last, my pets. To my two cats Delilah and Wanda, who mince across keyboards at the most inopportune moments, your concern for preventing carpal tunnel in me is touching. To the ever-present George, my pug shadow and adorable muse— I'm still not sure you could fight off an owl, buddy, but you're awfully cute.

# About the Author

Joy Jarrett enjoys imagining something creepy in every situation, starting with a fourth-grade theater production when she became convinced a monster lived under the stage. She might not let different foods touch on her plate, yet she's fearless when it comes to mixing love stories and horror in her scary good romances. Joy is currently a school librarian, but has worked in a pet store, a safari park, and vet hospitals and holds a Zoology degree. Animals always feature in her writing. On a good day, her two cats and pug make room on the couch for Joy and her family. They live outside Denver, where Joy experiences frequent shaming that she's never gone skiing in her life. She enjoys reading, traveling, board games, and going with her English husband to explore castles in Britain, where she finds plenty of romantic, spooky inspiration.